Up Like Thunder

Colin T. Nelson

Rumpole Press of Minneapolis, MN

ISBN: 978-0692444429

Library of Congress Control Number: 2015906634

First Edition: June 2015

Cover Photo by Russ Stanton

Printed in the United States of America

Rumpole Press of Minneapolis, MN

Dedication

To our friend and personal guide, Wah Wah Lwin,
a courageous and fascinating woman who gave us an old
Buddhist saying: *If we become friends in this life, it's because we
were already friends from a previous life.*
She and many other brave women will be the ones to lift
Myanmar out of tyranny and into freedom.

Also by Colin T. Nelson

Reprisal

Fallout

Flashover

The Amygdala Hijack

Acknowledgements

While writing this book, I received an immense amount of help and encouragement from the following people: Mary McCormick, Marilyn Curtis, Mary Stanton, my editor Jennifer Adkins, Doug Dorow, Jim Kuether—my local expert on Myanmar, and of course, my best idea-starter and supporter, my wife, Pam Nelson. Thanks to all of you; I appreciate your help!

"If you've 'eard the East-a-callin', you
won't never 'eed naught else.
No! you won't 'eed nothin' else.
But them spicy garlic smells,
An' the sunshine an' the palm trees
An' the tinkly temple bells;
On the road to Mandalay. . .

For the temple-bells are callin', an' it's
there that I would be—
By the old Moulmein Pagoda,
looking lazy at the sea;
On the road to Mandalay,
Where the old Flotilla lay,
with our sick beneath the awnings
when we went to Mandalay!
On the road to Mandalay,
where the flyin'-fishes play,
An' the dawn comes up like thunder
outer China 'crost the Bay!

—Rudyard Kipling

Up Like Thunder

Chapter One

Minneapolis, Minnesota

The regional manager of the US Export-Import Bank, Martin Graves, called Congressman Brian Holmes at five-fifteen in the morning—an emergency. Graves, who was never at his desk this early, dreaded making the call. In the dead of winter the heat hadn't been raised in the office building yet in order to save energy, so he felt the chill penetrate into his bones.

Graves needed a miracle. "Congressman, it's Bridget. She's missing." Graves spoke quickly.

"What? She's only been in Myanmar two months."

"We haven't had communication from her for three weeks. Something is wrong." Graves paused to take a deep breath. The conditions in Myanmar were dicey enough that he had hesitated sending Bridget there. She'd insisted, but Graves required Bridget to maintain contact every day. Graves didn't mention this to Holmes.

"Oh, my God. So where is my daughter?"

"I'm sorry, we don't know. She's always punctual with her reports."

"I'm sure she is. The police?"

"Not reliable. The government—or however you want to characterize the generals' dictatorship—is one of the most corrupt and brutal in the world. You know that."

Holmes agreed.

"She was conducting a due diligence investigation of Yangon International Timber Company before we agreed to extend credit to them. But her work didn't threaten the generals. In fact, we had their approval to do the financials on the company."

The Export-Import Bank (Ex-Im Bank) had been chartered in 1934 and tasked with providing loans and credit to developing world companies that the private banking industry considered too risky. The companies, in turn, provided a market for US exports.

Because of congressional concerns, the Ex-Im Bank had recently tightened their investigation of prospective loan clients to see if the companies were financially solid enough to warrant the loans.

Holmes' voice took on a sharp edge. "So, you don't think her work crossed their government the wrong way?"

"No. They want Western business. The generals came to us, and we followed all their procedures." Graves keyed his computer to life. He scrolled past the government forms that related to the work of the bank. He'd uploaded every form available.

"Marty, it's my child, for God's sake."

"We'll do all we can, sir." He leaned forward and pushed the cup of McDonald's coffee to the side. He could still smell the Egg McMuffin on the greasy wrapping paper next to the cup. Graves searched for recent posts from Bridget. Her last report had been filed six weeks earlier. Graves scanned it and found nothing suspicious or out of the ordinary. She was an accountant whom the bank had hired at the insistence of her father, the congressman, to work in the new markets opening in Southeast Asia. Fortunately, she'd turned out to be very smart and more than competent.

Myanmar was located on the west side of Thailand in Southeast Asia. For over fifty years, the country of Burma had been ruled by the military and completely closed to the world. The Burmese people couldn't leave, nor could anyone from the outside get in. In the destructive aftermath of a hurricane in 2008, the Myanmar generals, who ruled the country, had even refused to allow Red Cross and United Nations relief missions with food and aid supplies to enter the country.

In 2011 the generals, for unknown reasons, had decided to open the country to a small degree for Western trade and tourism.

Graves talked quickly to the congressman. "I'm checking her notes. Her last wire post was from the embassy even though she was staying at the Chatrium Hotel. You know that the Internet is pretty much non-existent in the country." He heard a rumble that meant the heat had kicked on, and he felt a warm draft surround him.

"Right. Even cell phones don't work very well."

"I'll get the embassy staff on the satellite now. They're about twelve hours behind us and—"

"Not good enough," Holmes barked. "I want feet on the ground right now."

Graves pushed back from his desk. He swiveled to look over the Nicollet Mall covered with piles of snow that looked dirty in the predawn light. Soon pedestrians would be struggling to climb over them to find the sidewalks. The street stretched out below him and crossed the Mississippi River. Turbulent, muddy water twisted between ice jams and fell over the falls of St. Anthony on its way south. What could Graves do?

"Marty, I want her found. We could contact the military. There's a detachment of Marines at the embassy."

"I'd advise against it, sir. How do you think those generals will react to that? No, we've got to do this our own way." He looked at the photo of his own family hanging from the tan sheetrock wall next to the door. What it if was his child?

The congressman breathed heavily into the phone. "Okay. I'll call the FBI."

"Uh, Mr. Holmes, they don't have jurisdiction there. Besides, do you know what's going on in that country?"

He paused. "I'm, uh, well aware of what's going on there."

"You know the generals are paranoid and fearful of everything. If we come in with a lot of muscle, it will make them nervous, and their reaction will be to shut down. They won't cooperate at all, and we'll never find her. No, we need something under the radar, but something effective."

"I don't know . . ." The phone went silent for a long time. "Wait a minute. Is Chandler still with you guys?"

"Yeah—" Graves thought of their investigator, in his mid-forties, who'd also received his job through the congressman. Pete Chandler had been a CID investigator with the US Army in Afghanistan and Iraq. He'd retired to work with the US House Committee on Banking, which Congressman Holmes from Minnesota chaired. Chandler had been extraordinarily successful and had done all the dirty work behind the scenes for the committee over the years. Something had happened to Chandler, and he'd quit the committee abruptly. The congressman hustled Chandler out of Washington and got him the job as an investigator at the Ex-Im Bank—guaranteed to allow Chandler a quiet glide into obscurity. "Uh, he's got international experience," Graves said, "but I'm not sure he's up to speed for something like this."

Holmes interrupted, "He's the best, and he owes me everything."

"Okay. But sir, he's not done well here." Holmes was obviously stuck on getting Chandler. How could Graves tell him the truth about the investigator? About how he was going to be bounced out of the bank soon?

"I don't care. I know how good he is, and I want him."

Graves sighed. He wanted to help in any way he could, but using Pete Chandler would be a disaster. Should he tell the congressman that Chandler was tired and disinterested? That he seemed so lost he didn't even go out to lunch? He ate alone at his desk every day.

"Listen, Marty. I worked with this guy for years. He's a fighter. And he's tough. I think he can still do that Tae Kwon Do martial arts stuff, can't he?"

"I don't know." Graves looked at the clock on his smart phone. "He usually comes in late, but when he gets here I'll touch base with him."

Holmes yelled, "*Touch base with him?* I want him on a fucking plane—yesterday!"

Graves wrestled with the decision to recruit Chandler. In spite of his drawbacks, there were some possible advantages to sending him. In the end, he was the only choice. "Yes, sir." Martin Graves hung up. He added more sugar and cream to his coffee and stirred it.

His mind pictured Bridget Holmes. Twenty-nine years old, dark hair, and dark green eyes that gave her an exotic look—nothing like you'd imagine an accountant to look like. But she had a cunning side to her also.

Graves had always worried about sending her to Myanmar, but she'd demanded the assignment—with her father's support. Bridget was one of the most ambitious people Graves knew. He lumped her into a younger generation who were handed everything and felt entitled to start at the top—just because they breathed. She had also gone with definite attitudes about the dictatorial regime. On the one hand, she despised their brutal activities, but she was also impressed by the potential fortune the bank and US exporters could make in the country.

Graves called Pete Chandler and left him a terse message on his voice mail.

Fifteen minutes later, Chandler responded. "What's the problem? You know how early it is?"

"I need you in here right now."

"I'm eating breakfast."

"Forget it. Bridget Holmes is missing in Myanmar."

Chandler stopped talking. After a few minutes, he said, "That's serious."

Graves knew that would get his attention. Chandler was a sensitive man and liked Bridget. "Her father asked specifically for you."

Pete grunted, "I don't know, Marty. I haven't been overseas for years."

"He wants you."

"I wouldn't know where to start in a country like that."

"With what you're facing here, Chandler, this might be a good break for you. We'll talk when you get in. And that better be soon," Martin demanded.

Chandler arrived in a half hour. He came directly to the regional manager's office at the corner of the tall building. He wore a full-length brown winter coat and a tan scarf. He untied and tugged it from around his neck. Martin could smell the cold, fresh air that clung to Chandler's clothing. He looked ten years younger than his age. He still had a trim body, not too muscular, but there was a hint of coiled energy inside of him. Pete's eyes moved slowly, and he talked in a languid manner while being careful to enunciate each word. Deliberate. "I'm worried about Bridget. Myanmar could be a dangerous place."

"The congressman is shitting bricks. Not that I blame him. If it were my child—"

"Doesn't sound good. That country is one mystery layered on top of another." Pete shook his head. "Maybe you should give it to someone at the State Department." His words trailed off like he was already tired of talking about it.

"I'd like to, but under the circumstances, we can't. The old man wants you."

Chandler's eyes opened for a brief moment before settling back into narrow slits. "Well, he's wrong." He tossed his coat and scarf across the leather couch by the door. Particles of snow melted off the collar.

"He's the reason you've still got a job. I wouldn't forget that if I were you."

Chandler's forehead arched in crinkled lines. He didn't respond.

"I'm not going to argue with you, Pete. Connie will get you booked on the first flight out of here. You'll need to fill out a GD 2035 and, of course, form INT 989. But you're going."

"What the hell do I know about Myanmar? Isn't that the old Burma?"

"Right. With your, uh, work here, you've barely used up our investigative budget. You'll have lots of money and the support of the embassy."

Chandler took a deep breath and let it out slowly. "Marty, I'm the wrong guy. Too rusty. I don't have the energy this would require."

"You don't have to tell me that."

"Well, there you go."

Graves stood up from his chair and came around to the front of his desk. "I've had a few minutes to check on your file. You're part Vietnamese, aren't you?"

"Half. My mother was Vietnamese and my father an American." He didn't look Asian. In fact, the only hint was his straight black hair and the slightly darker tone of his skin. "I grew up here; I'm an American." Pete leaned back. "What does that have to do with anything?"

"Maybe you'll have better access with the Burmese."

Pete snorted. "Ridiculous. I don't know, or care, anything about my Asian background. I'm an American."

Martin waved his hand between them. "I don't know what your history is with the congressman, and I don't give a damn what happened in Washington. You're the only one that Holmes trusts for the job. And we don't have time to stand here talking about it. Every minute we waste could mean her life."

Pete cupped his hand and ran it over the shine of his hair. It had started to creep backward over his forehead but still remained thick. At the mention of Washington, Graves had seen a squint of pain in Chandler's eyes. "Tell me what you know for sure," Chandler finally said.

Graves led him to a beige table in the corner opposite from his desk. Since the congressman's phone call, Martin had worked hard to assemble the details. Spread out on the table were printouts, some photos, and another open laptop. On the screen was a map of Myanmar.

Graves pointed to the map. "It's located in Southeast Asia on the Bay of Bengal. About the size of Texas. Borders Bangladesh on the west and China to the north. Received its independence from Great Britain in 1948, only to fall into a long line of military dictatorships that closed the country to everything from the outside world. Consequently, we don't know much about what goes on inside. The government and how it operates is a mystery."

"Isn't that where the Nobel Prize winner lives? Aung San Suu Kyi?"

"Right. Her father was the president at independence but was assassinated two years later. She left the country and married a professor from Great Britain but was forced to leave him and her children in order to return to her country. She heads the National League for Democracy party."

Pete laughed. "Democracy? She hasn't been too successful yet."

"No. The government normally kills any opponents, but since she's the daughter of their 'George Washington,' the government spared her life. Instead, they've kept her under house arrest for years.

She was finally released a short time ago and now holds a seat in their parliament."

"So she's got some power?"

"We think it's only as much as the generals allow her to have. From the bank's perspective, at least a door into the country has cracked open for investments." He closed the laptop as if to signal the decision had been made. "The embassy says you can coordinate with the local police. They seem to be somewhat on the up-and-up —at least for that country."

Chandler pivoted on his foot. He walked to the tall window that overlooked the Nicollet Mall. "I'm concerned about Bridget; I've got a daughter of my own. But it's probably too late. Don't tell the congressman that. I'd call in the cavalry—some special forces —and make a quick effort to grab her. I've seen this before in the Middle East. Doubt it'll work, but it's the only chance."

Graves didn't answer. Chandler's work in the past had been exceptional. Lately, it was as if he'd given up. Nothing seemed to motivate him. It was part of the reason he was scheduled for an employment review next week. Graves hoped to force Chandler into an early buyout and get rid of him. He said to Chandler, "Maybe you could start there by interviewing a guy named Jeffrey Sumpter. He works for an environmental group called Free the Oxygen. Apparently, he was a close friend of Bridget's."

"And what do you think I could possibly do?"

"We don't trust the government to do much to find Bridget. God dammit, you're an investigator, right?" He stood next to Chandler and smelled the comforting odor of hash browns on him. Winter food. Outside, snow swirled on a stiff wind. Across the city, gray fog had settled to obscure the brown and black lumps of buildings.

"Any ransom notes? Things like that?"

Graves shook his head.

"Great. The more you tell me, the more attractive this sounds." Pete sucked in a deep breath through his mouth. "I'd like to help, but I'm not up for it."

Without saying it out loud, Graves didn't blame Pete. It was one thing for Bridget to be invited to investigate the bookkeeping of a timber company; it was another thing to try and conduct a missing person investigation in a country like Myanmar. If the government disagreed in any way, Chandler could be toast in a moment and "disappear" himself. It could be very dangerous.

Martin turned to put a hand on Pete's hard shoulder. "Think of the congressman, and think of Bridget."

Concern flashed across Chandler's eyes. "I liked her a lot. But I can't help for all the money in China . . . er, Myanmar."

"Don't worry about money—they're one of the poorest countries in the world. And, by the way, that's *tea*. All the *tea* in China."

"Your jokes stink."

Graves, tired of Chandler's resistance, yelled at him. "You're the one always telling jokes. You should like mine."

"Sure I do." When Chandler smiled, his mouth opened wide to show bright, straight teeth, but he wasn't laughing. "When I think back to Washington . . . I do owe Holmes; he saved me when I was at the lowest point in my life." Pete changed the subject. "What's the weather like?"

"Huh?" Martin backed away and put his hand on the window. It felt cold.

"Check it out." Chandler motioned toward the computer.

Graves went to the table and scrolled through his Dell to find the weather site. "It's still the dry season, and the temp is in the nineties. Monsoons will start in less than a month." He thought of the snow removal crews from the city, who were down on the streets pushing gray snow blowers with spinning brushes. "It's better than here."

"I hate hot. Ever since Iraq, I don't do hot."

"God dammit, Chandler—"

"So I better find her quickly and get back here."

Chapter Two

Yangon, Myanmar (Burma)

A cool breeze clattered in the palm fronds and tinkled the bells at the tip of the Shwedagon Pagoda, the holiest spot in the country, as if to warn people of the impending midday heat. A closeness in the air caused even the orchids to droop forward from their perches in the Bodhi trees. Station Commander Lieutenant Moe Ma Kha of the Yangon People's Police Department raced across the marble floors of the terrace.

He hoped the lab people would get here soon—not that the police had much of a lab. Electricity ran sporadically even in the biggest city in Myanmar. He wanted them to remove the dead body before it bloated and split into an open mess in the tropical swelter.

He also wanted to beat his commanding officers, who would arrive shortly. Would they let him keep this investigation?

Moe watched the pilgrims and worshippers who had climbed the Singuttara Hill to the fourteen-acre elevated terrace that surrounded the largest pagoda in the country. Covered in a half ton of real gold, the dome squatted like a fat bell, reflecting the morning sun. In contrast, the center rose to an elegant tip hundreds of feet in the sapphire sky.

The faithful Buddhists walked clockwise around the pagoda, searching for the worship area that corresponded with the day of the week when they were born. Many carried offerings of rice, white gardenias on strings, incense sticks, and caged doves. When they spotted the body and the blood pooled over the marble tiles, they paused, shocked. But after fifty years of brutal military governments, when they noticed Moe's uniform, the worshippers dropped their eyes and hurried away.

As the first police investigator to arrive, Moe was in charge of the crime scene, but he didn't think that would last for long. Because violent crime was rare in Burma and because the victim was obviously a Western foreigner, the generals from the *Tatmadaw*, or army, would certainly take over. Moe was careful to avoid making any mistakes. With his family's history, he had to be especially circumspect.

He looked up to see three monks coming toward him. They had shaved heads and cashew-colored skin and walked barefoot while the breeze blew their burgundy robes to the side to expose their legs. They, too, looked at the body, then turned away. Moe saw a crowd of military men following the monks.

The lead officer wore the most medals, and large gold epaulets covered both shoulders. Behind him, in descending rank, colonels and captains wore fewer medals. Moe recognized his boss, Brigadier General Lo Win, the head of the Command Investigation Division. He had the broad shoulders of a Brahma bull. The fat man next to him was also a brigadier general for the Special Intelligence Department, another one of the five departments of the State and Divisional Police Forces. The group reminded Moe of a school of mindless fish because they all turned in precise and identical movements. In deference to the Buddha, they were all barefoot, as was Moe.

There were all dressed identically—creased pants, tight green uniform jackets, and flat caps with black bills that shaded their eyes. Most of them wore sunglasses also.

Moe lifted his chest and saluted one after another.

"What have we got here, Lieutenant?" General Win demanded.

Moe felt sweat dribble down behind his ear. "Appears to be a murder victim, sir."

The general raised small pig eyes at Moe. "We don't have murders in this country."

"Of course not. It's an accidental death by unfortunate means." He glanced at the other officers for help. He saw a circle of round faces with flat noses and olive-colored skin—different from Moe, who was taller than all of them and had a lighter complexion, a product of his family.

"When did it happen?"

"I was called right after the opening of the pagoda and notified my supervisors immediately." When General Win peered at the others, Moe knew what he was thinking—why had it taken over an hour for him to be notified? But Moe knew the answer to that also, contained in an old Burmese saying: *The monkey you're calling is still up in a tree.* No one ever answered the phones at army headquarters before they were authorized to do so.

Moe finished the answer. "It must've happened recently. If it was last night, the dogs would've been here." He referred to the packs of feral dogs that roamed all over the country.

"You've identified the body?" the general asked.

"Yes, sir. Jeffrey Sumpter. He has an American driver's license. Age thirty. We checked with the US Embassy already. Apparently, he works with a nongovernmental organization on environmental issues."

The brigadier general nodded slowly, his mind digesting the information. "Good work, Lieutenant. The Command Investigation Division has once again shown how capable we are."

Moe let out his breath. He didn't think the generals would remain long, but their presence made him nervous. He hoped they wouldn't ask him to roll over the body. He turned to the side and pointed toward a trail of blood stains that led to the western stairs. "The accident must've happened over there, and the body was dragged here."

The general frowned and looked back and forth several times. His cheeks were pockmarked, probably from one of the common childhood diseases. With a grunt, he kneeled over the body and studied it. He stood up and tugged on the sides of his jacket to smooth out the chest of medals. "Looks like something I'd find in the fish market." He grinned briefly.

Moe agreed, which made the general's insistence on an accident ludicrous. The American had been gutted in a deep cut that ran from above his pubic bone in a jagged line up to his chest. Already the bodily gases had split his chest cavity apart to expose red and gray viscera.

The wind shifted and blew the fragrant smell of burning incense over the group.

Local law enforcement and the state police/army often had jurisdictional conflicts over crimes. Moe assumed the Tatmadaw would step in immediately. He said, "You'll be taking charge, sir?"

For a moment, the general's stiff expression softened. "What?"

"I mean, considering it is a foreigner."

"Well." He turned to confer with two underlings. They whispered in harsh tones. Turning back, the general said, "The army of the People's Republic of the Union of Myanmar is in complete control."

It was no answer. Maybe Moe still had a chance to head this investigation. He felt the stifling closeness of the air and removed the glasses he wore. He waited and clicked the bows against one another.

"In the meantime, get the body removed to a government hospital for an exam."

Yangon had both public and private hospitals. Those persons who could afford them went to the private ones. Since the government didn't put any money into the public facilities, the poorest people went there and received poor medical care. But a government hospital was also the perfect place to hide a dead body until the generals figured out what to do about it.

The general snorted. "Any idea what he was doing here? Pretty unusual for a foreigner to be up here so early."

"You're absolutely right. How insightful of you," Moe assured him, even while Moe remembered the general hadn't gone beyond the eighth grade in school before joining the army. Moe could smell onions on the general's breath. Moe added, "With the world's finest police force and the help of the people, I am confident we can fulfill your orders. But I don't feel worthy of your confidence."

"Lieutenant Moe Ma Kha is one of the finest investigators I have," General Win said to the curve of officers behind him. "I guarantee he will take care of the body without further problems." The gold braid on the bill of Win's cap looked like a string of scrambled eggs.

While the others murmured agreement, the commanding general said, "Our esteemed leader has ordered that relations with the West must be improved." The group of officers went silent at the mention of President Thein Sein. "Therefore, I will assign another investigator to help you," he told Moe. "Captain Thaung has a good history and will relieve you in the near future."

Moe knew that the only reason for the captain's presence was to spy and report back to the generals.

The sun crested the green roofs covered with scalloped gold decorative peaks and flooded the area where they all stood. Moe felt the humidity rise. Two girls walked by wearing silk blouses. On the back of one was a portrait of a smiling Aung San Suu Kyi, who had been released recently from house arrest by some of the generals who now stood around the body.

Moe heard the slap of bare feet hurry along the marble as the police photographer ran up to them. He stopped and waited until one of the generals nodded. The photographer stooped next to the body and flashed shots from different angles with an old 35mm Canon camera.

Some of the generals stepped back into the shade of a covered shrine. Behind gold columns, the Saetawmu Buddha sat on crossed legs in the shadows along the back wall. The image was made of solid gold, topped out at eight feet tall, and wore a breast plate and headdress of intricately carved gold. The ears looked larger than normal—better for the Buddha to hear the supplicants.

His eyes were closed, and a peaceful smile curved the corners of his lips. Seven stakes of jasmine incense smoldered before him. Too bad he couldn't speak to Moe about the crime he had witnessed in front of him.

General Win asked, "Was there any kind of weapon found, Lieutenant?"

"We've searched around the platform at the entrance and the elevator and the stairway." They all knew that foreigners were allowed up here only by way of the south entrance. "I went as far as the Jade Buddha but didn't find anything." He wondered to himself —with all the hidden, broken-down buildings on the street below, why would the crime occur up here? Why in the Shwedagon Pagoda? The mystery intrigued him.

"Lieutenant," General Win said, "any sign of a fight or reason the accident occurred?"

Moe shook his head.

With nothing more to do, the general shifted from one leg to another. HIs uniform had gone limp. The other officers looked up at the gleaming spire stretching into the sky above them. Sun reflected off the thousands of gold surfaces, concentrating the heat on them.

The brigadier general slapped his hands together. "That's it. Must have been a robbery. That's the problem with these new Western influences. They bring crime and corruption."

Moe kept a stone face as he thought of the United Nations' assessment of the generals' influence on their own government— one of the most corrupt in the world.

General Win glanced at Moe and said, "Carry on for now, Lieutenant."

Moe saluted crisply but felt deflated. He really wanted to solve this mystery.

The officers, apparently bored, moved in a pack toward the elevator of the east entrance. Three skinny dogs with bite marks on their backs trailed the group, hoping for a handout of food. The human group went through the large open doorway, stepped behind a bamboo wall, and disappeared down the elevator.

Pushing past them in the opposite direction, two lab techs from the station came toward Moe on bare feet. They carried a nylon body bag. The photographer backed away and told Moe he was done. Moe could smell curry on the man's clothing from dinner the night before.

Moe wanted Captain Thaung to leave also. While he waited, Moe paced back and forth. He looked over the walls to gaze across the city and the hundreds of trees sweltering under a hazy mist of humidity. He could smell the Yangon River on the breeze from the west. He admired the Thazin orchids growing in the trees. A national treasure, they bloomed in the winter. The force of nature pushed through the fuse of the green stalks to ignite a profusion of white flowers.

Finally, the captain said he would check with Moe later, at the station. He walked the same path as the officers had, and Moe could see the dirty soles of his feet as he padded over the hot marble tiles.

The girl with the portrait of Aung San Suu Kyi on her blouse came from the direction of the Padashim Buddha image until she saw the damaged body. She stopped abruptly but didn't turn away.

Moe thought of the secret work he did for Aung San Suu Kyi's party, the National League for Democracy. If his commanding officer ever discovered that, Moe would "disappear" into the Insein Prison in northern Yangon. Built by the British when they ruled Burma and called the city Rangoon, the joke was there were still prisoners held there from the 1800s—no one ever got out, especially now. But in a land of secrets, he had his own share of them like everyone else.

He looked up and saw three people standing next to a brazier of burning incense. They surrounded a white marble statue of Buddha about the size of a monkey. The people repeatedly poured cups of water over his head to wash down over his face, which had a horizontal red slash in the middle to represent the lips. They were washing away their past problems.

Moe wished he could do the same with the incompetent and corrupt history of the police: simply wash it away. If he had only been given the chance to investigate this murder, Moe might have been able to make a small difference for his country.

He helped the techs gather the body so it could be squeezed into the body bag. He looked at the long blond hair on the victim and the prominent nose that came with all Westerners. Luckily, the commanding general hadn't asked to have the body rolled over.

As the techs lifted the sloppy remains into the bag, they both jerked backward at what they saw. One stood up and refused to touch the body again.

Moe scrambled over and grabbed the small doll on the tile. Free of blood, it was male and dressed in a black cloak with bright red silk lining. Long black hair surrounded a marble white face. It was a *Nat*, or Natural. Although black magic had been outlawed in the country years ago, many Burmese still practiced a popular form of magic called *yadawa*. The practitioners worshipped Naturals—people who had died violent deaths but were thought to have mystical powers of intercession.

It was known that many of the ruling generals also depended on astrology and alchemist monks called *auk-lan saya*, or "one who's chosen the way of darkness," for the generals' decisions on many issues. The official religion of Myanmar was Buddhism, but alternative religious practices, including numerology and animism, percolated below the surface of the society.

The height of the Nats' powers came in the month with two full moons called the "black moons." It was a rare occurrence, but Moe and everyone else in the country worried about the black moons that were scheduled to appear in less than three weeks.

Moe wondered what the American had been doing at the top of a Buddhist pagoda with a Nat buried underneath him.

Only by threatening the techs with their jobs was Moe able to get them to carry the bagged body to the southern entrance and off to the public hospital. One of the techs would remain to clean up the blood.

He delayed at the scene and thought of what the generals had done to his parents and to his sister, Mi Mi. A fury overcame him so strongly that he felt like his stomach was boiling. His thoughts were interrupted by a commotion at the doorway to the stairs. General Lo Win walked slowly toward Moe, followed by his adjutant general.

When General Win stopped, his adjutant bumped into him. Win's small eyes pinned Moe backwards. "I have changed my mind. The Americans will come soon. Get this entire investigation finished quickly; the State Law and Order Restoration Council will be watching us closely." He adjusted his cap. "You speak the best English." The general turned and hurried to the exit.

Moe felt shocked but elated. He'd be able to work on his own, for now, without the Tatmadaw taking away the case. He'd solve it —but not in the way his commander assumed. Moe would solve it honestly and expose the truth. In order to do that, he'd have to be extremely careful.

Chapter Three

Minneapolis, Minnesota

Pete Chandler walked back to his vacant cubicle, which had tan walls nestled in a space next to where the skyway entered the main office building. If he left for Myanmar, he'd be away from his daughter for several weeks. Would it make things even worse between them?

He glanced out the window next to his cubicle and saw the brown and smoky colors of winter. After a new snowfall, the humps of snow could gleam white under a bright sun, but today they were blackened from the dirt of the streets. To Martin Graves' credit, he'd started a program to add more green plants to everyone's office in spite of the budget restrictions from Washington. What did they know about the monochromatic winters in Minnesota? At least there was a living presence of something inside the drab, cold walls.

He booted up his laptop and studied what little information there was available about Myanmar. Pete had started to boil water on the credenza while he waited for the computer.

Kendra Cooper, the other investigator in the cubicle next to his, stepped around the wall to say good morning. Her forehead wrinkled. "What's wrong?"

"I'm that easy to read, huh?"

"You think you're a tough guy, but I can see the soft spots."

"I'm going to Myanmar." He looked up from the computer screen.

"Where?"

"Southeast Asia. Bridget is missing there."

Kendra gasped. "When? Maybe she's just lost."

Pete explained what he knew.

"I can't believe . . . Is it dangerous?" She charged into the cubicle. "When are you leaving?"

Pete stood up from his desk. He walked to the credenza and selected a tube of Via instant coffee. He shook it into the cup of boiling water and stirred it. "Graves wants me to leave tomorrow if I can get a flight."

"Well, if anyone could find her, it'd be you."

He shrugged. "I don't know." He swirled a plastic spoon in the cup. "But I owe the congressman a lot, and I'm worried about Bridget. She'll get eaten alive."

Kendra cocked her hip to the other side. She watched Pete blow on the edge of his coffee cup. Then she said, "So there really is a hero inside of you?"

"Shut up."

"Besides, it may be good for you. You need a change. I know you're bored to death with this place."

"You're a broken record."

"*You're* the one who's broken."

When Pete worked as an investigator for the banking committee in Washington, he had seen and uncovered some of the worst garbage to be found in the political backwaters of the capital. Corruption, payoffs, cheating, lying, and the results of extreme ambition had been his daily environment. And even though he was an excellent investigator, he'd rarely exposed the problems he found. Instead, he'd become an expert at covering them up. Then, when the tragedy occurred, he felt totally lost.

Julie—an image of her popped into his mind, so real it seemed like he could reach out and hug her. An ache for her crawled up inside of Pete, and he remembered the sound of her laughter. It was pitched lower than he'd expected from such a small woman. It came from deep inside of her and was genuine, as if she enjoyed the act of laughing as much as the reason that caused it.

She used to tease him about the dimple on his chin. It matched the two dimples that were low on either side of his back. "So low, no one else should ever see them—*except me.*" Julie had always had the ability to bring out the best in him.

Then her political opponents threatened her with a scandal. Pete had used all his skills to help Julie avoid it. He worked harder than ever, but eventually her history was exposed. It shattered her, and she committed suicide. Of all the success he had had in helping others, Pete had failed Julie. His own world crashed in, and he limped back to Minneapolis.

Kendra curled her arm around the dusty top of the cubicle wall and waited for Pete to respond. *Broken.* He didn't want to admit it in front of her, but she had a point. He was scheduled for a performance review in one week. He knew what would probably happen. The bank had been anxious to get rid of him since he'd started working there. *Unamenable to the working environment*, the performance report had said. It was his nature to fight them, but it didn't seem worthwhile anymore.

But if he left for Myanmar, that would delay the review. He might be able to put it off for several weeks. His head nodded toward Kendra. "Maybe you're right. It might be good for me."

He thought of his daughter, Karen, who lived in St. Paul. Pete had never married her mother, and years ago, she'd broken off all relations with him, saying he "brought her down"—whatever that meant. Pete had tried to get closer to Karen, afraid he'd lose her also.

Kendra said something to him he didn't catch and retreated around the wall. Pete thought of how he'd like a drink now. In Washington, he'd always had a bottle of bourbon in his desk for the times the Southern congressmen stopped in looking for gossip and dirt. In Minneapolis, no one would ever even consider having booze around an office. And if they did, it would be white wine, inexpensive, but not bourbon.

He remembered that his father had always stashed a bottle in a lower drawer at his work. He'd been foreman, years ago, of the last steel foundry in South Minneapolis. His father liked to work with steel because he could "get his hands on a solid product." He'd often say, "It's worthwhile to go the extra mile to produce a good product for the customer. Otherwise, why go to work day after day?"

What kind of a product did a middle-aged investigator produce by digging around in other people's crap? It seemed like he had wasted so much of his life. Pete hesitated to call Karen, afraid that he'd make a mess of things again. His Samsung phone sat on the desk, its vacant black face like a bottomless hole.

Kendra popped her head around the cubicle again and said, "What will you do when you get there?" Apparently, she was more curious about this assignment than Pete.

He blinked his eyes and looked at her again. "Bridget had a friend there named Jeffrey Sumpter. I'll start with him, of course. Then I'm supposed to make contact with some low-level cop."

"Good."

Pete shrugged. "I'm sure they're all crooked."

"Why the hell are you so negative about the cops there?"

Pete raised his eyebrows. "After what I saw in other third world countries, I can't imagine this place is any different. Since Myanmar's been closed to the outer world for almost fifty years, it could be even worse. Their law enforcement is probably incompetent from top to bottom. Here, look at this." He rotated his laptop so Kendra could see it.

"According to World Audit, which checks out the conditions of democracy in every country in the world, Myanmar looks pretty bad. The Audit ranks countries based on their conditions of democracy, like human rights, political rights, civil liberties, free speech, and public corruption. Myanmar ranked 132 out of 150 countries."

Kendra squinted at the screen. "But look, they have a 92 percent literacy rate. Can't be all that bad. And they have some of the most exotic orchids in the world."

He chuckled as a way of disagreeing with her. "Oh, yeah? Look at the Google map." He keyed it open. "Where else in the world do you see this?" There were blank spaces in some of the northern sections of the country.

She stepped back and adjusted her sweater. "And you're so busy here," she mocked him. "Look at yourself. That plant, for instance." She pointed to the carcass of a palm in the corner of his office. "It's dead."

Pete glanced at it. "You mean watering it with coffee doesn't work?"

"I know what's wrong with you. You've lost your song."

"What?" Pete focused on her.

"I mean, you don't know who you are. Why you're here."

Pete collapsed into his chair and glanced out the window. The sky had a pearl tint to it. "Maybe you're right. I feel unconscious much of the time. Like I'm sleepwalking."

His phone rang. It was Connie from Human Resources. She'd booked a flight on Air China for the next day. "Don't miss it. The ticket cost me half my month's budget. And we got the State Department to fast forward your visa application." She paused. "And don't forget you have to fill out form INT 989. Graves will blow a gasket if you don't."

"Put it on my bill." Pete laughed and clicked off.

Kendra straightened her back and gave him one last piece of advice. "You've got to listen for the music in your life."

Pete smiled politely and waved her off as he called his daughter's number. Karen worked as a barista in a coffee shop while she pursued a full-time career as an environmental biologist. Her phone rang several times until she answered.

"Oh, hi, Dad. Sorry, we just had a rush." She shifted the phone to her other ear. "But now I'm on a ten-minute break."

Pete told her, "I'm going to Myanmar tomorrow. I've got an investigative assignment. One of our people is missing."

"Myanmar."

"Yeah, it's the old Burma in—"

"I know all about it. I've been volunteering for an NGO called World Democracy Empowerment. They're not officially supposed to be there, but they've made contact with the National League for Democracy and are helping with some money and work."

"What a coincidence."

"Be careful."

"I will."

"No, I mean even though the government has opened the country to tourism and some business, they're still a repressive, brutal regime. What other government can you imagine that not only imprisons Buddhist monks, but also kills them when they get in the way of the generals?"

"Isn't the National League for Democracy Aung San Suu Kyi's party?"

"Yeah. You must've done some research. She's out from house arrest, but they've got her quieted down, unfortunately. Although she's a member of their parliament, she's gone soft on the military. Of course, I don't blame her. When she criticized the generals, they put her under house arrest. I'd probably go soft on them, too."

"Sounds like a wonderful place to vacation," Pete said. The more he learned about the country, the worse it sounded.

Karen detected the sarcasm in his voice. "Hey, it's supposed to be a beautiful place full of gentle and kind people."

"I don't think those exist anymore."

"Aw, come on. You've gotten too burned out in your old age."

"I'd call it realistic."

She didn't respond. Outside his office, Pete could hear the murmuring of people walking through the skyways combined with faint sounds from the musician who always sat in the skyway playing for tips. Pete couldn't make out the words.

"And maybe you can get in touch with our Asian background," she said.

"I'm not Asian; I'm an American."

Karen sighed. "Aren't you interested in where your mother came from? Your heritage? What it means to you today?"

"Not particularly." Pete was born in San Francisco when his father had returned from the Vietnam War with his new bride. Soon after Pete's birth, his parents had divorced and his father moved back to Minnesota and remarried. He brought Pete with him. Since then, Pete had had only occasional contact with his birth mother.

"I think you're missing something in your life," Karen said. "I'd like to learn more about my heritage since it means a lot to me."

"Ah, what difference does it make?"

"Maybe you should fall in love." Karen giggled. "If you weren't so old, I'd introduce you to some of my friends."

"Your *Asian* friends?" He kidded her. "Won't work. I'm not on Twitter. I actually talk to people, face to face." He drained the last of his now tepid coffee.

"Seriously, Dad, be careful. The government's been actively fighting with several of the ethnic minority groups around the country for years. Wherever you go in the investigation, don't get mixed up in that. When will you be back?"

"The monsoon season will start in a couple weeks. I hope to find Bridget and be out of there long before that time." He paused, hesitant to bring up a tender subject. When he considered that he'd be gone for a while, he plunged ahead and asked, "How're you and Tim?"

Karen didn't answer for a moment. Finally, she said, "Fine. He thinks he's got a shot at being the sous chef at a new place."

"Oh?" Pete tried to think of what to say. "What's it called?"

" 'Ticket to Ride,' after an old Beatles song."

"I know the song. Uh, good for him." Karen and Tim intended to marry. Pete liked Tim but worried that his pursuit of a chef's job was crazy. How could he add to the financial half of the marriage if he were in a restaurant? Of course, Karen disagreed and called him "just an old parent." But Pete looked at it from a realistic viewpoint.

"Please don't say anything," Karen added, "but he's sacrificing a lot to get his dream. I believe in what he's doing. It's important. I know it doesn't sound like much to you, but he's giving something of value to people."

"I know. But there's no future—" Pete stopped.

"Oh, Dad, shut up. You always ruin everything."

"It's called trying to be helpful."

"Well, it's not. You just crush all the dreams we have."

"No I don't." From the skyway beyond Pete, a woman shouted something. He couldn't make it out through the thick sheetrock walls around him.

"Listen, I can't talk about this anymore. When you're gone, you should do some serious thinking. It's like you don't think *any-thing* is worth going after."

"Not true. And I resent you saying that."

"You can resent all you want. You'll really resent it if I disappear from your life."

"Don't talk to me like that," he shouted.

"Why the hell do you think Mom boogied?"

Pete felt a thickening in his throat. He couldn't speak.

"Hey, sorry. Not fair. Forget I said that. Hey, take care of yourself over there."

He managed to squeak out a few words. "That's okay. Wish Tim luck for me. I'll try to contact you when I'm there, but they don't have the Internet or cell phone service out of the country. I'll try the embassy."

"Well, I hope you rescue the girl. You're kind of a grandfatherly Indiana Jones." Karen paused and finally said, "Love you, Dad." She hung up.

Probably had to get back to her customers. Had to make more mocha lattes. Run plastic cards through machines. Pete slammed his palm onto the desk. Once again, he'd managed to screw up the communication. A good relationship with her was probably hopeless. The conversations with Karen were always too short, and she hung up too quickly.

Chapter Four

Yangon, Myanmar

The Air China jet slanted down through the bright sun on its approach to the Yangon International Airport. Pete saw tan and lettuce green patches divided by muddy rivers. As they came lower, a layer of dense green trees carpeted the land. It was punctured by the domes of pagodas, dotted across the ground like fat golden bells. The lakes glistened like blue sapphires.

The plane lumbered to a stop on the short runway. Pete climbed down the stairs from the side of the plane and stepped onto the tarmac. A humid blast of tropical air slammed into him. The wind blowing from the south helped cool the perspiration that started to spread across Pete's face.

He always traveled light, so he pulled only a small suitcase plus a backpack. He was tired from the flight and wondered how long it would take to get through security. Even before he left Minneapolis, he'd received a text from the US ambassador's administrative assistant, Carter Smith, who offered the embassy's help with the investigation to find Bridget.

All Pete wanted at this point was to get to his hotel, get cool, and get started on his work. Hopefully, the people at the embassy would clear up things for him and help. He'd find Bridget as soon as he could and go home. He already missed Karen.

As Pete got closer to the low terminal, he stepped over some broken concrete on the tarmac. The left side of the terminal had been built by the British in 1947 and was still used for cargo deliveries. Now it looked deserted. A new sign in gold trim read: *Welcome to the Republic of the Union of Myanmar.* He mobbed ahead with the passengers from the plane and entered the newer side of the terminal. They lined up to walk into a large room with two customs desks in front of them. He smelled the copper odor of sweaty people around him.

From all his years working overseas, he'd come to realize that it was important to withhold judgments about a new country and its people until he had been immersed in them for a while.

Pete ducked out of the line to find the bathroom. He found three urinals and two stalls. The stall didn't have a toilet but had a large hole in the floor with an outline of a foot stamped into the concrete on either side. At least there was a roll of toilet paper.

Back in line, he got through customs quickly.

With his luggage, he came out through a wide door to the lobby. Thank goodness it was air conditioned. He looked for the ambassador's assistant. He would be easy to spot since there weren't any American-looking people in the lobby. The few Caucasians stuck out because of their height and pale skin. Most of the people were short, brown, and had small noses. Both men and women wore long skirts called *longyi*. They came in bright colors, and many had geometric designs printed into the cloth. Everyone wore sandals.

A tall woman with strawberry-blond hair pushed through the herd of people and came up to Pete. She was followed by a Marine in uniform. Her face opened in a broad smile when she saw Chandler, and she introduce herself as Carter Smith.

"Welcome to Burma," Smith said as she pumped Pete's hand. "*Mingalar par.* That means hello." She must have seen the surprise on Pete's face because Smith said, "Expecting a man, right? I know. My father always wanted a boy but got five girls instead. I'm the oldest, so I was named 'Carter.' It was tough when I was a kid, but I like it now. Makes me different."

She pulled him by the elbow toward a glassed-in booth. The sign read "Change" in English, as did many of the signs in the airport. "You'll need some *kyat*," she told Pete. She pronounced it "chat." "They'll take dollars, but it's a good idea to have both currencies. You heard about the bills you'll need?" Smith turned to look at Chandler.

"I was told they'll only take brand-new, unwrinkled American bills," Pete said.

"Right. They worry about counterfeiting, as it's quite common here."

Pete stepped up to the security window and removed a one hundred dollar bill. The clerk looked at it carefully and turned it over to make sure it was crisp and didn't have any folds in it. He proceeded to give Pete a thick wad of wrinkled *kyat* in exchange.

When he finished, Smith pulled on his elbow again. "Let's get the hell out of here. It's getting hot."

Pete followed a step behind her into the crowd. The chattering noise of the Burmese language filled his ears. Sing song, it sounded like clanging bells, and it irritated him.

Smith wore a silk pineapple-colored blouse with the tails hung out over tan slacks. Her height masked her wide shoulders. Pete knew that she had worked for years with the ambassador, G. Anderson Popham, when he had been president of the University of Texas. Brown freckles splashed across Smith's pointed nose, and her pale skin was burned red. Her large teeth made Smith look like she was smiling all the time—even when she wasn't.

They walked outside to be assaulted by humid air again. Palm trees circled the edges of the parking lot. The fronds fluttered in the breeze. A few Japanese tourist buses slumbered in the morning heat, their engines running. Several of the tourists stood outside the vehicles, posing beside the front tire while their friends took endless photos. Then the person with the camera would trade places with the others, and more pictures were shot. Within a few feet of the parking lot, brown fields rolled off into the hazy distance.

"Here we go," Smith said as she opened the back door of a Mercedes for Pete. "Compliments of the President of the United States." She spoke with a Texas twang in her voice. A US Marine removed his hat and climbed into the driver's seat. He turned through the lot and was onto a bumpy three-lane road in a few minutes.

"We'll help you in any way we can. You're staying at the Chatrium Hotel, right? A nice, refurbished colonial place where Bridget was staying. When Hilary Clinton visited, she stayed there also." Her eyebrows pinched together. "This whole thing is dreadful. I didn't know Bridget well, but I'm quite worried about her." Smith's eyes refused to make contact with Pete's.

"Why don't we go directly to the hotel? It was a sixteen-hour flight."

"I'll get you there. In the meantime, I have to warn you about some things up front."

Pete sighed. "Can I meet with Jeffrey Sumpter tomorrow?"

Smith jerked to the side. "You don't know? He was just murdered at the main pagoda here. He and Bridget were close." She waved her hand in the space between them. "I know that's not your problem; we're working on it ourselves." The skin around her face tightened, and she explained the details of what was known about Sumpter's death.

"Murdered? I was going to start my investigation by questioning him." Pete slapped the arm rest. "Already things are worse than I imagined. Local police know anything?"

Smith looked at him and raised an eyebrow. "I thought that's why you were here—to conduct your own investigation. We don't trust anyone from the government." Her left eye ticked at times, like it was somehow broken.

"What about this local cop I'm supposed to meet?"

"A lieutenant named Moe Ma Kha. They've got the most mixed-up names in this country. Sometimes they take the father's name, sometimes the mother's, sometimes a new name altogether. How the hell they keep relatives from the big families straight, I don't know." Smith's demeanor changed as she drifted off into a different subject. Her attitude seemed inappropriate in light of Sumpter's murder.

The road narrowed as they drove across a flat plain of farms. At the edges of the road, ebony colored trees mixed with others that had yellow trunks with brown splotches. They passed a brick pagoda where Pete saw a dozen burgundy-clad monks lined up in front.

"Waiting for alms," Smith said when he noticed Pete looking at the monks. "Unlike the clergy in the States, these guys don't work, but instead, study all the time. They certainly don't 'minister unto the poor.' It's the reverse: the people support the monks by offering gifts. That could be food or money. The Burmese people feel strongly about the monks, and you're going to see hundreds of them. More than anywhere else in Southeast Asia."

They passed the Myanmar Golf Club on the left side of the road. The curbs on both sides were painted white, although most of the paint had flaked off. The traffic became heavier with buses, taxis, cars, pedal cabs, horse-drawn wagons, and small covered trucks. Dozens of people crammed inside the back end of one of the trucks, with a handful of men and women standing on the narrow bumper in the rear. They all wore flip-flops for shoes.

"Cheapest form of taxis," Smith explained. "It only costs them a few cents. And years ago, one of the generals got mad, so he banned motor scooters from Yangon. You'll see them all over the country except here." Smith waved her finger toward the traffic that buzzed around them.

"I'm really tired." He didn't want to tell her, but he felt depressed again. It was like he was living under a blanket and couldn't hear or sense much of what was going on around him.

They approached a large lake filled with green water.

"Inya Lake," Smith announced. "Built by the British as a reservoir. Now it's surrounded by this beautiful park." A white iron fence guarded the park from the people crammed onto the narrow sidewalk next to the fence. Inside the park, it was empty.

Pete noticed that unlike the brown countryside, the city was unusually green. Frangipani trees and flowering bougainvillea vines tumbled over walls, grew out of pots, and hung down the sides of buildings as if people had hung ruby-colored carpets to air out. They even grew in the vacant lots between dilapidated buildings.

They hurried alongside the lake for blocks until the traffic started to clog the streets and slowed them down. A low white wall ran beside the road with large letters that said *Yangon University*.

Smith offered more tour guide information. "Built by the British. It used to be called Rangoon University, the original British name for Yangon. When the democracy uprising occurred in 1988, the generals cracked down, shot about 3,000 student demonstrators in the streets—including children—and closed the university for over twenty years. It just opened again."

A headache threatened Pete.

The traffic closed in and stopped them all. Hundreds of people crossed the street and walked along the sidewalks. Many carried umbrellas to shade them from the fierce sun. Coming from bland Minnesota, Pete was happy to see all the colors in the clothing: bright blues, yellow, green, red, and burgundy. That interested him. "I didn't know there could be this much color in the world. Especially compared to Minnesota in the winter."

"Pretty, huh? It's like everything else that's smashed together in this country. Colors, smells, tastes, different people, with the beautiful next to the ugly." Smith seemed cynical about the government of Myanmar but genuinely happy with the people of the country. When Pete asked her, Smith said, "Many of them have entrepreneurial instincts that drive them like cattle heading for feed. Lately, the government has allowed a certain amount of low-level business to occur."

The traffic opened up, and the driver circled a roundabout. They headed east on University Road. Large mansions lined the street, shaded by broad-leafed trees. White iron fences separated the buildings from one another. A pack of three mangy dogs wandered between the store fronts on the opposite side of the road. People ignored them and walked in all directions over the broken sidewalks. Many of the stores were deserted and had tin roofs but missing doors. Bamboo shades hid the dusky interiors.

Smith continued, "It's important for you to understand that we estimate about thirteen to eighteen extended families control all the military. They've also divided up all the major industries and own everything. For instance, the Lo family may own all the cement companies or the battery manufacturers, so you've got some frickin' rich people hidden here. In the past couple years the generals have turned to the West for increased trade. That presents tremendous opportunities for American business, and that's what we're here to do—encourage that opportunity." Smith looked at him closely. "Are you okay?"

"Jet lag," he replied. That was partly true. Also, he felt despondent. Like his life, this mission, looked hopeless.

The Mercedes slowed at a mansion, waited until the steel gate rolled open, and pulled into the grounds of the United States Embassy. A narrow strip of grass struggled to grow in the dusty yard while a row of deferential frangipani trees shaded the flushed front of the building. The trees had fragrant flowers with pale yellow centers that changed to pink and white at the edges.

"Did you see that Lamborghini that passed us?" Smith asked Pete. When he shook his head, Smith continued, "That's unusual because the rich people don't flash their money or power. The Asian way is to be discreet about it. Hidden behind a plain wall, you might find a housing compound worth millions of dollars. We're convinced that some of the richest people in the world live here."

They all got out of the car, and the humid air doused Pete again. He realized it might take some time to acclimate to the humidity. What the hell was it like during the monsoon season? He hoped to be out of here by then. The sound of traffic carried through the fences, and he could smell the odor of diesel fuel from the trucks.

They entered the side of the sprawling building. Pete saw tennis courts in the back and wondered how anyone could play in this heat. Two Marine guards stiffened and saluted to them as he and Smith came through the door into the cool of the interior. Although the embassy had opened recently, the décor looked like something out of the 1960s—colors of orange, gold, avocado green, and rich wood tones. The end of the hall disappeared in dusky shadows.

"I bet you're hungrier than a baby calf stuck on the range in a blizzard. Let's go to the Teak Room for something."

"No, I'm really just tired. Listen, I appreciate your help, but I'm not going to be here very long. I don't need to know about all the details. I'll do my work and get the girl and get out."

"Of course. But you have to eat." Smith turned abruptly. "Here's the ambassador now." She lowered her voice and whispered into Pete's ear. "Don't ever call him Andy. It's always Mr. Ambassador or Anderson."

A large man appeared from the darkened end of the hall and came toward them. He had steel-colored hair that stuck up from a cowlick on the back of his head, and he walked with a slight limp. He stuck out a dry hand to Pete, smiled, and said, "Welcome to Myanmar. I'm Ambassador G. Anderson Popham." He gripped Pete's hand tightly. Muscles bulged out of Popham's arm as it extended from his short-sleeved shirt.

"Thanks," Pete said. "This must be quite a change from the university."

Popham shrugged. "I don't think so. We're still in the same business—trying to educate people. These people are wonderful, but they're far behind the rest of the world. They need our help desperately." He turned and pointed across the hallway toward the dining room. "You must be hungry."

"Tired."

"Carter will feed you first." Popham nodded at his assistant. "I hope you find Ms. Holmes. I only met her once. Nice young woman." His voice dropped to a lower pitch. "But I'd do it quickly. The generals won't like you poking into anything that might threaten them." As he leaned closer to Pete, Popham focused his jungle green eyes. "This place is wilder than an east Texas bayou and full of the same wily swamp adders." He stepped back and smiled briefly.

His eyes remained fixed on Pete, giving Pete an uncomfortable feeling.

Then Popham turned and walked down the hall in a rocking motion caused by his limp. He disappeared back into the shadows. But he left in his wake a sense of strength, a steel will, and a friendliness that seemed false to Pete.

Smith led Pete through the facility to a small, plain room in the back. It had several teak tables, each surrounded by four chairs. A few people were eating and said hello as they entered the room. She and Pete sat in the corner. "You've got to try the local beer."

"I'm not much of a beer drinker. Bourbon?" He thought of his father, who had never touched a drop of beer, preferring bourbon.

"Cocktails aren't popular with the locals. But as tourism grows, the restaurants are starting to stock some for the foreigners. I'm from Texas. Bourbon and branch water, usually. But the beer is great. It's a mild lager style."

Pete agreed and watched as a uniformed Burmese waiter set down a bottle with a glass. The label said *Myanmar* in yellow lettering over a bamboo-green background. In this hot climate, an ice-cold beer tasted perfect. Music played over the PA system, but Pete couldn't make out the details.

"So, let's get right to the problem, Chandler." Smith propped her elbows on the table and leaned forward. She lowered her voice. "Three years ago, Jeff Sumpter and Bridget Holmes wouldn't have been here. Our government had some of the toughest sanctions against this country. Since the new president, Thein Sein, took control in 2011, there have been reforms—but not much. We still remain deeply concerned about the lack of transparency in business here, the human rights violations, and the heavy-handed dominance of the armed forces in all aspects of the society."

"I know." Pete was bored with the talk and wanted to get some rest at the hotel.

Her voice took on a sharp edge. "Don't you think it's important you understand what you're getting into here?"

Pete waved his hand in front of his face to get her to stop talking. "Whatever."

"But you're of Asian descent. I thought that's why you were assigned here. Aren't you interested in your heritage?"

Pete snapped at her, "Not much. I'm an American."

Smith lifted her face. Her eyes stared down the length of her nose to search over Pete as if she were conducting an investigation. "Okay. Bridget didn't work for the embassy, but we helped her research in any way we could. There are a lot of mysteries in this country, and the government is very paranoid about outside interference with anything."

"Bridget's work for the bank was to investigate an agri-business company called the Yangon International Timber Company and prepare a financial report for our lending committee," Pete explained.

"That's what I understood. We were able to open a few doors for her."

"Did you get much cooperation?"

Smith leaned back and grinned. "One thing about the cowboys here—they all want more money and power. But at the deepest level, they all crave international respectability. Once you figure that out, you can work with 'em. And believe me, there's money to be made. The Chinese are running all over the locals. In fact, we think that's one reason the generals are willing to do business with the West. They're desperate to counter-balance the influence of the Chinese."

"And we're happy to help," Pete added. He hoped the cynicism in his voice was apparent to Smith.

She ignored him. "It's part of the President's 'Asian pivot' strategy for the region. We are working closely with more Asian countries like Vietnam, the Philippines, and Malaysia to increase trade and defense preparations to counter the Chinese hegemony. But be careful. Just below the surface that the tourists see, the government here is still as brutal and oppressive as they've been for decades." Smith's blue eyes hardened. "And the Chinese are equally ruthless."

"Thanks, but this doesn't help me find Bridget Holmes." He changed the subject. "What about Jeff Sumpter?"

Smith sipped on her beer, then lowered the glass. "I liked the young man. Engineer. One of those 'do-gooders' who go out in the world. Occasionally, they actually accomplish something. He was working with an NGO that advocated for environmental precautions. The generals are raping this country of natural resources at an alarming rate. We've made arrangements for the body to be shipped back tomorrow. They were engaged, you know."

"What?"

"Sumpter and Holmes were secretly engaged. Well, the American community here knew all about it. They were inseparable." Smith studied him closely.

Pete was surprised. Although the people in Minneapolis knew the two were friends, they didn't know about the engagement. That meant there was certainly a connection between the murder and Bridget's disappearance. "Have you done any investigation yet?"

"We've protested to the Myanmar government through the correct 'channels' but haven't received any help from them. Don't you worry about Jeffrey Sumpter; we'll handle everything through the State Department." By the tone of her voice, she dismissed any effort Pete might want to make.

He changed the subject. "I thought the country was rich in resources. Why are they so poor?"

"The country has more natural products than Texas has oil. Gold, precious gems—some of the most valuable rubies in the world—teak, minerals, and now oil and natural gas."

"So, what's the problem?"

"There's been a civil war going on for sixty years." Smith flicked a quick smile. "Because the majority people, the Burmese generals, want the natural resources located at the edges of the country. And the minority people, like the Shan or Kachin or Karen people who live there, don't want to give 'em up."

Pete sighed. It sounded familiar. He'd seen it in so many of the third world countries where the rule of law was non-existent. Governments used armed force to control things. For a moment, a wave of despair swept over him. It never changed in these backwater places. "How does the embassy fit into this?"

"For business to work, there must be stability—something that's threatened in this country right now."

"The civil war?"

Smith lowered her head and looked from left to right. Not that anyone was listening, but she dropped her voice. "Yes, but a bigger problem is the democracy movement."

"But our government supports that, don't we?"

"Of course—officially. But it leads to instability, which threatens trade and business and really is counterproductive to the creation of democracy. That's because when the generals get nervous about the movement, they clamp down harder on people's freedom."

It sounded ridiculous to Pete. Typical, convoluted behavior of politicians and third world dictators.

The waiter approached and set down a plate of stir-fried vegetables piled over rice with chunks of chicken on the side. "Hope you like curry," Smith said. "The Indians who came here with the British brought it." She used her knife to maneuver the food onto her fork. Smith chewed quickly and offered more unsolicited advice. "About your investigation? I'd start with the cop."

"I was told you'd provide a car and a cell phone that works."

"Yes, yes, of course. I'll get it set up before you leave here."

"What about local law enforcement?"

Smith grunted, "Worthless as balls on a mare. There's actually very little crime here, so the government doesn't put any resources into law enforcement at the local level. But don't believe much of what they tell you. Culturally, they will defer to you and they'll say whatever they think you want to hear." She took another bite of food. "Now, on the national level, that's a different color of cotton."

"What do you mean?"

Smith stopped chewing. "The army's doubled in size to an estimated 400,000 or more soldiers and keeps growing. But the thing to watch out for is the *Lon-Htein,* the riot police. Basically, they're thugs drawn from the poorest sections of the country to enforce the general's illegal dictates." She looked into Pete's eyes. "Whatever you do, don't get mixed up with them." Her left eye ticked twice.

Pete started to eat. The food tasted fresh, and the cold beer complemented it perfectly. The more he learned, the more hopeless his mission sounded. He'd stick to the original plan—try to find Bridget. He wouldn't spend time on Sumpter's death unless it had something to do with Bridget.

Smith pushed her clean plate away and signaled the waiter for another beer. "You could also check out Bridget's room at the Chatrium. I don't think it's been disturbed since the bank continues to pay for it."

"I've done a little investigation before. I can figure it out." He studied Carter Smith. Although she seemed helpful and friendly and concerned about the situation, she wasn't devastated like he thought she would be if a young American had been brutally murdered. From the kitchen, he heard the clatter of plates.

Smith leaned forward. "There's something else you should know." Her voice changed to a hoarse whisper.

"Oh?"

"Even though we're the embassy of the United States here, we can't always protect you. The wrong people could break you with as little concern as snapping a piece of bamboo in half." She drained the last of her beer while watching Pete.

Pete dismissed the warning since he didn't plan on doing anything to get himself in trouble.

Smith folded tan arms across her chest. "You're just like all the reports said. You seem disinterested. I hope you can handle it."

"I'll do my job." From the kitchen he heard the sound of plates clattering against each other. People shouted. "I wasn't close to Bridget, but I liked her and owe it to her father."

When Smith stood, she pushed back from the table, and the chair legs scraped across the wooden floor.

Pete stood also. He asked, "But why would this young guy be murdered and Bridget disappear? Did they find something that got him killed?" Pete realized that he might not be able to get out of Myanmar quickly. The more he learned, the more complicated and dangerous it became. He heard the crash of dropped plates smashing on the floor in the kitchen.

Smith's eyes lifted up to the left for a moment. They came back, dry, to look at Pete. "I'm sorry that I can't give you an answer about them. It's so unfortunate." She turned to the side to let Pete pass. Although Smith smiled and her dusty blue eyes followed Pete, he knew that Smith was lying.

Chapter Five

Chandler got back to the Chatrium Hotel late. Night dropped swiftly in the tropics and brought cooling relief. There were few lights along the Nat Mauk Road. Tomorrow, he'd be rested and could finally start on the investigation and finish what he'd come to do.

Across from the hotel, Bogyoke Park stretched off into the dusk under hundreds of tamarind trees. In the rental car, Pete stopped at the stone entrance to the hotel. Two uniformed guards came out from the bushes and used flashlights and mirrors on handles to search under the car. Satisfied there were no bombs, they waved him through the gate. Pete circled up an incline to the immense front door. He got out and felt a noticeable decrease in the heat. Fishtail palm trees swayed from the breath of the wind.

Another man, dressed in a short blue jacket and a red and blue *longyi*, welcomed Pete. "*Mingalar par*," the attendant said, and his round face split like a melon with a big smile. "Good evening, sir." Before Pete could act, the man grabbed his luggage and insisted on carrying it inside to the reception desk. "I take care of car, sir."

"Hey, hello. Okay." In the lobby Pete registered and turned the corner into a long open hallway. His shoes clicked across polished teak floors, and he noticed that the darkened wood continued halfway up the walls. Fans above him turned slowly in the damp air, which helped spread the air conditioning.

To his left, he looked out over a series of descending gardens overflowing with mounds of flowers. Royal palms soared into the deep blue of the evening sky, their fronds illuminated from underneath by spotlights. An L-shaped swimming pool reflected the lights back up to Pete. He stepped outside through the glass door in the hall and smelled the fragrance of gardenias.

The huge city around him had gone to sleep, and he could hear a soft wind, like someone breathing, above him. Standing on top of the highest hill and dominating the city, the Shwedagon Pagoda was lit up with bright lights. It glowed golden against the backdrop of the night. Pete had learned that it was fifty feet taller than the US Capitol in Washington. Tonight, it looked immense. Pete turned back into the hall, rode the elevator up to the fourth floor, and went into his room. It, too, had a polished teak floor, paneled walls, and a double set of French doors that led to a small balcony.

He found a Myanmar beer in the refrigerator and sipped on it slowly. He thought of his daughter, Karen. Would she be happy with Tim? Would they have enough money to live on? Would their cars continue to run through one more tough Minnesota winter? Halfway around the world from her, Pete felt powerless to undo the damage he'd done already.

He knew his obsession about Karen's problems stemmed from the vacancies in his own life. Karen had told him repeatedly that he needed someone. Of course, but that became harder as one got older. The few times he'd dated had gone badly. Pete recognized it was his fault. Inevitably, his thoughts always went back to Julie. In comparison to her, the new dates were pale and uninteresting. Besides, he often felt like he lived inside a bubble, unable to hear anything outside of it or to comprehend the world around him.

Pete left half of the beer unfinished, brushed his teeth with bottled water, and in the quiet coolness, he fell into a comforting oblivion.

The following morning, he went down to the dining room that flanked the gardens and pool. As at most hotels in Myanmar, a large breakfast was included with the room. He found a hot cauldron of *mohinga*, Burmese soup. It reminded him of Vietnamese *pho*, and he thought of his birth mother. He must have inherited his love of the soup from her. In his bowl, Pete added sprinklings of scallions, peppers, and lime juice to the noodles, vegetables, and meat. Two cups of black coffee filled him up. He was anxious to find evidence about Bridget's disappearance.

His first instinct was to check Bridget's room, but the hotel told him it was unavailable until he was authorized by some officials —whoever they were.

The appointment with the local law enforcement was scheduled early to avoid the worst heat of the day. Pete ordered his car brought around to the front entrance and got into it. He steered around the curve to exit onto Nat Mauk Road. The air was soft, and the broad leaves of banana plants, still cupping the night's dew, glistened in the pink sunlight. He merged into the flow of traffic and headed toward the downtown area. Along the side of the road, lotus plants floated in ponds and ditches. The flowers had opened to the day—pink, white, and blue.

Above the tree line he spotted the gold spire, or stupa, of the immense Shwedagon Pagoda. At the very top perched an "umbrella" from which hung precious jewels, all of them glittering reddish-gold in the morning sun.

The streets and sidewalks were packed with people moving in every direction and at different speeds. Most smiled from round faces and waved at him as he passed. The explosion of life all around impressed Pete. He glanced at the map spread out on the passenger seat. Although the streets ran in every direction imaginable, the main ones were easy to follow. He would have used GPS, but there wasn't any Internet access here.

Pete had been directed by the embassy to the Central Kyauktada Police Station and told that he could park in the small space in front of the building. It had once been used as the stables for the mounted police. Street signs were labeled in both Burmese and English. When he reached the station, it was a concrete building with little ornamentation. He parked and walked to the front door, guarded by windows on either side with heavy mesh screens. A blue sign in Burmese above the door was the only identification Pete could see. The Burmese alphabet was composed of many curved, twisting letters that all ran together without a break, making it look like the words were curled-up snakes.

He walked indoors, and it felt like a police station anywhere in the world—militaristic, orderly, surprisingly quiet, and so much testosterone in the air he could almost smell it. It felt comfortable. Pete identified himself and asked the three men who sat at a low desk for Lieutenant Moe Ma Kha. They all stood up when he mentioned the name. One man made several phone calls while the other two studied Pete's passport and the Ex-Im Bank identification for ten minutes. Finally, the lieutenant appeared from around the corner.

Chandler noticed right away that he was taller and more muscular than the average Burmese man. He also had a different look in the face. Not as round, longer, and with slightly lighter skin. Pete tried to shake his hand, but the man merely nodded with a brief bob of his head. He glanced at Pete's face but didn't look him in the eyes. "Welcome to Myanmar, Mr. Chandler." He spoke English.

"From the little I've seen so far, it's a beautiful country."

"You come at pleasant time of the year. By April, it will be, how do you say it? *Scorching* hot and is followed by monsoons. They come soon." Ma Kha wore the same uniform as the other men: blue trousers with a blue-gray shirt, blue epaulets on the shoulders, and a shield on the right shoulder containing the Myanmar flag. He wore a pair of black framed glasses which he swiped off his face while he chatted.

They both tried to make small talk, but it was difficult, and finally, they agreed to start the investigation. Pete wanted to get the entire meeting over with as soon as possible. He was certain this low-level functionary couldn't do much to help.

"I drive to—"

"Thanks, but I'll drive myself." Pete didn't want to be stuck in a small car with this guy for too long. The sing-song cadences of the lieutenant's voice irritated Pete.

Moe's head bobbed again. He replaced the glasses on his nose. "That is acceptable. Please, you follow Moe Ma Kha. Do you want to see crime scene or body of Mr. Sumpter first? We must hurry, Moe have to leave for other investigation."

"Let's start with the body." Although he wasn't officially investigating Sumpter's death, Pete thought it was a place to start. He followed the small black-and-white police car as it slalomed through the tight traffic. In ten minutes, they pulled up in front of an old red brick building. When he got out, Ma Kha was already moving toward the front door. He called over his shoulder, "One of public hospitals here. Main one Yangon General, built by the British. This one is smaller and used not much."

Pete followed him down deserted corridors into the basement. At the far end of the building they came to an abandoned kitchen. Wooden counters and lifeless steel ovens stood quietly surrounded by worn brick walls. It was cooler down here.

"This is place to store bodies. Old walk-in refrigerator work well."

Chandler laughed to himself. This is what they called their morgue? A damn kitchen? He'd view the body and get out quickly. Besides, the embassy was coming to get it later this afternoon for shipment back to the family in America.

He followed the cop into the largest refrigerator. They pulled humid air from behind them to create a cloud of steam that obscured Ma Kha as he tugged on a steel table with rollers. Pete brushed the cloud away as he leaned over the body, covered by a white sheet. The cop rolled it down slowly and carefully. A young face appeared, blond hair, waxy white skin, and then, below that, an opened chest lined with purple and blue colors. Although he was an experienced investigator, Pete turned away. He could never stand the sight of violent death.

And it had certainly been a violent death. In America, any medical examiner would be able to examine the body for signs of a struggle. The type of weapon used might be identified. Perhaps, scrapings from underneath the fingernails or blood transfers from the killer to the body would reveal the identity of the assailant. But in order to do that, one would need an up-to-date lab, qualified technicians, and a database of DNA samples—all of which Pete doubted were available here. A forensic psychologist might even be able to identify some of the personality aspects of the killer based on such a crude and violent murder.

He stepped back as Ma Kha reverently rolled the sheet up over the face. "Don't suppose anyone did an autopsy or a forensic exam of the body?" Pete asked.

The cop shook his head. "Cannot do such a thing on foreigner unless given permission. Besides, scientists are at conference in Mandalay." He removed his glasses and wiped the condensation from the lenses.

Scientists, Pete scoffed to himself. How many? One? Probably some kind of a voodoo witch doctor.

"But you do not understand how things work here." Moe interrupted Pete's thoughts.

"Huh?"

"The government scientists not get paid well. So, many record false test results and then sell chemicals on black market to have enough money to feed their families."

The state of law enforcement here was abysmal. "Anything found around the body? Any possible clues, something unusual?"

Ma Kha glanced at Pete for a moment and said, "No."

"Okay. I've seen enough." At least Pete had learned the death hadn't been a routine murder. Someone had gutted the body with violence. Unusual. That in itself could be a clue to be used later.

As they came out of the cloud of humidity, the lieutenant closed the door with a snap and looked up at Chandler. "Please, what is wrong? Your face has expression."

"Huh? Nothing. Let's go."

"I think you do not feel we are very competent here." He opened and closed the bows of his glasses, clicking the ends together each time.

"No, that's not it," Pete lied. He didn't want to get into it with this guy.

The cop stopped and propped his fists on his hips. "I normally do not meet with private citizens for official investigation. But commanding general ordered Moe cooperate with Americans." Ma Kha's face didn't reveal anything, but his voice betrayed his frustration.

"Humph. Kind of like my situation," Chandler said. He let out a big sigh. "Can we see the crime scene?"

"Of course." Moe Ma Kha led him back up the stairs, down the hallway, and out to their cars. He directed Pete to the Shwedagon Pagoda, which stood above everything else in the city. "Drive behind and you can find parking on side street. Most pilgrims come later today."

It took twenty minutes to cover the few blocks to the pagoda because of the twisting streets and dense foot traffic. Pete turned left on a street crammed with broad-leafed trees that hung over the sidewalks. Palm trees at the end of the street lined up to point the worshippers toward the base of the pagoda. He parked behind the cop's car and lifted out his leather briefcase. They walked along the narrow sidewalk past storefronts selling silk cloth, food, bicycles, hardware, and a few pieces of Western women's clothing.

The lieutenant stopped before a storefront that had several photos of Aung San Suu Kyi for sale. They were displayed along with pins, pens, and calendars all stamped with her image. High above, a red sign said in English, *National League for Democracy*. Under that it read, *Party Headquarters*. Moe peered into the dim interior.

Pete also saw a few tables with people sitting behind each one. A placard on one table read: *Health Care*. Another read: *Education*. A large stainless steel pot of rice balanced on a chair with an electric cord running from it across the floor to the wall.

Moe Ma Kha glanced back and forth along the sidewalk. "My sister work here when she can sneak in and not be detected. She will meet us." He started to walk quickly toward the pagoda.

Pete said, "What for?"

"Moe Ma Kha cannot be with you for investigation all the time. My sister need job, so Moe pay her to help sometime. She will be guide and interpreter."

"I don't need—"

Moe Ma Kha stopped and looked up at Pete. " 'Pardon me,' as they say in England. But you do not know much what is going on here now. Please, you must be careful."

"Okay. I've only been in Afghanistan and Iraq with the US Army. I'm only an expert in Tae Kwon Do self-defense, but you try to tell me what to do?"

The lieutenant blinked his eyes and said, "Moe Ma Kha is at your service." His head bobbed imperceptibly. Then he turned and started walking.

Pete followed and tried to stay on the sidewalk, but it was so crowded that everyone spilled out into the street. There were no lanes marked, so the vehicles swerved and sped up to get ahead of each other. People, clothed in a riot of color, walked in every direction. Packs of dogs ducked between the small houses and shops. As they came closer to the pagoda, Pete heard chanting from five monks. They sat in a row on the sidewalk with their eyes closed. Dirt from the street dusted their burgundy robes. One held a shallow lacquer bowl in his outstretched hands. Two *kyat* were crumpled in the bottom along with a plastic baggy of rice.

At the corner, next to a stinking sewer, three wagons with braziers mounted on the top offered grilled food. One dish looked like strips of pork, and the other two were blackened fish. Hanging off the front of each cart in a dented metal box were open bottles of dipping sauces. The food smelled wonderful, but Pete didn't dare eat anything.

Both of them finally reached a grassy area at the foot of the Shwedagon Pagoda. Pete felt drenched from the heat, but Ma Kha didn't seem to feel it at all. "We wait for sister," he said.

In ten minutes, a woman came from the opposite direction. She had beautiful, smooth skin, large brown eyes, and even though she was wrapped in a yellow *longyi*, Pete could tell she had a fuller figure than most Burmese women. She was the same height as her brother but had a lighter shade of skin. She carried a flat bag of striped colors over her shoulder. The lieutenant held both her hands in his and turned to Pete. "Moe's sister, Mi Mi Zaw."

She shook Pete's hand like an American. She smiled slowly but didn't show teeth. Under the broad brim of her straw hat, he could see that her cheeks were touched with pink from the heat.

"I am pleased to meet you. I like Americans," she said in a voice that was harsher than Pete had expected from the soft look of her features. She spoke with a slight British accent. It reminded him of his stepmother. She'd affect a British accent when she was trying to impress someone, in contrast to Pete's father, who was straightforward and earthy and talked like a steelworker. Pete had inherited his father's directness—sometimes to Pete's detriment. Although he liked to think of it as a dedication to honesty.

"Mi Mi like foreigners because our grandfather was British. Mi Mi study at Oxford in England. That is one reason we are both larger than other people here. Also, we are Shan."

"What?"

"Shan are one of minority groups in our country. Burmese are majority, but we are from northern part in mountains. There are also Karen, Kachin, Chin, and many other groups in our country."

"Yeah, like the US. We got African-Americans, Latinos, and—"

"And like us they, too, are discriminated, right?" His eyes, slightly magnified by the glasses, peered at Chandler for a moment.

Pete didn't like where the conversation was going. He changed the subject. "I want to see the crime scene."

"Of course. Let us go to work," Moe said as he turned toward the long covered staircase that led up the hillside to the pagoda above them. It looked high enough that it might snag on the cumulus clouds that floated across the blue sky.

Mi Mi said to her brother, "I only have enough petrol for today."

"That is not enough," the lieutenant sighed. He pushed back his cap and thought.

"Can I help?" Pete offered. What was the problem?

"Yes." Moe waved his hand at the dozens of cars snaking their way through the street. "All these cars running on black market gas." When Pete frowned, Moe continued, "We are allotted four gallons of gas, bought at official government station, per week. So people are forced to buy on black market at over ten times official price. Most of extra gas is 'leaked' from government officials who have access." He turned to Mi Mi. "Moe check later." He never answered Pete about how he could help.

Pete noticed that Mi Mi's right arm was bent slightly. She must've noticed him looking because she said, "I'm a bit gammy. Broke it in an accident years ago, and it was never set correctly." She smiled but covered her mouth with her hand.

"How did it happen?"

She didn't answer and looked away quickly.

As he walked next to her, Pete asked, "Do you have a family?"

"No. I would like to someday. But I am not married by my own choice." She didn't say anything more.

"What kind of work do you do?" He smelled wood smoke coming from inside the small shops next to them.

"I have a doctorate from the University of Oxford in olericulture."

"What's that?"

She laughed and her eyes teased him. "It's about the production and marketing of vegetables. In our country, we have a blooming abundance of them but are not able to take full economic advantage of this fact. I want to help develop that industry and bring our country into world trade system. I also love to garden."

"Makes sense. Did you teach in Great Britain?"

"No. Actually, I was offered a teaching position at the University of Wisconsin. That's near Minnesota, isn't it?" When he nodded, she continued, "Maybe I'm barmy, but I turned it down to come back to my country. I thought I could do more good here."

"So, what are you doing now?" Pete said.

Moe interrupted and pushed himself between them. "We must go to right here and take elevator. Pilgrims will use the long stairway. In Buddhism, effort to get to top of pagoda, like Nirvana, should be a difficult journey." He pointed ahead at a long tunnel of steep wooden steps covered by a series of overlapping roofs. Several decorative golden carvings crowned the top of each roof. His cell phone rang. Before answering he said, "Sometimes we have service."

Moe talked for a few minutes. He frowned and took a deep breath. When he clicked off, he said, "That was call from Captain Thaung." A quick glance passed between him and his sister. "He may have new assignment and cannot spend time on Moe's investigation."

In ten minutes, they emerged from a small elevator on the south side of the monument. They all removed their shoes, setting them on wooden bookshelves. Moe and Mi Mi wore sandals. Pete removed his leather shoes and socks. Then they entered the religious area.

Pete stopped walking and took a deep breath. The heat bore in on him, making him miserable, but the marble floor felt cool and dry on his bare feet.

Immediately in front of him rose the golden spire of the pagoda, squat at the base, wide as a mountain, in the shape of a bell, and rising gracefully 326 feet up into the sky. Surrounding the main stupa were dozens of small replicas, each one twenty feet tall and covered by gold. Anything that wasn't gold was pure white marble that reflected the blinding sun. As far as Pete could see, pagodas of different heights dotted the immense terrace. He'd read earlier that the complex had 4,000 bells and more than 83,850 precious gems either hanging from the spires or imbedded in the statues.

Monks strolled all over, including some dressed in pink with shaved heads—female nuns. Hundreds of people circled the edifice. Some had serious expressions; others waved cameras and smiled as they posed in front of various temples.

Moe stood silently while the monks passed them. Then he said, "Please, over here."

Pete hesitated for a moment, stunned by what he saw. Finally, he followed Moe to stand in front of a small temple. In the dark recesses, he saw a Buddha sitting with crossed legs. The entire statue was covered in gold. Before it, lotus flowers on delicate strings, birds in cages, rice, and sticks of burning incense had been offered for the "merit" of the faithful.

The beauty and serenity of it all dazzled Pete. It reminded him of old cathedrals in Europe—all the intricate ornamentation, the gold, the immense size of everything, and the grandeur of the artistic design.

Moe Ma Kha waited, then said, "Please to follow me." He led the other two around the corner of the temple. He looked down at the marble and said, "Here we find body. And blood went back in direction we came from." He took off his glasses and clicked the bows together.

Pete was astounded. He couldn't believe there wasn't any crime scene. "Where is it?" he demanded.

"What?"

"The tape to protect the integrity of the scene, the markings where the body was found, the analysis of the area around the body for forensic clues. The blood is gone—"

Moe looked back and forth over the marble as if he were trying to find something. He looked up finally. "Yes. Samples taken. Then we move everything."

"Figures," Pete muttered.

"Would you like to look at picture?" Moe reached into a red cotton bag that hung by a strap from his shoulder. He pulled out a stack of photos clipped together in an organized manner. "Taken after I got here and discovered body. Nothing was touched," he said proudly.

Pete took the crisp photos and paged through each one. When he finished, Pete looked up and said, "You call this a crime scene?"

"Yes. In Moe's country it is not common to have death like this—unlike your country. Therefore, we do not have resources for investigation. We will do orderly search for truth with harmony and discipline according to procedures."

"What the hell do you expect me to do now?"

"You do what you need, please," Moe said. "Moe has been authorized to help you." He stared at Chandler for a moment before turning his eyes away. "What do you want?"

Pete ran his cupped hand over his hair and turned around while he thought. "I learned that the victim and my missing lady were engaged. So, it makes sense they might have been together up here." He looked at Ma Kha as if to ask for his opinion. The man didn't respond. Pete continued, "Did you talk to any of the people at the stairs? Show them pictures of Jeffrey Sumpter or Bridget Holmes?"

Moe frowned. "Yes. We know nothing about missing person."

He must have meant *No*. "Talk to any witnesses?" Pete asked.

"There no witnesses."

"How do you know if you didn't ask?" Pete's voice rose again, and he slapped his arms along his sides. This seemed even more hopeless than he'd expected. "Okay, let's forget the crime scene. I've got to find some evidence, something to work with. Let's start by talking to any possible witnesses." He paged through the accordion file he carried in his briefcase until he found a rumpled eight-by-ten blow-up of Bridget's face. Three uniformed soldiers came around the corner of the shrine and walked past them.

Moe watched the soldiers until they passed and then studied the photo. "Good. Moe must now leave. Moe report to divisional commander and work on other case. But Mi Mi will go with you to interpret." Moe dipped forward toward Pete in a shallow bow while he placed his palms together in front of his chest as if he were praying. "You contact Moe Ma Kha any time." He left on silent, bare feet.

Pete forced himself to remain calm. Was this all the help he would get from the local law enforcement? He remembered the original plan and, as he got more involved in the case, he determined that the plan would be exactly what would happen—a quick investigation to discover Bridget and rescue her, and then the flight home. He looked at Mi Mi. She smiled at him, and she didn't seem to be affected by the tension between him and Moe.

"By the way, why do so many people here bow with the folded hands?" he asked.

"It is a sign of respect and friendliness."

"Huh? After the way I've treated your brother, he still does that?"

"We don't get argy-bargy. Instead, we respect all people and wish them good luck."

"Hmm. Let's go. Take me to the end of the stairs so I can show this photo around. I'm trying to find out if anyone spotted the girl and her boyfriend coming or going."

They spent the next hour moving from one entrance of a stairway to another. They talked to the guards at the elevators. They stopped janitors who swept the vast expanses of marble and polished wood of the floors. They questioned some of the vendors who sold offerings at the foot of each stairwell. Mostly, they were met with silence.

Pete felt the sweat running down the middle of his back. He realized that the dark golf shirts he'd brought and blue jeans were the worst clothing he could wear. Tomorrow, he'd have to buy something cooler. Crowded by cumulus clouds, the sun crested the sky and started to drift down the west side of the golden dome. Three soldiers stood against a palm tree and watched Pete and Mi Mi.

As if to confirm that, she whispered, "*Lon Htein.* They're smarmy, come on."

They worked their way around the outside of the pagoda, questioning everyone Pete could stop. A half hour later, the three soldiers were still following them. Pete and Mi Mi came down the steps between two immense white lions, two stories tall, that guarded each side of the south entrance. The lions had green eyes with red eyeliner and open mouths that could be either grinning or menacing.

At that point the street made a sharp turn. The soldiers had maneuvered to their left and approached. One larger man appeared to be the leader. He wore a camo-green fatigue jacket, creased pants, and jump boots. He looked directly at Pete for an accusing instant.

Pete realized that it wasn't a coincidence that the soldiers happened to be there. He looked back in the direction of his own car, calculating how far it was and how long it would take to work his way through the crowds to reach the car. Would the crush of people buy him enough time to escape?

Don't run, he told himself. When he was younger, he wouldn't have hesitated to fight. But that instinct had gotten him in unnecessary trouble. Particularly if he felt the fight was for the underdog. When he was in high school, he'd found a mob of guys in the back of the bus garages. They'd circled another boy who was teased a lot. The crowd taunted him to provoke a fight. When Pete saw it, he exploded. With barely a minute to think of the odds against him, he plunged into the group to protect the lone boy. Pete saved the kid but suffered a few punches himself. Since then, he'd learned to think and react by talking his way out of trouble.

As the soldiers surrounded Pete now, he hoped that he and Mi Mi could fade into the crowd.

He grabbed Mi Mi's elbow and turned to the right. Without looking back, Pete started a forced march toward the narrow side street. He'd gone a half block when he felt someone grab his shoulder. His first instinct was to swing on the guy, knock him off, and run. He flattened his right hand to prepare a martial arts chop.

Before he could attack, the soldiers surrounded him. The leader shouted at Pete, "You violate Code 47. We question you." A bright streak of sweat coursed down his cheek.

The heat made it feel like an elephant was sitting on Pete's lungs. "Hey, buddy. You got me wrong." Pete smiled in a lazy way as if to say it was a mistake. No big deal. He pulled out his driver's license. "American citizen," he said, hoping that would deter the soldiers. They were small and looked almost like children except for the Chinese automatic weapons cradled in their arms.

"We watch you. You come for question. We promise not keep you to miss dinner at fine Chatrium Hotel."

How did they know he was staying there? "No, I think something's wrong. I'm not going with you."

They closed in on him. Pete worried about Mi Mi. When he looked for her, she'd disappeared.

The soldiers pushed Pete around a corner into a quiet, deserted street. It curved in an "s" pattern. Small, empty shops fronted the street. They had tin roofs and no doors, and some had sheets of torn plastic hanging from the sides. A silent pack of dogs shadowed the group as they trudged along. Two people stood before a brazier in the street. Pete could smell something greasy. They refused to raise their heads when the group passed.

The road narrowed as they moved deeper into the neighborhood. The soldiers prodded him around more corners, around holes in the street, and turned again and again. Pete tried to remember the route but was soon lost. Piles of garbage were strewn across the old pavement, forcing the group to zig-zag to avoid them. Pete saw an old man lying in the broken remains of a storefront. He looked like he was either sleeping or dead. He was the last civilian Pete saw.

The angle of the sun changed to throw the streets into deepening gloom. The soldiers finally came to a stop. Wire fences prevented them from going further. It was a dead end. The group turned to the right, and the men shoved him toward an open door in an old shop. The inside was dark, and he couldn't see anything. From somewhere he could smell smoke, and it stank.

As he stood at the edge of the door, one of the soldiers slammed his rifle butt into Pete's back. He pitched forward into the room, his brain going as dark as the interior.

Chapter Six

When he woke up inside the building with his face on the floor, Pete could see mold growing along the wall, green, black, yellow, and orange, some fuzzy, some with a sheen. Coming in from outside, he didn't think it could be any more humid, but it was. He tamped down the bubbling of fear in his belly that almost made him throw up and tried to figure out a way to escape.

There were two couches set at an angle to each other. A small TV with rabbit ears was balanced on an overturned box between the couches. Two ashtrays spilled light gray ash onto the floor. As he was heaved up onto one of the couches, Pete heard two of the men laugh. One soldier slammed a hand into his back. Pete's neck jerked, and he flopped onto the couch. He sank down, and it seemed like he was sitting on the ground, so low he could see the layer of dirt across the floor. It made him feel defenseless.

God damn Moe and his sister. They must've tipped off the Lon Htein. Why else would Moe leave suddenly and Mi Mi disappear? If Pete ever got out of this alive, he'd find them and take his revenge.

Another soldier went to the open window and turned on a circular fan. It scraped to life and blew hot air around.

All of them lit cigarettes. One sat on the arm of a couch with his leg hooked over the edge. It dawned on Pete that this was an "R and R" spot for the soldiers. They could come here to relax. The thought made him feel slightly less nervous. Except that it was hidden. They would be free to do whatever they wanted to Pete, and no one would ever find him.

The leader looked at a thick watch that was too big for the size of his wrist. "Okay. Start," he grunted in poor English. He studied Pete briefly with soft brown eyes. "What you do?"

"Huh?" Pete stalled for time. He scanned the room. The only ways out were the door behind one of the soldiers and the window with the squealing fan. Could Pete bolt toward either one? Knock down a soldier and escape? And even if he did, where would he go? The shop was hidden in some shit-hole neighborhood. He decided to play dumb and hope they'd grow tired of the interrogation and let him go. This had happened to him twice before in Afghanistan. He'd made it through those sessions; he could make it through this one also.

"Why you go Pagoda?"

"I'm a tourist."

"Not funny." The man stepped closer and shouted in Pete's face. "We watch you for long time. No tourist ask questions."

Pete had time to look at the far side of the room. A metal file cabinet with a dent in one side stood beside a desk. On the wall a calendar boasted the photo of a beautiful woman. Next to it was a series of male photo portraits. Each head was shaved, and the bodies were cloaked in burgundy robes. Were these the top five monks in the country? Like a series of movie stars? A small statue of Buddha rested on the far desk, smiling, with closed eyes. He'd never be a willing witness to what might happen to Pete here. The two other soldiers jabbered in Burmese. The sound of it irritated Pete.

Pete smelled the smoker's breath of the man before him. "I'm here because I'm curious about your beautiful country and temples," Pete said.

The soldier slapped him across the face. When Pete straightened up, the soldier motioned for Pete to give him his wallet. He handed it to the soldier, who cracked it open and fingered his way through it. "Where is passport?"

"Back at the hotel."

"Passport," he demanded again.

"It's back at the hotel." Thank God Pete had left it there. Without the passport, he would be stuck in this country for a long time—something he didn't want to think about.

"Okay." The leader nodded and stepped back beside the TV. "Okay. What you look for at Pagoda? You talk many people."

Pete hesitated and looked around at the group. They all looked aggressive. And Pete had been around military men long enough to know they were usually bored. So when they had an excuse to get rough, they jumped at the opportunity. What would they do here? Maybe if he gave them a sliver of the truth, it would satisfy them and he'd get out. "I was looking for someone."

"What name?"

"A person I work with."

"Who?"

"Her name is Bridget Holmes."

The leader looked from one soldier to the other. One shrugged. The gesture made Pete relax. Maybe they weren't Lon Htein but just local cops checking on suspicious people. From behind the leader, the soldier came forward and pulled out his weapon from the holster. The leader didn't stop him. Unconsciously, Pete tried to sit up. He couldn't and slipped back down into the couch, which made him feel even more vulnerable.

It looked like a Chinese M77B pistol, and it looked new. The Chinese had stopped using it in the People's Liberation Army years before and, instead, exported them around Asia.

The fan pulled in the smell of bird shit from outside the window.

From his training, Pete knew that he should stay calm. But he felt sweat covering his chest. He moved his eyes away from the gun. The leader jerked his head toward the man sitting on the couch, who rose to follow the first one into a dark corner. They talked between themselves. They came back to the couch.

The leader cleared his throat. "This warning. You not go."

The man with the gun pushed it into Pete's face. If there hadn't been three of them, he would have been tempted to grab the pistol and take his chances wrestling it out of the soldier's hand. Pete remained still. He nodded.

"You violate Article 47. No more. We watch you."

"Okay, okay, I got it."

The leader raised Pete's billfold and pinched all the cash between his fingers. "You pay fine in Myanmar for violating."

"Sure. Of course. A fine." He was surprised at first. He felt his chest relax. This was just an Asian version of a speed trap—although a lot more scary. Would they leave him here? If so, he'd never find his way back.

The one who had been on the couch stubbed out his cigarette in the ashtray, dislodging a gray clump onto the floor. They seemed ready to leave. Pete heard the squeal of car brakes outside the door. Now what? The soldiers looked as surprised as he was, and Pete thought of making a jump out the window, but they still stood too close for him to make it.

There was shouting from outside, and two more soldiers came through the door. These were older men and must have been officers by the look of their medal-clad uniforms. They all wore flat hats with shiny black brims. After they entered the room, they stood off to one side and waited.

In a few minutes, another officer was at the door. A general. Pete could see the pockmarked cheeks under his wrap-around sunglasses. He came in slowly, as if his bull-like shoulders could hardly fit through the narrow door. He took a few steps to stand in front of Pete, stared at him for a long time, and finally said, "You violate Article 47."

"Yeah, somebody told me that before." The minute Pete said it, he regretted the tone of his voice.

The general stepped to the side and, with a faint nod of his head, looked at the "passport" soldier. He came back over, stood in front of Pete with his legs braced wide apart, and took a professional swing at Pete. The blow hit him high on the head and knocked him to the side of the couch.

"Passport" moved over and lifted Pete up into a sitting position again. Pete's head rang and he fought to avoid blacking out.

"General not like Americans," the general said. "You bring filthy sex practices and corruption. Why you at Pagoda?"

Pete's brain struggled to understand the words. He mumbled, "Looking for someone I work with." He thought of how Moe and his sister had led him there and probably positioned him so the Lon Htein could grab him easily.

"You ask for young man?"

"No, not really. I'm here to find Bridget Holmes."

One of the soldiers circled around behind the couch. The general said, "We investigate young man. You do not need to."

"I told you, I'm not particularly interested in the guy."

"Why you look for woman?"

"Her father is a very important man in our government. He wants her found."

The officer took a deep breath. "General know of woman. Boyfriend dead. General not know where she go. Like you say, disappear." He chuckled again. "General's problem is you. Our country is peaceful democracy. People bring trouble. That is you."

Pete started to protest but didn't want to get hit. He waited.

"This is gentle time. You want water?"

When Pete nodded, one of the soldiers brought over a hollowed-out gourd. Inside, dirty water sloshed around. He dipped a dented cup into the mess. Pete decided to ignore all the health warnings he'd heard about the water in the country. He gulped as much as he could. It tasted warm and metallic.

"You stop investigation." The general sighed as if he were already tired of the questioning.

"I'll think about it."

The man behind the couch grabbed Pete's chin, and jerked it backward to pull his body upright on the couch. At the same time, "Passport" came in low and swung his fist into Pete's exposed stomach. The breath burst out of him. He fell forward and tried not to throw up. When the coughing stopped, he gasped to get some air into his lungs.

The general removed his sunglasses and came closer. He had small, pig eyes. "You think we not serious? General warn you. Go Chatrium Hotel, pack suitcase, and leave our peaceful country. There is nothing more you do. This time General warn you. You not look for woman. Forbidden by Article 203 of People's Democratic Code of Conduct. Instead, you leave country." The general leaned closer to Pete's face, and he could smell heavy cologne. "Understand orders?"

Pete's voice rasped, "Is she dead?"

The general stood back and didn't say anything. The officer on the left side leaned closer to the general and said something into his ear. He blinked several times and nodded. He turned back to Pete. "What trust do General have you leave country?"

Pete felt a fury growing inside. Like the teenage brawler he'd been, he didn't like being pushed around and decided to fight back. "I don't plan to leave your fucking country until I find the girl."

The general's eyebrows dropped low over his squinting eyes. Then a faint smile turned up the corners of his mouth. He looked over at "Passport" and nodded. Passport came back to stand in front of Pete.

He braced for the next blow.

"General decide of a way to make sure you stop investigation." The general laughed to show gray teeth. "Now, you chose to not leave country—ever." He stepped back and turned around to walk toward the door. "Passport" waited.

Outside, Pete heard tires scraping, car doors slamming, shouting. He thought of trying to slither out of the couch, get on the floor and try to scrape his way to the window before the reinforcements got there. They'd probably kill him before he got close, but he wouldn't die lying on this stinking couch. As the soldiers in the room all turned toward the door, Pete made his move. He rolled over the edge and hit the floor. It hurt all along his side.

He heard more shouting and expected that at any moment, the new soldiers would finish him off for good. A thought of his daughter flitted through his mind. Someone barked, "United States Marines. Stand down!"

He heard people speaking perfect English. They shouted and the soldiers shouted back in Burmese. Pete used his elbow on the edge of the couch to raise himself off the floor. His eyesight was blurring, but he saw three US Marines in full uniform take command of the room. Even after all his years in the Middle East, these guys had never looked so good. He saw two of the Lon Htein jump out of the window, knocking the fan onto the floor, where it whirred and blew dust all over.

Pete didn't see the general. He must have escaped outside. The room went quiet except for the rasping fan. A dove cooed next to the open window.

In a few minutes, Carter Smith stepped through the door. She came over to Pete, called for two of the Marines to help him get back up onto the couch, and kneeled beside him. "I tried to warn you, Mr. Chandler." Her left eye ticked a couple of times.

"Thanks," he croaked. "How'd you manage to find . . ?"

"Moe Ma Kha called the embassy. He said he couldn't get involved, but tipped us off about the grab and suggested they'd taken you here."

"He called you?"

"Right."

Pete shook his head. He couldn't believe the news. "Okay." He tried to stand, couldn't, and was helped up by a young Marine. Pete finally stood on shaky legs.

"What the hell happened here?" Smith asked.

"They tried to warn me about continuing the investigation for Bridget. Told 'em to go fuck themselves. That's when they got rough."

"You just can't avoid a fight, can you?"

"Now I'm mad. If they want a fight, I'm ready."

"You're going to die the next time they get you," Smith corrected him. "I told you about these thugs."

The Marine helped Pete stumble to the door, step outside, and walk to the Mercedes parked under the frangipani tree. Delicate white petals had drifted down to cover the roof and the street around the car in a circle. It looked like snow.

Pete propped himself on the side of the car. Smith followed him. "Listen, Chandler, I don't particularly like you, but let me tell you something. This country's a mess. Your lone search is going to be tough, and now, it looks like it'll be dangerous."

"Maybe." He took a deep breath of fresh air. Even though he still didn't trust her, she had saved him. Pete would at least listen to her advice. The heat was leaking out of the day, and he didn't smell the wood fires anymore.

Smith asked him, "So, what did you find?"

"Huh?"

"At the Pagoda. What did you find?" Her eyes searched across his face.

"Not a God damned thing." How did she know he'd been at the pagoda?

She sighed and backed away.

Smith had four Marines with her, all of them armed. Two helped him climb into the Mercedes with diplomatic markings on the side and an American flag mounted on each of the front fenders. He described where he'd parked his car near the National League for Democracy headquarters.

"You're at the NLD?" Carter asked while her eyes opened wide.

"That's where Moe told me we could find space to park."

"Of course. Volunteers and workers don't advertise their presence there, so the parking is usually open. No wonder the Lon Htein followed you. What the hell did you think?"

It hurt to turn his body in the back seat, so Pete just said, "How did I know? Don't they have a fuckin' parliament in this country? Isn't that woman, Aung San Suu Kyi, elected by the people?"

Smith sighed. "You don't know a damned thing about this country."

"But this taught me two valuable things." He waited until she got into the other side of the car. "One is that we're obviously onto something important here. Why would a general be interested in beating me up? Unless he's worried I will uncover something really big."

Smith didn't respond.

"And the best news is that Bridget is still alive."

"They told you that?" She looked out the front window of the car.

"Not in so many words, but the guy with the pig eyes didn't say she was dead when I asked him. So, I think she's probably alive— somewhere."

"That may be true, but you should go back to the States. Take care of yourself; this'll be a waste of your time."

It was tempting, but he said, "I'll go back soon. I'm not going to give up my life for something like this, but now I'm pissed off. I want to check on a few things. What about Jeff Sumpter?"

"Don't worry about him. We'll take care of it."

"Funny, that's just what the general told me."

She waited for a minute, then looked over at Pete. "All right. Have it your way. But I can offer you valuable help about Bridget. We'll look for her together."

A Marine started to shut the door on Pete. He took a last look around at the dark, abandoned buildings. Pete hesitated, then said to Smith, "Yeah, I guess I could use some help."

Chapter Seven

The following day, after three gin and tonics and dinner in the open-air lobby overlooking the hotel pool that led to ten hours of sleep, Pete felt pretty good. One of the best legacies of the British occupation of the country was the gin cocktail which they convinced themselves prevented malaria. Pete took the modern anti-malarial pills but thought the tonic still must have some benefit—he had assured himself as he drank them.

He'd previously been inoculated against yellow fever, hepatitis A and B, dengue fever, typhoid fever, and Japanese encephalitis. If one of those wild dogs bit him, he'd need the series of rabies shots also. This was a country that didn't even have clean drinking water —anywhere.

He wanted to get into Bridget's room as soon as possible. Several weeks had already passed since her disappearance. Any evidence had probably already been taken by the government. The hotel management finally said he had permission to look at the room and that a maid would open the door for him.

Since he'd arrived in the country, Pete had realized he'd need more help but didn't know where it would come from. In spite of Carter Smith's help, Pete didn't trust her.

He ate his breakfast in the garden near the pool. From the tops of the palm trees hundreds of birds chattered, and Pete watched pigeons and zebra doves dart in and out of the green shelter formed by the drooping leaves. He drank some of the good coffee that was offered everywhere. He didn't believe that he could ever give up his Starbucks coffee, but this was pretty good.

From the tamarind trees behind him, Pete heard the tinkle of bells. Several strings of brass bells hung on sagging lines from branch to branch. When a breeze blew, the bells shivered and chimed in response. A man stepped out of a palm-roofed shelter in the corner of the garden. He walked to the edge of the pool, turned around and, like a symphony conductor, raised his arms toward the roof. He waved them several times. The pigeons roosting there were startled and flew off. Ten minutes later the birds returned, and the man came back out to scare them away again.

It reminded Pete of a job he'd had as a teenager at the local swimming pool. He was required to keep the facility clean. It was part of a string of monotonous, repetitive summer jobs where he worked hard. His parents had often disagreed about those jobs. His father felt they were necessary to "build character." His stepmother had objected and said her children were "above manual labor." She felt Pete should be taking music lessons, dance, or theatre.

Thank goodness his father had won. The jobs had toughened him, as had his time in the military. Ironically, it was Julie who had re-awakened the dreams Pete's mother had had for him. Julie had encouraged Pete to take up oil painting. Landscapes. He'd only had a few lessons, but they gave him a heightened sensitivity to colors and light. Too bad his bouts of depression dulled everything in his world now.

Pete drained the last of his coffee and walked through the lobby to the elevator. He was scheduled to meet the maid at the room where Bridget Holmes had stayed. On the third floor, he left the elevator and padded down the carpeting to reach room 312. The thugs that had roughed him up yesterday had made him mad. Part of Pete wanted to stay and fight. But now that he was in Myanmar, the hopelessness of the mission was apparent. He'd do what he could and get out.

A maid waited for him. "Hi," he said to her with a slight nod of his head. He didn't fold his palms, nor did she.

"Good morning, sir." She had latte-colored skin and large eyes. "Welcome to the Chatrium Hotel." She smiled briefly and covered her mouth with her hand.

"Your English is so good."

"Most of the younger people learn it in school. We also watch American films and learn more from them."

"I haven't seen any movie theaters here."

"Yes." She smiled. "We go to the shops. Many people pirate the films on DVDs, and we rent them at various kiosks. Then we have all our friends over."

"Does the government allow it?"

She glanced down the empty hall. "Not really. The government has a visitor's law. If we want to have friends over, we must report their names on Form 10 to the Law and Order Restoration Council before nine o'clock in the evening. Otherwise, we may all be subject to fines or prison. They have the right to check at home any time during the night and compare the guests there with those listed on Form 10."

He studied her face for a moment. She reminded him of Mi Mi. Sparkling dark brown eyes and a wide white smile. Many of the Burmese women were beautiful. He saw she wore a cream-colored paste across her cheeks. He'd seen it on many of the women. "Do you mind if I ask about that?" He pointed to her right cheek.

She blushed slightly and said, "It is called 'thanaka.' It comes from the root of the thanaka tree. We scrape off some and mix it with water and apply it to our faces like a cream. It's not only fashionable, it's also therapeutic and protects us from the sun. You'll see it used all over Myanmar."

Pete nodded and thought of his own deeply lined face. Maybe he should use some to repair what the years had done to him. When she unlocked the door, he followed her into the empty room.

It felt cool, like the air conditioning had been running over time. He moved to the middle of the room. Pete felt as if he were invading the privacy of Bridget Holmes. While he stood for a moment, he could picture her and felt a stitch cross his chest. She had inherited the face of her father—a stolid Minnesota farmer. But Bridget's personality and the way her eyes wrinkled when she smiled had always made her look attractive. Pete thought of the way she walked because it reminded him of a cat: self-possessed, graceful, and sneaky.

Now the room was quiet. He could hear birds calling faintly to one another outside the French doors. What if he were standing here looking for evidence of his own daughter's disappearance instead of Bridget's? He started a methodical search.

In the teak closet, Pete found one suitcase resting under wooden hangers. Three cotton blouses hung from them. One blouse had a logo on the chest pocket in curving letters that read *US Export-Import Bank*. He lifted the suitcase out, opened it, and discovered it was partially full—as if she had been preparing to leave. T-shirts, white cotton blouses, and long tropical-weight pants—it was disrespectful for women or men to wear shorts in Myanmar in spite of the heat. The drawers in the closet contained more clothing, but certainly not enough to last a woman who would be working in the country for months. Where was the rest of her clothing?

The maid helped him open the room safe. It was empty. Back at the closet, he saw three hanging *longyi*. Made of silk, they looked limp, as if they had died.

He burrowed through the drawers under the desk and didn't find a laptop or any phones. Next to the desk Bridget had lined up a pair of pink flip-flops, and Pete saw a faint yellow outline on the carpet. It looked like dried mud from a pair of missing hiking boots. Why would she need hiking boots in the city? A baseball cap with a curled red bill and a Minnesota Twins logo sat on the desk. Pete turned it over and saw a single long strand of black hair caught in the hatband.

He canvassed the area around the bed. Nothing except a rotary phone. Out of habit, he ran his hand behind the nightstand and found a square object jammed against the wall. He pulled out a paperback mystery. Pete fanned through the pages and found a folded map of the country. He opened it and sat on the edge of the bed. It was a map of Myanmar bisected by the Irrawaddy River—one of the four major rivers in Southeast Asia. It started in the Himalayas and ran south through the country to submerge into a wide delta that flowed out to the Sea of Andaman and, ultimately, into the Indian Ocean.

Pete saw the towns on the river: Sinbaungwe, Bagan, and Mandalay. Mandalay had been circled with a red pen. A red arrow pointed to the northeast of the ancient city. There were some notes scratched in the margins, but he couldn't read them. He re-folded the map and put it into the briefcase he had brought with him.

Had Bridget been planning a trip into northern Myanmar? Had she found something about the Yangon International Timber Company in the northern part of the country that she went to investigate? Maybe she'd left already and hadn't been with Jeff when he was killed. But everyone said they were inseparable. Also, wouldn't she note her movements in her daily posts to the bank back in Minneapolis? She hadn't said a word about leaving Yangon.

But the map sure made it look otherwise.

He stood and decided to check the bathroom. In there he found the same clear-glass shower, large tub, and sink as in his room. A shopping bag from a store at the market lay crumpled on the floor. Pete stooped down to dig through it. He found a pair of athletic socks, two silk scarves folded between gauzy paper, and a shiny, black lacquer container about the size of a salad bowl.

He started to stand when he noticed a second bag on the floor hidden behind the first one. He pulled it out. It was a silver travel bag, zippered shut.

Pete opened it and found two black bras and a handful of thongs. Bright red. He thought of Bridget for a moment and pictured her body clothed, so to speak, in one of these thongs. Then he remembered she was about the same age as his daughter. He zipped it shut but noticed it felt too heavy for just underwear. He opened it again and dug through the tangle of straps until his fingers came to the bottom. He felt a hard, oblong object and pulled out a smart phone.

Why would she put it in this bag? A woman her age would never be without her phone. Was she trying to hide it? Was it a second phone she forgot?

He turned it on and watched the screen come to life. It beeped twice. He looked at the screen saver—a monkey with a white crown of hair clapping his hands together. He started by opening her contacts. Hundreds of names came up. Pete didn't have any idea what they might mean. He looked through her e-mails. Most of them were recommendations about restaurants and films, messages from

Jeff and her family, or notes from Director Graves at the bank. Since the Internet wasn't available in most parts of the country, the messages were all dated weeks earlier.

Pete tapped on the camera icon and brought up photos. All of them were of Jeff, and Bridget and Jeff together. They stood in the parks, by golden pagodas, next to a noodle restaurant, and beside two BMWs in front of the Strand Hotel. They smiled, held hands, and kissed each other in a few of the shots. Clearly, they were in love and must have been inseparable as people had said about them.

Then the subjects changed. There was a photo of a small prop plane and Jeff poised to climb up a metal stairway into the back end of the plane. He waved at the camera. Two more shots were from the interior of the plane, looking down on a muddy river that flowed through green fields.

The next shots must have been on a river. They showed a long, brightly-painted boat with open sides and a sagging wooden roof. From bow to stern, the boat was painted turquoise, green, and blue. From the shadowed interior, two crew members with dirty faces smiled broadly and waved.

Then Bridget had shot dozens of pictures of something that looked like a raft of tan logs that rode low in the water. A long pole stuck up at an angle from the back end. It must have been some kind of a rudder. A frame lean-to covered with straw sat in the middle, and three people crouched beside it. They didn't wave. By their size, Pete estimated the raft at enormous dimensions—about a block long. The Myanmar version of Huckleberry Finn? A family moving like the dust bowl days of the Great Depression in the US?

For some reason Bridget had taken dozens of shots of the raft from different angles, more than everything else combined. She had video of it, and Pete could see the people duck into the lean-to when the camera found them. A wisp of smoke came through the roof and flattened in the breeze behind the moving raft.

What was so interesting about it for her?

He shut off the phone and placed it in his bag along with the map. Maybe someone at the embassy could pull out more information from the phone than he could. Normally, a forensic expert could extract everything, but Pete didn't trust the police here—if they even had such an expert.

He came out of the bathroom and nodded to the maid. He followed her to the door. She stood aside, smiled, and said, "*Chei zu bah.* Thank you."

"Uh, yeah. Thanks to you." He turned back to look into the room one last time. The space was chilly, and he couldn't hear the birds anymore. They must have flown away.

A half hour later, he drove slowly on the street, looking for the Swel Noodle Restaurant. Moe Ma Kha had said it was his favorite and he would meet Pete there.

The traffic pressed in around Pete so tightly, he couldn't make any progress and was late. Maybe he should start taking taxis. The narrow sidewalk had two broken sections. He saw a large billboard that said in black letters: *Oppose those trying to jeopardize stability of the State and progress of the nation.* Beside the restaurant was a tea shop. It was open air, and several men sat on low wooden stools with their *longyis* tucked around their ankles. Some smoked cheroots, a crude cigar made of herbs, honey, and crushed plant leaves. Pete could smell the sweet smoke when he entered the restaurant.

There were a few tables with red tops separated by carved wooden panels to give the diners privacy. A lighted sign on the wall showed a white elephant covered up with the name *Myanmar Beer* in green and yellow letters. Pete spotted Moe in the corner.

He stood, bowed quickly, and offered Pete a seat. It was noisy with talk, and Pete could smell the damp odor of boiling noodles with spices so exotic he couldn't identify them.

A young waiter delivered a cup of mocha-colored tea and black coffee.

"Mi Mi will join us soon," Moe said. "Did Mr. Chandler experience power out last night?"

"No. Did it go out?"

"The hotel has generator. Yes, electric goes out quite often, even here in largest city. It is frustrating for us." He held the cup in two hands and took a tiny sip.

Pete watched him, noticing the broad shoulders and the thin arms that tapered to long, brown hands. He could see muscles bunched in his hands, hidden beneath smooth skin. Although Pete still didn't think much of the police here in Myanmar, he owed Moe for rescuing him. "Thanks for showing up with the cavalry."

"What?"

"A group of Marines rescued me. Thanks."

Moe glanced to his left. "You are welcome. Mi Mi called Moe when they forced her to leave. Moe Ma Kha not in position to stop those criminals."

"But you're a cop, as we call police in America. Why can't you stop them?"

"Please keep voice down. Partly, it is because my family history."

"What do you mean?"

Moe's face darkened. He appeared to be thinking. "Moe cannot say more now."

"Mi Mi?"

"Yes. Do not question about our past." He looked up when the waiter delivered two menus.

Pete reached for his menu and pretended to study it. This country was in worse shape than he had imagined. He thought of all the things it didn't have: movie theaters, shopping malls, beach houses, casinos, fast food chains, theme parks, the Internet, freeways, big-box stores, concert venues, and libraries. He wasn't hungry, but the smells from the kitchen were tempting. "When the soldiers had me, there was a general who questioned me about Bridget and why I was looking for her."

Moe looked up quickly and frowned. He changed the subject. "Noodle shops start all over Yangon. They quick and cheap like this one."

Pete scanned the choices. Noodles in seasoned oil, steamed chicken and noodles, and fried or steamed dumplings, $2,000 *kyat* each. He also saw the Burmese soup, *mohinga*. He asked about it.

"It is one of our favorite dishes. Fish stew that people eat for breakfast—when they can manage find fish. It is made with coriander, garlic, chilies. A squeeze of lime juice and you have wonderful meal," Moe said proudly.

"How about these dumplings? Aren't they Chinese?"

"They are popular because there are many Chinese in our country now. They own many businesses. We have old saying: 'Save like an Indian, then work hard like Chinese, and do not be lazy like Burmese.' " He smiled. "My parents told me this, and I live by it. So, Moe Ma Kha is successful."

They both ordered and in a few minutes, bowls of soup with noodles arrived. In the middle of the table was a tray of hot sauces that could be added. Moe leaned his face close to the bowl and slurped up the noodles as he ate.

"Can you talk about the investigation?" Pete asked.

"Since Moe has been ordered to help you, yes."

He still didn't trust Moe enough to tell him about finding Bridget's smart phone. As he started to talk, Mi Mi arrived. She wore a white cotton jacket and a dark blue *longyi*. As she walked, her narrow legs peeked out, and he saw she wore flip-flops. Her hair was tied in a curved ponytail. She smiled and sat next to Moe. When the waiter came by, she ordered tea. "I will take it sweet and rich." Mi Mi turned back to Pete and told him, "In Myanmar, tea shop sitting is a national experience. We don't order Earl Grey or green like they do in England. We order it mildly sweet, sweet and strong, and sweet and rich. That means they add condensed milk to the tea. You should try it."

"Tea shop sitting is *only* pastime in Myanmar." Moe laughed.

Mi Mi added quickly, "Oh, tosh. For the men, that is. They're lazy while all women are working." She waved her arm around them. She was right; the shop was filled with men.

"I prefer coffee, but I'm getting used to your tea," Pete said to her. "Also, I should thank you." He was happy she'd not been arrested with him and realized, with surprise, how deep his concern was for her. But he still hesitated. She was the sister of a government cop. Probably as crooked as everyone else in the government.

"Usually, when they look dodgy, we can avoid the army easily. Not this time." She frowned. "Sorry for you."

"I'm okay. We were just talking about the investigation. I'd like to ask about the death of Jeff Sumpter. Do you have any clues as to what happened? Did you find anything unusual at the crime scene?"

Moe waited until a clot of men moved past them to take a table in the other corner. "No. This is country where murder rare except killing of political prisoners. There is only one possible answer."

Pete chewed on his chicken dumpling. It was bland, and he shook hot sauce on it.

"Generals ordered or, at least, allowed to happen."

Mi Mi nodded in agreement. "This kind of brutality is not common. It is very dangerous for you to investigate his death. You are better to look for the missing girl."

"The American embassy will investigate Sumpter's death as much as they can. But why would anyone kill him?"

Moe shrugged to indicate he didn't have an answer. "But Moe is certain generals will take over case if they worry I cannot control it."

It didn't surprise Pete. He'd seen this kind of unchecked power in many third world countries, but it still made him mad. "So, they can get away with this?"

"Yes," Mi Mi said. "They do whatever they want. We purposely met you here because it's so loud. We know the government spies on us, particularly me." She didn't explain further. "If someone protests, they will disappear. A year ago, a group of monks was protesting, and they were arrested and some were killed. The generals are very nervous at this point."

"Why?"

"Some want to open the country and agree to the restoration of a few rights, but many others and cronies don't want to let anyone from outside world in here."

"*Cronies?* Who are they?"

"The generals run the government and all the businesses. But they can't bloody do everything, so there are business people outside the Tatmadaw who bribe the generals to allow them to take a share of the business. They are called cronies."

Pete finished his dumplings and asked for more coffee. None of the information surprised him. It was a pattern repeated the world over at the expense of the local people and their freedoms. He wondered why Moe and his sister persevered. He asked about that.

"Moe not dreamer," Moe said. "Goals are clear, and Moe Ma Kha work toward them objectively. I see opportunities in future and want to work for freedoms. For Moe and people of country."

Pete didn't think he was serious about helping the country. Moe seemed too cynical, and it renewed Pete's distrust of them. "And being a police officer will do that?"

"Yes. In small steps. For instance, all police stations are given quotas of crime they must report. The quotas set so other, lazy stations not put to shame. When government first opened country to foreigners a few years ago, they want to demonstrate reduction in crime." He pushed his empty bowl away from him and wiped his hands on a small paper napkin. "So they simply lowered numbers of crime."

Mi Mi laughed. "Pretty soon, we will have 'negative' crime." She hid her smile, but when it broke out it shone white in her tan face.

"If Moe keep case, I do honest work without corruption. And we may find girl," Moe added.

Mi Mi said, "There are many small business owners now. They are all chipping away at the power of the generals. Have you ever heard about the writings of Gene Sharp?"

"No. I'm not at all political. I don't even vote anymore in the US. A waste of time."

"Gene Sharp has written some books on political defiance. I've read all of them. But we have to be careful. In Mandalay, nineteen political prisoners were tried on charges of 'high treason'— they possessed books by Gene Sharp. They went to prison for seven years." She looked around the restaurant and whispered, "I've taken some of his political defiance courses. They were smashing."

"Well, good luck." He noticed that Moe didn't say they would *solve* the case—merely find the girl. Now it was Pete who was cynical. He'd seen this too often, met with too many young and naïve people like these two, and had seen too much disappointment and death as a result. Still, he felt a stirring within him. If the cause was something Pete could believe in, he was the first to jump on board. So much that his actions had often gotten him in trouble. As a kid, he had been a brawler, defending friends who were loyal and were underdogs. He was almost kicked out of high school, and it was only through the discipline of college and the military that Pete could now control some of his instincts. It had taught him to think before acting, to use newfound verbal skills instead of fighting.

"Do you have any idea where Bridget may have gone?" he asked.

Moe and Mi Mi looked at each other. "There is always possibility of Insein Prison." Moe pronounced it *insane*. "But she is foreigner; Moe do not think that happen to her," he said. "Moe has listened around the stations, but have not heard anything. I think she is not in Yangon anymore."

"Hmm." Pete wrestled with the idea of revealing the existence of the map he had found in her hotel room. How much could he trust these two? For all Pete knew, Moe was a spy for the Tatmadaw, sent to stop Pete from going too far in his own investigation. Then Mi Mi smiled at him. She probably did it merely to make him feel better about the situation, but the effect was strong. Something traveled between them, and Pete decided to show them the map. He explained how he had found it.

"You have it here?" Mi Mi asked.

Pete nodded and reached around behind him to his leather briefcase sitting at the corner of the chair. He pulled out the map and opened it halfway. After pushing his bowl to the side, he flattened it on the table. His finger traced the red marks up the middle of the country.

"That's Mandalay. And the arrow points to our province, the Shan Plateau. The mountains start there, up from the central river plain," Mi Mi explained.

Without mentioning the photos of the raft, Pete asked, "Is the river used to move cargo?"

Moe laughed. "That Irrawaddy River is the 'Road to Mandalay' Rudyard Kipling write poem about. It has carried most of goods from the north to south and back again for centuries. Since we still do not have many roads, the river is also main way of transportation except for air."

Pete paused for a moment. How much could he say? "Do you think she's gone up the 'Road to Mandalay'?"

Both of them studied the map. Pete bent his head over it in a subconscious motion to match their lowered heads. "What company you say Bridget investigate?" Moe asked.

"The Yangon International Timber Company."

"Their headquarters is up river to north, at Mandalay, but they have a small trade office here. We start there." Moe looked out the smudged window to the busy street and became silent.

Pete wondered if he'd made a mistake and gone too far by showing them the map.

Moe jerked around to face Pete. "Tell Moe again what general who questioned you looked like."

"Huh? I don't know. Pockmarked face, small eyes, short."

"Shoulders like bull?"

"I guess."

Moe turned to Mi Mi, and a look passed between them. He said to Pete, "That was General Lo Win. He is Moe's boss."

Pete sucked in a breath. He'd made a huge mistake trusting these two. They were all in it together with the general. He shoved back his chair to leave. "Hey, gotta run."

"Please, stay," Mi Mi said. "Just because he is Moe's boss, that does not mean we agree with him."

A new police officer appeared next to their table. Moe twitched in surprise and introduced him as Captain Thaung. "How did you find me here?" Moe asked.

"You were followed. General's orders," the captain said.

In a whisper, Mi Mi translated for Pete. His stomach grumbled with worry.

Moe sucked in a deep breath. "Why are you here? I am working on the case right now."

Captain Thaung's eyes traveled over Pete and in a sarcastic voice said, "That is most obvious." He shifted his weight to the other side and continued, "I must leave Yangon for a few days."

"How can you leave the investigation with me alone?" Moe's own sarcasm was evident.

"You are aware of the new freeway they built down to the delta?" Before Moe could respond, the captain continued, "I have been temporarily assigned to the Department of Pleasant Scenery for the Esteemed Commander in Chief."

"What does that mean?"

"Our beloved President is being driven on the new road to the delta. Ahead of his motorcade, we have planted trees, erected new signs, and planted flowers. Once he has passed, we work through the night to move and re-plant everything for the next part of his journey. Captain Thaung in charge of the crews." He looked at Pete for a long time, saluted to Moe, and turned sharply to leave. "But I will be back to help you as ordered."

Pete stood and pushed his way outside onto the crowded street. The noise of traffic was deafening. Moe and Mi Mi hurried after him. Pete took a deep breath. They were jostled by the surging mob on the sidewalk, and Pete felt Mi Mi fall against him. He sensed her weight and size. Then she stepped back and was looking up into his eyes. "We will help you investigate the company." Mi Mi glanced behind them. "We think it definitely has something to do with Sumpter's death."

"No, thanks." Pete was even more worried since the captain had spied on Moe.

"You need our help," Moe insisted. "By yourself, will be like tossing sesame seeds into the mouth of elephant. You do not understand anything here. General Lo Win owns Yangon International Timber Company."

Chapter Eight

Moe held Pete's elbow to move him along the sidewalk. "Hurry. We must leave."

Pete twisted his arm from Moe's hand and tried to find a quiet spot out of the crush of people moving in every direction. A half block away, there was a vacant lot with a low stone wall separating the lot from the sidewalk. Pete stepped over it. Moe and Mi Mi stood on the other side. To their left was a small storefront that advertised the services of a fortune teller. Four people waited in the sun to learn their futures.

Pete felt the heat bearing down on him. He'd have to get different clothes soon. But he also felt hot inside. "Don't push me around," he yelled at Moe. Two dogs with lowered heads crept toward them.

"Besides Captain Thaung, there were two Tatmadaw following us. We must get away." Moe took off his glasses and folded them.

Pete looked around them. All he saw were hundreds of people dressed in bright clothing pushing along the sidewalk and spilling out into the street. "Look, all I want to do is figure out what's going on in order to find Bridget." He moved under the shade of the strawberry-colored leaves of a crape myrtle tree that grew next to the low wall.

"The timber company has a small trading office down by the river," Mi Mi said.

"But this not easy." As Moe led them to his car, he didn't look at Pete. They climbed in the small Toyota, and he pulled away from the curb into the surging traffic. The car didn't have air conditioning, so Moe rolled down all the windows, letting hot air blow through the car. He spun around a corner and almost hit a small street cart.

Pete could smell pork grilling on the cart. "If your commanding general owns this company, don't you have to be careful?"

"Of course. But Moe ordered to investigate Jeffrey Sumpter death. Therefore, have to look at timber company."

"But how do you know Sumpter was involved?"

Moe glanced at Pete and flashed a quick grin. "Because his NGO concerned about environment problem caused by timber company. Since he friends with Holmes, I am certain they shared information. And Moe Ma Kha know General Win want his ownership protected in any way." He turned down a quiet street lined by six-story apartment houses. Palm trees fronted each building. In the breeze, their leaves slapped the sides of the building. Bougainvillea bushes looped around the doors of each apartment to form ruby-colored arches.

Between the sidewalk and the street, the torn-up pavement revealed a brown gash of dirt almost the full length of the block. Five men in a row held a long piece of black plastic pipe which sagged in between each man. They waited while three others fed the pipe into a culvert dug under the intersection. On the far side, two more men tugged at the pipe to pull it through the hole. Next to them, three men squatted so low their butts touched the ground. Pete had seen this resting pose all over Asia.

"They lay drainage line," Moe explained. "Our system built by British to handle fifty thousand people. Now we have six million, and we have serious problem during rainy season, which is almost here." The red light changed, and Moe sped through the intersection while the motor of the car whined like a lawn mower engine. He almost brushed one of the workers on the shoulder. All the work was done by hand without the help of machines.

"The trade office is near the Yangon River," Mi Mi said from the back seat. "Since the mid-2000s raw timber can only be shipped from Rangoon Port on the river."

Moe turned onto a one-way street of three lanes and was able to gain a little speed. Pete saw a billboard that advertised UV White Oxygen Skin Care. A smiling Caucasian-looking model offered proof of the beneficial effects of the product.

He looked up to his right and saw the Shwedagon Pagoda gleaming golden in the hazy heat. What an irony that in such a poor country, this expensive pile of gold dominated everything about the city and was visible from almost every point.

They turned into a roundabout and headed through a tree-lined street toward the river. Beside them, a large brick building looked solid and permanent. "British Supreme Court," Moe shouted above the noise of the wind and traffic. The streets became narrow, old lanes that were laid out in a rectangular grid. This had been the center of the British colonial city. Most of the buildings were abandoned, the windows broken out. A curved sign on a two-story building read *Telegraph Office.*

Moe said, "We still use. It is only way to contact Northern provinces at foot of Himalayas." He came to the edge of the river and turned right on Strand Road.

Another golden pagoda stood on the corner. It seemed out of place. Pete asked about it.

"The 'One Thousand Generals Pagoda,'" Moe said. "It has been there for centuries, before British here and develop river front. Please look at Ferris wheel." He smiled and pointed as they raced past it.

Pete saw children fidgeting in an irregular line, waiting to ride. Two men in flip flops climbed up the structure to the top, hung on, and swung out to the side. The metal wheel creaked into motion. Two more men grabbed the steel struts, and the combined weight of all the men brought the wheel down in a fast revolution that continued turning. Even the Ferris wheel was human powered.

The river flowed swiftly, and Pete could see the far bank. Small wooden boats that looked like Chinese junks chugged back and forth across the water, throwing up muddy wakes behind them. They were ferries shuttling people to the far side. Several cargo ships, labeled with Chinese and Indian names, were moored along the wooden docks. Tall cranes arched over them, laboring to fill the holds of the ships. The cranes were the only mechanized equipment Pete had seen on the waterfront.

They came to a paved industrial lot with a small office set in the middle. It was surrounded by a chain-link fence and a gate. A street sign read *Lan Thist Street Jetty.*

Moe pulled up to the closed gate. He got out and checked to find it padlocked. He waved at the office. In a few minutes, a soldier opened the front door and came down the two steps to the parking lot. He started toward them.

While they waited, Mi Mi said, "Our country has a bloody problem with raw timber. In the last four years it is estimated that our forests have been decimated from both legal and illegal logging. Maybe as much as eight billion dollars' worth. Of the remaining teak in the world, we have about fifty percent."

"You said legal and illegal?" Pete asked. In the distance, bells chimed faintly and ended in pleasant harmony.

"Yes. About three quarters of the timber is smuggled out illegally. This company is a legal operation, but we don't know how much of their trade is suspect."

Moe interrupted and said, "Myanmar Forestry Department denies any illegal smuggling happens, of course."

"But an environmental watchdog group from Great Britain accused the government of 'rampant criminality and corruption' and questioned the five billion dollars in timber missing from the government books," Mi Mi added quickly.

Pete could see the heat from the asphalt quiver around the soldier's feet as he walked slowly toward the car.

Mi Mi continued, "The Myanmar Timber Enterprise is supposed to regulate the timber trade. But they cocked up everything—most timber leaves the country without their approval. Under international pressure, the government decreed on April 1 that only sawn wood could be exported, not raw timber. It's an effort to keep jobs and industry here in our country. They have also invited foreign businesses to invest in timber processing in our country."

Pete said, "Which is what the Export-Import Bank came here to do—possibly lend money to the Yangon International Timber Company. That's what Bridget was checking on. Are the new regulations working?"

Moe scoffed. "Yes. Watchdog group say seventy-two percent of timber left without approval of Timber Enterprise."

"And that's because the generals own the companies. Like this one," Mi Mi said. "For years, they have plundered the forests with their crony businessmen, and that has led to deforestation in massive areas. Pretty soon, we will be as manky as your Detroit." When Pete twisted around to look at her, she smiled. "I visited it once."

The soldier reached the fence. Moe got out again and showed his police ID. The soldier glanced at it, opened the gate, and stood back to allow Moe to drive through. Inside the fence, they rolled to a stop before the office. Pete could smell the river close behind. He was glad to get out of the stifling car.

He followed Moe inside while Mi Mi remained with the car.

One other soldier sat behind a teak desk while a second fiddled with the controls on a window air conditioner. It hummed and blew tepid air into the room. Moe talked to the first soldier in Burmese for a long time. Finally, Moe turned to Pete. "They say cannot open records for you, even if you from the US Export-Import Bank. Need authorization."

"Ask them about Bridget." A radio on the desk played music, but Pete couldn't understand any of it.

Moe turned back and spoke to them again. Five minutes later he said, "Can you describe her?"

"Oh, for God's sake. She was the only Caucasian foreigner to come here. All right. She is about five-eight, thin, long black hair, with white skin, very pale."

Moe related the information. The two soldiers talked between themselves for several minutes, then said, "We do not know about woman. When was she here?"

Pete felt his patience draining away like the sweat that dribbled down his sides. "Probably a week ago. No longer than two."

Once again, the soldiers talked. One picked up the black handset from a rotary phone and called someone. He talked for another ten minutes on the phone.

"What the hell are they doing?" Pete whispered to Moe.

"Permission to talk with us." He avoided eye contact with Pete.

"But they're already talking with us," Pete said louder.

Moe patted the air with his palm to get Pete to shut up. Moe listened to the soldiers. He frowned and pulled Pete off to the side. "This not good. I leave quickly."

"Now what?"

"They call State Law and Order Restoration Council. That is top governing group. President Thein Sein is boss." Moe's face drained of color.

Pete felt Moe's fear and glanced back at the two men behind the desk. Their black eyes searched over Pete.

One of the soldiers shouted at them, "The woman you look for was here. She was here with a young man about one week before now. That is all I know."

"Did she look at their books?" Pete urged Moe to ask them.

He hesitated but talked to the men again.

The soldier's eyes became smaller. "Yes. That is all." He threw his arm to the side to dismiss them.

Pete couldn't keep quiet any longer. He shouted, "This is a bunch of crap. You know all about her. Where did she go?" The soldiers didn't seem to understand the words he said but could figure out the tone of Pete's voice. One of them picked up the phone again.

Moe spun on his foot and hurried out the door. Pete followed. They got into the steaming car, and Moe drove back through the gate, throwing up gravel as he went.

Between the heat in the car and his frustration, Pete shouted, "Why the hell don't we go back there and force them to talk? These two-bit little jerks must know all about Bridget. She would have spent a lot of time in there, looking at the books. These ass-holes won't admit it, and I'm not going to put up with their crap."

Moe agreed. "Yes."

Mi Mi shouted, "Tosh. That would be a bad idea—"

"I've been in backward countries like this before. What they understand is brute force. I should come back here with a platoon of Marines. We'd get our answers about Bridget, Sumpter, and the damn company real quick."

"It isn't that easy. We've got to work together." Mi Mi leaned forward from the back seat.

"I'll take a few guns in there with me. I don't need your help for this anymore." The car felt claustrophobic to Pete. He wanted to get out and into someplace cool. But he really wanted to personally smash the faces of those idiots at the office.

"You are becoming just like the generals," Mi Mi warned. "That is exactly what they do. Kill and torture to get what they want. We can't have any more of that in our country. Don't you understand?" Her voice ratcheted up to a shrill level. She flopped back into her seat.

Moe drove quickly down the street from the way they'd come earlier. He stopped for a red light and removed his glasses. Ticking the bows against each other, he said, "I think is time we separate. We risk much to do this with you."

"You said the general ordered you to investigate the case."

"He does not mean *honestly*. That is Moe's motive, not from boss. We must all be cautious. Even soldiers may be spies for government. You work on your own now."

"Hey, I'm sorry, Moe. I didn't mean what I said. Well, I did mean it, but I certainly won't do that."

The light changed, and Moe lurched forward. He drove through the tangle of streets and traffic to the north, back to Pete's car. After a long time, Moe said, "At least we know few things now."

"Yeah, like Jeff was with Bridget at the timber company," Pete said. "That's the closest we've ever tied them together. His death must be related to her disappearance."

"Yes. Soldiers had to call State Law and Order Council mean someone at timber company is worried."

"Which makes it much more dangerous," Mi Mi added, "but also tells us how threatened the general must be about Bridget's investigation of their company. What are they hiding?"

"And it makes sense that the NGO Jeff worked for would also be investigating the company for environmental problems," Pete said.

"His NGO called 'Free the Oxygen.' " Moe said, "No wonder General Win wants Moe work on case—to cover over and protect him."

"But the timber company wants the loan from the Ex-Im Bank," Pete said. "Why would they get worried about Bridget? They knew she'd have to complete the due diligence work with their books."

"It is obvious." Moe glanced to his left, saw a tiny crack in the traffic, and floored the Toyota. It gave off a high-pitched whine and surged forward. "She discover something."

Moe made several sharp turns around corners, slowed down, sped up, and kept watching in his rearview mirror. He must have been trying to make sure no one followed him. Pete sensed how dangerous the investigation was for these two—and for him, also. He turned around and looked at Mi Mi. She watched out the window, but he could see a sprig of wrinkles across her skin that grew from the corner of each eye. Her brown eyes were clear and reflected the sun as it bounced around inside the moving car.

How much could he trust them? After all, it was the Marines from the embassy who had rescued him, not Moe and the police. And although Moe had seemed worried in the timber company office, how did Pete know it wasn't faked? Maybe Moe and Mi Mi had staged the entire show—Moe worked for General Win, for God's sake. The general probably needed to learn how much Bridget knew, and now, what Pete knew. The company wanted Western loans, so they didn't want too much dirty laundry to get back to the bank.

Moe finally reached the area where Pete's car was parked.

They pulled to a stop beside the car. Moe stared ahead and didn't say anything. Pete looked from one to the other. "Are you serious? We don't work together?"

"It is best, Mr. Chandler," Moe said.

Mi Mi didn't say a word, and Pete thought of never seeing her again. He said, "I'm sorry. Look, I've got something to show you. It doesn't make any sense to me, but you might see something. Let's have tea."

Moe took a deep breath. He spoke slowly. "Our freedom is long struggle for us, even though you do not care about our country—'

"I never said that," Pete interrupted. "My mother was Vietnamese. I've got a sense of what it must be like for you."

Moe glanced at Mi Mi and he continued, "Aung San Suu Kyi gets Western attention in media. And she is hero to us, but reality is different. Tourists do not see underneath the golden pagodas. Even if we want to make small step forward, it is risky."

"I thought Aung San Suu Kyi was just released from house detention. Democracy's on the rise. Wouldn't the generals go easier on you two also?"

"If her father had not been hero in Burma, she would be killed long time ago. With our history," Moe gestured with his head toward Mi Mi in the back seat, "they would like excuse to get rid of us."

Something quivered in Pete's chest. He hadn't seen this kind of sacrifice in a long time. Could he trust them? "Okay. I think I understand. Let's get tea."

Moe parked the car, and they walked across the street to an open air market. On one side in the shade stood a refrigerated cooler with four tables and stools without backrests surrounding it. None of the stools balanced. A tiny kitchen exhaled breaths of exotic smells. Mi Mi ordered black tea, very sweet, and a doughy pastry for each of them. Pete, tall as he was, had to squat to get down to the level of the stool. Once there, he felt like it would tip over at any moment.

The tea was served from an ancient, blackened steel pot by a girl with chalky thanaka spread across her cheeks. She had flawless skin and smiled as she poured a combination of coffee and condensed milk from one dented pot to another before serving it in cups that didn't match. Pete agreed to try some. He sipped the delicious tea. In weather this steamy, hot tea actually made him feel a little cooler.

Moe took off his glasses and set them on the table.

Pete reached down into his briefcase beside his feet. He pulled out Bridget's iPhone and showed it to them. "There are some images on here I want you to look at. Tell me if they mean anything to either of you." He swiped at the screen until he brought up the series of photos of the rafts. Pete shifted his stool to the right, closer to Mi Mi, and showed the images to both of them. As he went from one picture to another, neither person said anything. When Pete looked at Moe, he could see concentration on the detective's face. Pete played the videos. After he'd gone through everything, Pete said, "Looks like Huck Finn on the Mississippi."

"Who?" Moe asked.

"Never mind." Pete noticed Moe's eyes flick over to Mi Mi and caught the look she passed back to him. "Okay. What's going on?" Pete asked. He smelled fresh-cut kale spread out on the ground next to them, for sale from the market.

Moe cleared his throat and put on his glasses. He glanced to either side and motioned for them to move to a deserted corner of the tea shop. When they were seated in the private spot, Moe said, "This is bigger than we suspect."

"What?"

"Those are teak rafts on Irrawaddy River. Raw timber cut up river and made into rafts that float down to Yangon."

"Is this some of that illegal stuff you told me about?"

"Yes, I think. I am surprised Bridget was able to photograph rafts. We suspected they move only after sunset. There no lights on river, and it is dark at night." Moe looked out from their corner to check on unwanted visitors.

"Could this be what she discovered in her investigation?"

"These could be rafts for the Yangon International Timber Company. But it also means this is much more serious than we thought," Mi Mi said. "You know how big the raw timber business is in this country. We are looking at the looting of possibly millions of dollars of teak." She pointed at the iPhone.

Pete leaned back to absorb the new information. On one hand, he was relieved to have solved the mystery that Bridget had uncovered, but then he remembered the mission—to find her. "So, where is Bridget?"

Mi Mi finished the last of her tea. Limp leaves clung to the bottom of the cup. "I'd guess that she went up river to continue her investigation. To Mandalay, where the main office for the Yangon Timber company is located." She turned to Moe. "We really should follow up with this."

Lines furrowed across Moe's face as he listened to Mi Mi. He reached into his wool bag and lifted out a small hardbound note-book. He licked the tip of his finger and paged through the book. When Moe came to one page, he stopped, read carefully, and leaned forward in the posture of prayer. When finished, he brought out a black candle from his bag and set it in the middle of the table. He lit it, watched the flame dance for a moment, blew it out, and lit it again. Moe repeated this several times. Then he used a pen to write several numbers in the margins of the book pages.

Pete looked around to see if other people were watching. No one seemed to pay any attention. His eyes found Mi Mi's as if to ask, "What's going on?"

She leaned forward and whispered. "I don't believe in this, but Moe thinks it can help. It's called *yadaya*. It's a form of magic called numerology. It can be used to predict events and the future. The book he has helps him. He has lit the candle nine times, and now he waits for answers."

In five minutes, Moe blew out the candle for the last time and raised his head. He looked into Pete's eyes and nodded once. Moe was ready.

With a grunt, Pete stood up from the low stool. "*Chei zu bah* for agreeing to help. What are we waiting for? Let's get going."

Chapter Nine

Pete was anxious to get started up river. There were few roads, so the only way to go was either by broken down train, slow boat, or by air. Rangoon Airways offered sporadic one-hour flights each day. Would he be able to reach Mandalay soon enough to find Bridget?

Before they could leave, there were many things to prepare.

They decided that Mi Mi would go back with Pete to the Chatrium Hotel, where the images on the iPhone could be uploaded to his laptop and enlarged for Mi Mi to study. Maybe she could recognize some landmarks on the river. Moe would book the flights and get clearance for them all to go.

Mi Mi and Pete got into his car, and she directed him back to the hotel. On the way, he called Carter Smith on the cell phone the embassy had provided. It worked in small areas of Yangon. He left a voice mail about what he'd found.

Smith called back in five minutes. "Good work, Chandler. I have to admit that considering your history, I'm surprised."

"Hey, they screw with me, I screw with them. I've got a job to do and I'll do it."

Before he could say any more, Carter interrupted him. "I'd love to help you there, but we're very busy on a new trade deal."

"Have any investigators from the State Department gotten here yet to check on Jeff Sumpter's murder?"

Smith paused and said, "No. I've requested help, but they seem to be dragging their feet. I don't know why. It's unusual." She cleared her throat. "Nevertheless, you've done good work. You can go home with a clear conscience that you tried."

Pete paused. "Uh, I'm not ready to go back yet."

"We're worried about Ms. Holmes as much as you are."

That struck Pete as odd. In earlier conversations, Smith hadn't seemed very upset about either Bridget or Jeffrey Sumpter. "What does the ambassador think?"

Smith paused for a long time. Then she said, "He's concerned about all American interests in the country. It's his job to protect them."

"But he's never available to discuss it," Pete said. Typical government-talk, he thought. What was really going on? He clicked off the phone.

Pete drove through an area of small shops, restaurants, and an open park to one side. "This is my neighborhood," Mi Mi said. "You can't see it from here, but I live three blocks over there." She pointed to the right. Cold air from the air conditioning vent blew her hair across her shoulder. He noticed how long it was and shiny and the deep levels of color that even black hair could hold.

"Do you live with your brother?"

"I did when I was younger, but after I came back from England I was 'liberated,' as you Westerners put it. I wanted to live alone. Luckily, he was able to find me an apartment on the second floor of a six-story building."

"Wouldn't you want to be up high? See the view? This park is beautiful." He nodded to the left.

"Yes it is. It's used by lovers. Only in Yangon can people be together regularly in public. They may hold hands and even kiss. But not anywhere else in country."

Pete looked over at her. "Another government restriction?"

She laughed. "No, that one is cultural. The cities up north and into the mountains are smaller and more conservative. When a man and woman become engaged, they must wait 'three monsoons' before they marry. Three years. Divorce is allowed but is rare."

He thought of her smooth skin and how she smelled and what it would be like to kiss Mi Mi. "So, tell me why you're on the second floor."

"None of the buildings in Yangon, except the hotels and some government buildings, have elevators. The best floors are near ground for obvious reasons and are the most expensive."

Pete couldn't believe it. Coming to this country was like stepping back in time about fifty years—or longer. "No elevators? People have to carry everything up? What about old people who can't afford the rent for the lower floors?"

Mi Mi looked out the window. In a few minutes, she said, "Look over there. See the man with the basket of food strapped over his shoulder?" When Pete followed her pointing finger, she continued, "The person up high rings a brass bell, and the man with the food comes over to take the basket lowered from the top floor with cash inside it. The merchant will fill it with produce, for instance, and even leave change for the buyer, who pulls it back up with a nylon rope."

In ten minutes, they turned around the driveway to the entrance of the Chatrium. The attendant insisted on taking the car for Pete. They walked into the cool lobby while wooden fans turned slowly above them. An ATM machine had been installed in a corner of the lobby. They walked over to it. "There's one of these on every corner in the US."

"Same in England. I miss them here."

"Can't you use this one?"

Mi Mi laughed. "Bollocks. That's another reason you need me. None of these machines work."

"What?"

"The generals place them in all the big hotels to impress the tourists, but they never have cash. They're fake." She must have sensed his disbelief and she said, "Try it."

Pete pulled out his debit card and inserted it in the machine. All the buttons worked and lights blinked, but no matter how often Pete tried it, the machine said, *Temporarily Out of Order*. Luckily, the Ex-Im Bank had provided him with plenty of cash.

She said, "There's no banking system. No credit cards. You'd think people would hoard cash, but generals have demonetized the currency three times in the past."

"What's that mean?"

Mi Mi shook her head. "They declare all cash worthless and issue new bills. Every *kyat* I have in my bag must be thrown out."

To their left, a narrow bar pointed to an open-air patio overlooking the gardens and the pool. A gin and tonic would be perfect.

He offered and she said, "I drank a little when I was in Great Britain. I'd prefer an iced tea."

They settled into a small love seat with curved wicker arms. The roof arched over them. A revolving fan hung down, creating a soft flutter of fresh air. It wasn't cool, but Pete was getting used to the weather. At least this felt comfortable.

The uniformed waiter delivered sweating glasses of gin and tonic and iced tea. "To finding Bridget," Pete said as he clinked his glass against Mi Mi's. He could smell the half-moon of lime wedged onto the rim when he tipped up the glass.

Mi Mi drank and laid her head back against the seat cushion. She hummed a song.

"What happened to your family here?" Pete interrupted.

She wouldn't answer at first, looking up at the palms bending in the breeze. Finally, Mi Mi stopped humming and said, "My parents were educated. My father was a law professor at the Rangoon University. During the Socialist time, he was forced to choose— join the government faculty or leave. My parents fled to Thailand and lived in a refugee camp for years."

"Did they ever come back?"

"When they were finally allowed to return, new generals tortured them to make sure they were 'correct' in their thinking."

"Did they torture you?"

"Not too bad. They broke my arm, and it was never set correctly." She looked at it briefly.

Pete set down his drink. He had seen this kind of brutal treatment in other countries. It had never affected him much before. Now, he sat beside a woman who'd suffered from it with lasting scars. It made him feel angry.

Mi Mi looked back at him. "Afterward, my father was offered his old job back. He was knackered, exhausted, so he declined. Both of my parents died shortly afterward under mysterious circumstances. I had to work extra hard, and I set aside my hatred for the generals. I left to go to school in England."

Pete didn't know how to respond, so he sipped his drink. Mi Mi continued, "Buddhists believe that if a person dies without the correct preparation for death, they enter a realm called *peta,* or hungry ghosts. They remain trapped on earth as they work on more merit in order to move on. Many times when I've been in the country, I have heard my mother's singing coming across the paddy fields. Once, I looked up and saw her legs dangling from a coconut tree. She was smiling at me." Mi Mi blinked her eyes. "Because of their positions and their work, our entire family is forever tainted in the eyes of the generals. Now, I must be very careful what I do."

Pete didn't know what to say. He stared at her, marveling at the courage and determination of this woman. "And what about Moe?"

"He remained quiet also, but studied and took the tests to become a police investigator. Through hard work, he managed to be accepted." Mi Mi shrugged as if to dispose of years of oppression against her family. Maybe that was the best attitude.

She continued, "Today, things are somewhat better, but behind the façade for tourists, not much has changed." Mi Mi took another drink. "The first pro-democracy movement happened on August 8, 1988. It was an uprising by the people. Just before then, Aung San Suu Kyi came back to the country from Great Britain to take care of her sick mother. The results of movement was brutal repression. Ten thousand people were killed and tortured. There was no rule of law, just repression. The times were mad as a bag of ferrets."

"When did things change for the better?"

"Aung San Suu Kyi was asked to become active in democracy movement. I don't know if she was that committed until then. She formed the National League for Democracy party. By 1990, the generals allowed an election, and the NLD party, our party, won eighty percent of the seats. The generals were so surprised they declared the election invalid."

Pete had seen a lot of this kind of government brutality in the world, but Myanmar shocked him. "But Aung San Suu Kyi is still here in parliament?"

"Yes. In fact, her husband in England contracted cancer, and the generals told her she could leave to visit him, but she would never be allowed back into Myanmar. In a supreme act of courage and commitment to her people, she stayed and sent him and her children a video of herself—which arrived two days after his death."

Pete looked around the vacant patio. The wind had died, and even the birds were missing. "You and Moe work for her party?"

"Secretly. If the generals found out that either of us did, we would probably be jailed, especially since Moe is a police officer."

"But everyone I've met here seems happy. They're so gracious to me, even when I don't treat them well."

"That is our culture. But underneath surface, our country is gutted, devastated." She stared at him, and her eyes went hard. "That's why I'm so committed to improve the production and marketing of vegetables. Our country could lead the region, which would lift our GDP and the standard of living for everyone." Her face flushed as she talked faster.

"Is the violence reduced now? Any good news in the country?"

Mi Mi took a deep breath. "The Chinese have sold the army over two billion dollars' worth of weaponry that the generals use against the people. That figure has dropped now. I don't know where new weapons are coming from, but they're buying less from the Chinese. I am hopeful the generals are not buying them at all."

"Are there more people like you and Moe?"

"Of course. We can gather in the NLD, and since the Saffron Revolution in 1988, we are slowly gaining more freedoms. But compared to somewhere like Great Britain or the US, it is a joke."

As so often happened to Pete when he encountered this kind of repression, he thought of the way most Americans took their freedoms for granted. And he was impressed that in spite of all the brutal treatment the people had suffered, many of them, like Mi Mi and Moe, were so patriotic and wanted to improve their country. They were proud of it.

She said, "For years, your country and the European Union refused to recognize the generals' government and imposed trade and travel sanctions. Now, these are being relaxed."

"Some people in the US are angry about the human rights abuses here."

"I know, but the dropping of the sanctions and the increased trade has actually helped to pry open some doors we never thought would budge a few years ago. It is helping us."

Pete slid closer to her. She was so Westernized, but like many Asians, she looked delicate and fragile in physical appearance. Underneath, he could sense one of the toughest people he'd met in a long time. And courageous. He was attracted to the combination.

The chimes in the garden down by the pool tinkled in response to a fresh breeze. It also carried the smell of incense from somewhere beyond the walls of the hotel.

Mi Mi finished her drink and shifted her body away from him. She asked, "Now, what about you?"

He shrugged. "I worked with the Army in the Middle East for years. Probably lost the mother of my daughter as a result of all the time I was gone." He didn't want to tell Mi Mi the real reason. "I was assigned to work in our Congress for many years after that, doing more investigative work." A smile creased his face briefly. "In fact, I'd say Washington is just about as corrupt as things are here. After that I went back to Minnesota."

"Why did you leave Washington?"

His throat pinched tightly. Melted ice puddled at the bottom of his glass. A part of him wanted to explain, to let it out, but the urge was soon smothered like a candle blown out, and he didn't say anything in response. It was still too painful, even after all these months.

Instead, he lied. "Uh, my daughter lives in Minneapolis. I wanted to take care of her."

"When you are finished here, will you go back to your job in Minnesota?"

How to answer that one? Pete wondered. He stood up and stretched. He wanted to change the subject. "Hey, let's look at those photos on my laptop. Maybe you'll spot something."

Mi Mi delayed getting up. "But you are part Asian. I can see it in your hair and your eyes."

"Uh, I'm half Vietnamese." He explained the story briefly.

"You are close to your heritage here."

Pete shrugged.

"You don't care?" Mi Mi stood up quickly. "We put great emphasis on our family and our culture that contribute to each of us."

"Yeah, well, I live in America."

"I am shocked that you are so cavalier about this. You are not even interested?"

"My daughter is," he said as if to offer something to Mi Mi. He wanted to change the subject, so he led her to the elevator in the hallway. The teak doors slid open with a grinding sound, and they got in. At the door to his room, Mi Mi stepped in front of him, and he smelled sandalwood perfume. She was so confident about the place where she fit into her world. Pete was envious. He felt lifeless and lost in comparison.

They booted up his computer and transferred the images, and Mi Mi settled into a chair to scroll through them. In ten minutes, she announced, "It looks like this is just south of Mandalay. I recognize one of the pagodas along the river. And the mud up there has an unusual yellow tint to it. See in the video how the people on the raft duck into the shack? They must have seen Bridget filming them."

Pete studied the film and agreed. "If you weren't right on the water's edge, you could miss this even in the daylight. It rides pretty low in the river."

"This film is hard to see. If we could get a clear video, I could leak it to the media and to the outside world."

"Like the NGO Jeffrey Sumpter worked for? Free the Oxygen."

"Right. The generals want more international legitimacy. They've been reacting well to this kind of outside pressure. It won't change overnight, but anything we can do to help is worthwhile." She leaned back in the chair and used her hands to lift the hair off her shoulders. She fluffed it and let it drop back down.

Pete was tempted to run his own hand through it, but that wasn't the message Mi Mi sent. "And what about Bridget Holmes?"

"I bet she's up around Mandalay somewhere."

"Then why wouldn't she report?"

"Remember, there's no Internet, and most phones don't work well."

Pete walked to the French doors and looked out onto the small balcony. He didn't hear any birds calling. "Or she's *unable* to report," he said over his shoulder into the silence of the room.

Mi Mi's phone rang, and she answered. It was Moe, telling them he had three tickets to Mandalay, scheduled to leave in two hours. She relayed it to Pete. "Smashing. We'll meet him at a temple on the way to the airport. He will drive from there."

"Aren't you worried about your phone getting tapped?"

Mi Mi chuckled. "In this country? The generals are prats, idiots. They'd never be able to figure out how to do it."

Pete called the embassy to tell Carter Smith about the flight and their plans at Mandalay.

Next, Pete assembled an overnight bag. He tucked $3,000 cash from Ex-Im funds into a thin cotton belt that he strapped around his waist, then covered with his shirt. He brought Mi Mi back to her apartment, where she packed, and they drove north along Kabar Aye Pagoda Road. At a large intersection, Pete saw a dozen shops selling precious gems clustered around the Myanmar Gems Museum. On the far side stood the Cherry Pann Royal Palace restaurant.

"One of our richest natural resources is gems," Mi Mi explained. "Especially rubies and sapphires that are mined up north of Mandalay. Also, we mine gold. Much of that is purchased in stamp-sized thin pieces to offer to the Buddha. After centuries of people sticking gold on the statues, some of their shapes are unrecognizable as Buddhas."

Pete kept the speed down as they passed the shops and came to the Kabar Aye Pagoda. The car crunched into the small gravel parking lot. To the left a golden dome rose out of the ground among the palms and mango trees as if it were an alien spacecraft that had recently landed. Some of the mangos were over one hundred feet tall, with glossy red leaves that drooped over the dome of the pagoda.

They parked and looked for Moe. He came out of the pagoda and hurried to a long, low building that sat in the corner behind a huge brass bell resting on the ground. A wooden log leaned against the side of it. He waved at them and ducked into the building. Mi Mi looked at Pete with a queer smile and told him to follow her.

The building was empty except for a large glass case that ran the entire length of the right wall. Behind the glass stood several statues that looked like big dolls. Some were made of gold and dressed in colorful clothing. Each one had a different face and stood in a different pose. The facial features were exaggerated and grotesque. Some had mouths gaping open; others had hideous smiles with green and red teeth. Some looked like ogres. Another one straddled the back of a bleeding Brahma bull. The largest statue wore a black beret and a black cape with red lining. Worshippers had placed house slippers on his misshapen feet. A pink silk scarf dangled over his shoulders, and he leaned against a golden lion with a snarling mouth larger than his head. The face on the statue smiled to reveal black teeth.

Pete saw Moe walk halfway down the row and drop to his knees while he bent forward in prayer.

Mi Mi whispered, "Naturals, or nats. These are representations of real people who died violent deaths. They are thought to have supernatural powers to intercede in daily life. The worship of these magical figures is outlawed, but many people still practice it—like my brother."

"I thought Buddhism was the official religion," Pete said.

"It is, but most of the generals believe in numerology, astrology, and animism, so they tolerate worship of the Nats. For instance, a person's date of birth is essential to diagnosing problems. That's why our former leader Than Shwe's birth date was always kept secret—so that he would be safe from lethal magic that could be practiced against him."

Moe bobbed his head one last time and rose. He came to them and patted Pete on the shoulder. "Are you ready to go?" He looked at his watch. "We must hurry to catch flight."

"They're on time?" Pete asked.

"This is last one of the day. We cannot be late."

The three turned to leave. Pete finally asked Moe, "I thought you were a Buddhist?"

"Moe is a Buddhist." He grinned and looked into Pete's eyes. "But belief in magic and supernatural things run all through our culture. It explain why many things happen. Moe Ma Kha also use magic in my investigations to try and figure out why people act the way they do. Maybe Nats can offer answer to the mystery of Mr. Sumpter's death. But we need to hurry."

"Why is that?"

He hesitated. "Month of Black Moons will be here in two weeks. Many bad things happen then. We want to be finish with work before that time."

Pete stopped walking and stared at Moe. "You're educated. You don't really believe this stuff, do you?" From the distance, he heard the hollow sound of the large brass bell he'd seen before. Three times it rang.

A flash of anger crossed the detective's face. And for once, he didn't avoid looking Pete in the eyes. "There are many things in country you Westerners never understand. They are so old we do not remember where come from. Do not make joke of them as it bring danger for you also." He looked behind them, frowned, and ordered, "Hurry."

Mi Mi kept her eyes down on the path before them and said, "Two full moons in one month—'Black Moons.'" She wasn't smiling.

Back in the car, they raced north on the Pyay Road to reach the airport.

They hurried into the lobby. Pete's long legs put him in the lead until he saw Captain Thaung inside the door. Pete stopped as Moe and Mi Mi came up behind him. Moe saluted to the captain.

"Captain Thaung back and have been ordered to accompany the three of you," he said.

"It is not necessary," Moe assured him.

Thaung blinked once. "Orders. Unfortunately, there are no seats left on the last flight. I will meet you in Mandalay." He forced Moe to give him the hotel address in Mandalay. With an odd look on his face, the captain called after them, "Enjoy your flight."

Pete approached the metal detectors. A thin young man sat behind the x-ray screen, and Pete could see the colors flicker in reflection on his brown skin.

He looked up at Pete and motioned him forward.

Pete placed his suitcase and backpack on the conveyor belt. He didn't take anything off, nor did he remove any clothing. He walked next to the moving belt. The young man glanced at the screen and waved Pete on again. At the far end, he lifted his suitcase off the belt and swung the backpack over his shoulder. Pete noticed six car batteries sitting under the conveyor belt. Two wires ran up to the machine the young boy watched. Pete realized the batteries were the only source of power for the apparatus and, at best, they only ran the belt itself and didn't have enough power to run the x-ray machine in addition. Fake security.

Moe used his official ID to slip through the checkpoint, and he rushed Pete outside onto the hot tarmac. The small prop plane looked bulky and heavy as it sat on the runway, its propellers turning lazily. Men in military uniforms loaded the luggage and cargo into the belly of the plane.

Pete followed a line of passengers out to the plane and came around the tail. Another man stood there holding the tail up in the air with his hand. He must have noticed the look of concern on Pete's face because the man said, "Just until we get cargo adjusted for weight. We have to be careful." He smiled and called to the crew filling the hold. Pete followed the other two up the aluminum ladder into the rear of the plane. As he was about to step inside, he saw the man at the tail had left, and the plane remained level. He shook his head and remembered the fake x-ray machine at the airport when he'd first arrived. What a damn primitive place this country was!

Inside, Pete tried to sit next to Mi Mi, but the flight attendant directed him across the aisle. "To balance the weight in the plane," the woman explained. He sat next to the window, looked out, and was surprised to see Captain Thaung standing on the tarmac watching the plane.

In twenty minutes, they had risen through humid skies to reach their cruising altitude. Pete stretched his leg into the narrow aisle. The old prop engines were noisy, unlike the quieter jet engines. Sunlight flooded the cabin, and the air conditioning, thankfully, was working well.

The flight attendant, dressed in a tight uniform, walked down the aisle offering a basket of small hard candies to the passengers. Her glistening black hair was wrapped in a bun on top of her head. Her face had perfect make-up, with red lipstick and lavender eye shadow.

A siren clanged and the plane pitched hard to the left. Mi Mi strained against the seat belt and flopped over to the side, hanging into the aisle. The plane corkscrewed down as if slipping through a children's slide. People screamed and luggage fell from the overhead bins. The interior lights flickered off. Pete could hear a sickening creak along the entire fuselage as it twisted beyond the normal shape.

"Cargo shifted," the flight attendant screamed as the plane nosed over into a dive toward the ground.

Chapter Ten

The plane fell with only the clouds to slow it down. Cushions, baggage, people, trays, water bottles, and iPhones flew throughout the cabin. Whenever the body of the plane groaned, people screamed even more. The pilots struggled to right it.

Pete saw Mi Mi wedged between the aisle and a seat in an unusual position even though she was still strapped in. He wanted to help her. Her hair flapped around her head and her eyes bulged. He thought of unstrapping himself to reach her. That would endanger him, and he wasn't sure he could save her anyway. He remained in his seat.

The noise got louder. The plane shuddered and rolled back to an upright position. It dropped lower. Pete thought of the possibility of dying. His one quick regret was not being able to patch up things with Karen. Would she ever know that his last thoughts had been about her and how much he loved her?

The fuselage squealed again, but the pilot was able to stop the free fall.

They leveled off close above the tree tops. Pete heard a roar as the engines received more fuel and the plane managed to stabilize on a straight path. The screaming stopped, and he wiggled out of his seat belt to find Mi Mi. He felt bruised along his entire back. He found her thrown forward in her seat. Her face was blanched white, but otherwise she seemed okay. They hugged tightly. Pete helped to straighten her into the seat.

When the plane started to climb, the passengers gave a nervous cheer and applauded for the skill of the pilots.

In twenty minutes, they came down over the Mandalay airport. It was located far out of the city in the middle of a vacant pasture. Gold and white pagodas dotted the landscape. Pete could see the terminal with peaked roofs that had decorative gold filigree around the top. One other plane was on the tarmac, and they landed alongside of it. When the plane stopped moving, the passengers gave another, more confident cheer. The pilot stepped from the cockpit to apologize to everyone. "We promise to investigate this immediately," he said in both English and Burmese.

Pete followed Moe and Mi Mi into the new airport. It was an hour outside of Mandalay.

Mi Mi explained, "The rumor is a crony owned this land and was able to get airport built out here with government money." They waited for their bags to be brought in from the plane.

Pete watched as two men in light blue overalls wheeled a flat cart out to the plane and started to lift the baggage out of the belly of the airplane. When they had piled the wagon full, one tugged at the handle to move it back into the terminal. Humans powered almost everything in this country.

Moe left them while Pete helped Mi Mi. She felt weak, so he carried her bag, and they moved to the lobby of the terminal. They came through the older, gray part where people shoved into a narrow hallway. There was only one bathroom, and Pete waited a long time for Mi Mi to get through the women's side. He felt exhausted from the ordeal, but he wanted to get to the main office of the timber company as soon as they could. There were only a few hours of light left before the tropical night brought total darkness.

When they made it to the lobby, Moe had already beaten them there. He scowled and looked around constantly. "I learn cargo had been misplaced in plane. It was loaded to guarantee plane would be too heavy on one side and crash. Only skill of pilots save us."

"A mistake?" Pete asked.

Moe shook his head. "You remember soldiers who load plane? It was meant for us."

Pete jerked backward. He looked around but saw only dozens of Burmese people hunching forward toward the exit door. It felt hot, and he could smell incense burning from a Buddhist altar somewhere behind them. "Captain Thaung? But your general wants you to investigate the case. Why would—?"

Moe shrugged. "While some events explain with certainty, there is much remains unknown. Moe not sure who is responsible. Soldiers could have been ordered by different general who is opposed to my general. Orders for Moe are to continue investigation of Mr. Sumpter death."

"Then we better get to the timber office as soon as possible," Pete urged. "I've got to find Bridget." Then Pete could get out of the country and back home.

They walked out of the terminal to the parking lot and hailed a taxi. Two ragged dogs trailed after them, growling for handouts. Another one circled from further away.

Pete thought back to the dirty shop in Yangon where he'd first met General Win. Pete remembered the utterly indifferent brutality the general had shown. Pete was sure that, like bullies and assholes the world over, the general was fully capable of downing an airplane just to stop an investigation. Pete looked at Moe and Mi Mi—two people struggling to make a small change in their country. Underdogs. Pete's first impulse was to "fight fire with fire." But he knew that approach wouldn't work in this country. He'd have to work within the culture to help. That challenged Pete.

At least the taxi had air conditioning, and they bumped over the two-lane road into Mandalay. At a roundabout, Mi Mi pointed to the white four-lane road that stretched into the wiggling heat of the distance. "Our blooming freeway," she said proudly. "It connects Mandalay to Yangon and is the first and longest in the country."

The taxi turned through the roundabout and drove onto the highway. The tires chattered, and they couldn't go faster than fifty miles an hour. For a new freeway it was horrible, but Pete didn't dare criticize anything. When Moe told him it had been built entirely by hand, Pete understood why it was so rough.

"When we get into town, can we stop for me to buy some new clothing?" Pete asked.

"Your Western jeans are too hot?" Mi Mi laughed.

"Yeah, I'm dying in these. And the shirt has to go, too."

In ten minutes, the cab turned to the right and drove along fields of rice, garlic, and soybeans. Acacia trees flanked the road, creating large circles of shade underneath them. Pete saw a man in a field guiding two gray Brahma bulls that pulled a wooden plow. The black soil was so choppy the farmer stumbled through the furrows as if he were drunk.

As they got closer to the city, Pete could see small homes on the outskirts bunched together, almost on top of each other. Neighborhoods were intersected by dusty dirt lanes. People walked along the sides of the roads, some with bikes, some on motor scooters, and some rode wooden carts pulled by oxen. Small groups of burgundy-robed monks strolled toward the monastery in the city. Their bare right shoulders exposed brown skin, and in spite of the dust, their robes were immaculate.

The variety of colors stunned Pete. He'd never seen so many different shades of green. And the houses were painted saffron, mint, cinnamon, cherry red, and lemon.

The traffic slowed down. Off to the left, gleaming in the lowered sun, was a section of the Irrawaddy River. In the distance, it looked as blue as the bright sky. Up close, it revealed muddy, stagnant water. Pete could smell burning wood, pungent feces from the oxen beside the road, and exhaust from the trucks. Even the heat had a smell—dusty and ancient.

They came into the business section of the city. A billboard said, *Crush all Internal and External Destructive Elements as the Common Enemy.* Drainage ditches ran parallel to the sides of the road. Long sections of wood covered them to protect people from falling in. When the cab stopped at an intersection, Pete saw a tractor dealership that offered several palm green tractors. He asked Mi Mi about them. "Looks pretty prosperous," he said.

She scoffed. "It's all fake. No one here has the money to afford even one of those. The cronies display these to impress the tourists." As they left the intersection, she pointed. "Like this car dealership. No one can afford BMWs in this country."

"*Most* of us cannot," Moe said. "*Families* can afford anything."

"What families?" Pete asked.

"Eighteen extended families own everything in country. They unbelievably wealthy and corrupt."

Pete recalled that Carter Smith had also said that.

As they drove deeper into the central city, the buildings became newer, and Pete even saw what looked like western-style shopping malls. The contrasts in the country astounded him. Less than three miles behind him, a farmer pushed a plow by hand, and here there were BMWs sitting in vacant lots—but none on the streets. Instead, hundreds of cheap Chinese motorbikes whined around them.

The taxi stopped before the Royal Palace Hotel. With just enough time to drop off their luggage, they got back into the cab and kept moving.

In five minutes, Mi Mi said, "We'll stop here for your new clothes."

On a narrow street that climbed up a gentle hill, the cab pulled to the side and stopped. They all got out, and Mi Mi led Pete into a tiny shop. Inside, the clerk gave him a thin smile with white teeth. "*Mingalar par*," she said and nodded. He placed his hands together and bobbed his head once. She led him between narrow aisles to find two pairs of cotton pants with drawstrings at the waist and three white, long-sleeve shirts that, at first, seemed much too large. With Mi Mi's translations, the clerk explained the size was necessary to let cool air circulate around the body. Pete bought all of them and a pair of leather sandals. He couldn't go so far as to buy rubber flip-flops like all the locals wore. At the last minute, he plucked a pair of sunglasses off a rack and put them on.

"You look like—what do you call those blokes, NASCAR drivers?" Mi Mi chuckled.

"This may help my image." Pete came out of the shop into the heat of the street. A small truck whizzed past, piled to overflowing with dirty white bags of rice and three people who perched precariously on top of the mounds. They waved a cheery greeting at him. In the dusty wake of the truck, four dogs wandered across the street.

Mi Mi waved back at the riders. "They must think you're Burmese," she joked and pointed at his new clothing. She reached forward to adjust the loose shirt over his shoulders. When she finished, her fingers lingered along the sides of his arms, touching them lightly.

"Yeah, I blend. At least it feels cooler." He hurried back to the taxi. "Let's get going; we've got a lot to check into."

The driver wound his way through tangled streets all crowded with vehicles and scooters and wagons. There were a few deserted brick buildings with a wall or two that had fallen in on themselves. A spreading ficus tree climbed out of the rubble of one and, with its groping branches, threatened to bring down a third wall.

"What are those?" Pete asked.

"Colonial buildings," Moe said. "Most people in Myanmar want to erase evidence of occupation by British." He looked out the window as he spoke.

Pete didn't understand. "But that was over sixty years ago."

"It does not matter. We value our independence that much. We all live close to nature, but it is useless to try control nature. It always grow back. We learn to co-exist with plant world."

"Sure." What would Moe think if he were to visit Manhattan? Pete wondered.

The cab turned into a long street and traded sides of the road with oncoming traffic so they could pass each other. On both sides for as far as Pete could see, there were Buddha heads sitting on the ground. Small shops, divided by hanging fabric walls, made and sold the statues. The heads were of all sizes, some large enough to place before a temple; others were small for inside a home. Bulky pieces of raw marble stood next to completed heads gleaming in the afternoon sun. Marble dust filled the air and made it difficult to see into the shops. Few workers wore face masks, but they smiled and waved as the taxi drove past them. Tracks of sweat stained the white dust that covered their faces. This street must represent the entire Buddha construction industry for the country.

"We come to main office of timber company," Moe announced.

Pete felt excited. He'd come too far to give up now. When the cab stopped before another small shop, Pete was disappointed. After all the build-up about the evil company, he had expected a huge edifice, something large and sinister.

A bamboo office sat at the edge of the road. A flat tin roof sloped down under a ficus tree that hung protectively over it from behind. Through yellow-framed windows, silk curtains fluttered out as if they were trying to escape. Three wooden steps led to the closed wooden door in front. On one side of the office, an open-air noodle shop offered lunch. Above the restaurant was a billboard that advertised Alpine bottled drinking water with a bright blue cap lying in a field of snow.

The taxi parked in front of the office. A sign read *The Yangon International Timber Co.* in English and in Burmese. No one was inside.

Pete walked in a small circle in the road, frustrated. They'd come all this way for nothing. The entire country was so screwed up, he might as well quit and go back to Minnesota. For all he knew, Bridget had been killed, like Jeffrey Sumpter, and would never be found.

"It is not important," Moe announced. He put on his glasses and started to get back into the cab.

Pete shouted, "Nothing works in this damn country."

"We find evidence at river. Please come," Moe urged him.

Pete looked at Mi Mi and watched as a puff of wind pressed her *longyi* against the back of her legs and butt to outline her clearly. He decided to at least go to the river with them. In a cough of dust, the driver sped off and turned at the next corner.

"In Bridget's video, I recognized one of the pagodas on the river," Mi Mi said. "It's just south of here. Maybe we could see the rafts from that spot."

Moe agreed.

They left the tangle of traffic and followed a tar road along the edge of the muddy river. The banks sloped down in bare patches of earth. They passed a field where five women in conical straw hats bent under the fading sun and hoed furrows into the soil. They straightened, smiled, and waved as the taxi passed.

Between the fields, wood-frame houses with brown straw walls balanced on stilts that reached out over the water. There were long wooden planks that led from the road over the slope of the river bank to enter each house. An occasional cow grazed on the little grass that grew nearby. Colorful clothing hung from wooden racks built next to the houses, and Pete could see into some of them through windows without glass. They looked vacant because there wasn't any furniture inside, but he saw kids running in and out of the rooms. The only doors were in the front, wood-framed and also made of straw, and always closed. Several fires smoldered on the ground underneath the houses.

Mounds of garbage lay between the houses, mostly plastic bags strewn along the river bank. Popping up amongst the trash were discarded plastic chairs, pieces of wood, and twisted metal debris.

At the next intersection, the cab rocked to a halt. The road was blocked by a white barrier. Behind it stood four soldiers in uniform who carried Chinese automatic weapons. They didn't smile and they waved the cab to the left, down another road away from the river.

"This is recent," Moe said as he looked back and forth. "Try to come from south," he ordered the driver. When they had circled through fields of rice to return to the river from the south, they encountered more road blocks. "We get out and walk," Moe said. The taxi stopped. The jungle crowded right up to the edge of the road.

He told the driver to retreat to a hidden spot on the road, park and wait for them. The driver refused. Moe accepted his hesitation and came back to the other two. "He is frightened. We catch ride from someone else. People always willing to give ride. Mr. Chandler like sitting in ox cart?" He laughed at Pete.

"I've done things here I've never done before. Why not an ox cart?"

Moe led them from the road into the jungle that grew up to the edge of the river. The minute they entered the green space, Pete felt claustrophobic, and sweat broke out across his body. He heard monkeys chattering high above but rarely spotted them. He followed the others over a hard-packed yellow mud path that twisted through the bushes. In a few minutes, he was lost. In ten minutes he could smell water. They must be close to the river.

The jungle was so dark, it looked black instead of green. Pete thought of cities like New York, of how humans had harnessed monster nature and eliminated it for the most part in favor of concrete. Here, it was reversed: nature was monstrous and unshackled. Menacing.

Ahead, Moe asked Pete to duck down and crawl the rest of the way. Pete agreed and could hear the rumbling of big engines and the squish of mud from somewhere in front. He caught up to the others and squeezed in next to Mi Mi. Her legs stuck out behind her, and Pete noticed her thin ankles and small feet and the pink flip-flops. Her toenails were painted two different colors.

Moe whispered, "Look there." He pointed down a slope before them.

Pete pushed aside a branch and saw a line of trucks. Each one had an engine in the front that looked like a baboon's snout. Each had a bed full of cut teak piled so high he wondered how the truck could even move. The engines were crude and had a big fly wheel on the side. He commented on them to Moe.

"Chinese motors. Three hundred dollars each. Very tough. You see all over country. They use for trucks, carts, and even outboard motors for boats."

The trucks lined up, pointing at the river bank. At some signal, the next in line groaned forward to slide through deep ruts down the muddy incline. Several soldiers stood at the edges of the operation with guns held at "port arms" position.

"Please we move close?" Moe said.

Pete scuttled after the other two and came within sight of the river. It flowed by in a muddy, choppy current. Tied up along the shore were two huge rafts made of teak logs. Several men, dressed only in shorts, worked on the rafts. Other than the trucks, there were no other machines to help them move the logs. They used the steep slope of the bank to roll the teak toward the river, and once the logs splashed into the water, the men waded after them. They floated the teak into position along the assembled rafts, adding the new logs. At the perimeters, more soldiers stood guard.

The carcass of a dead cow lay off to the side of the line of trucks. Moe speculated that it had unknowingly wandered away from the owners into the operation. Rather than lead it out, the soldiers had shot it. It could easily be the family's main asset.

Mi Mi said, "They must build the rafts up river and add to them as they come south."

Pete sat back on folded knees. Part of him felt satisfied—they'd found proof of the illegal activity. But he was still discouraged. They hadn't found Bridget, and even with this proof, what difference would it make here? The generals and cronies would continue their crooked businesses, and nothing would change. The wind shifted, and Pete smelled exhaust from the trucks and the primeval mud he squatted over.

Mi Mi felt differently. She raised her iPhone and clicked several photos. "I'll get these distributed as soon as I can," she said. "Look at the trucks. They've got the bloody name of the Yangon Timber Company on the sides."

"They don't even try to hide that." Pete shook his head at the brazen attitude of the generals.

"It's not much, but people are upset with corruption. Every little bit we can expose helps things," Mi Mi said.

Pete disagreed but admired the determination of these two people.

When they'd finished the photos, they backed up along the path. In a few minutes, they worked their way close to the road. The jungle was silent, but it wasn't a peaceful silence. It was the stillness of something huge that was waiting for humans to leave and let the jungle return to its dominion. As they turned a bend in the path, four men appeared out of the undergrowth to surround them.

They weren't dressed as soldiers but looked like they'd been in the jungle for a long time. From his military training, Pete assessed them as some kind of soldiers—but they were Caucasians.

"Find anything?" one of the men asked. He stood with his hip cocked to one side, and he tilted back a floppy camouflage hat that was sweat-stained around the brim.

Moe became deferential and bowed his head. "Yes, activity behind us. I do not understand many English words."

"What?" a second man asked. His voice was deep.

Pete pushed his way to the front. "What the hell are you doing here?"

"Hey, cowboy, we'll ask the questions," the first man said.

"Who are you?"

"Okay. We got nothing to hide. We're with an NGO. Maybe you've heard of 'Free the Oxygen'?"

"Jeff Sumpter. What . . .?"

"Yes. Unfortunate. We're investigating what happened to him," the first man said. "The question is, what the hell are you doing here?" The sun fell below the jungle top, infusing crimson and blue colors into the space around them.

Pete studied his face. Scraggly beard, black eyes, and a sunburned nose. These men didn't look like any NGO people Pete had ever encountered in his work. "I'm with the US Export-Import Bank. I'm looking for an American named Bridget Holmes. She was engaged to your partner."

The man's eyes opened suddenly, and he shifted his weight to the other hip. "Black hair? Tall woman?"

"Yeah. Seen her?"

"You're too late. Three days ago in Mandalay. With two men. Burmese soldiers. The world's biggest pieces of shit as far as I can tell."

"Prisoner?"

The man shrugged.

"Where did she go?"

"You're way too interested." The man straightened and reached behind his waist to pull out an American .45 caliber automatic pistol. He pointed it at Pete.

Chapter Eleven

Pete raised his hands with palms out toward the gunman. "Take it easy, man."

"I always take it easy."

Moe stepped forward. "Please, Moe Ma Kha handle this."

Pete ignored him. "What do you want? Money?" he asked the leader.

The man snorted and looked at his partners. "Do we need money?" he asked them. Two of them chuckled but continued to stare at their prisoners. "What we need is for the three of you to get the fuck out of here."

"People keep telling me that," Pete said.

"It's good advice."

"What the hell kind of an NGO do you work for that you carry guns?"

"Hey, pal, this is a shit-hole country that doesn't make any sense. The Tatmadaw don't screw around. They're armed; so are we."

The second man pulled out a small radio from a canvas bag strapped over his shoulder. Holding it in one hand, he tapped the keys with his free fingers. "Hey, Rob. We've finally got tracking again. Dude, we're back on mission."

"We can work on solution," Moe said.

"I thought you were worried about the environmental problems in Myanmar?" Pete tried to keep the man talking as long as possible. He surveyed the other three and considered what a fight might look like—not good with these bad odds.

At Pete's comment about the environment, two of the men laughed out loud. The leader said, "Oh, we're worried about the environment, but not the kind of environment you're thinking about. This is a lot bigger than you can even imagine."

"What are you talking about?"

"Dude, that's enough," the second man hissed. "Let's get rid of them." He placed the radio back into his canvas bag.

A painful tightness gripped Pete's spine and spread heat throughout his chest. He looked beyond the NGO men and realized they were all embedded deeply in the jungle. Monkeys chattered just above their heads, and a strong wind shook the tops of the fishtail palm trees. Their trunks curved down gracefully into the soft soil. A green coconut was smashed open on the ground where an animal had eaten the tasty pulp inside. In spite of all the pulsating life around them, it was very quiet.

"Wait a minute," Pete said. "Were Jeff and Bridget aware of the teak smuggling?"

"Probably."

"Is that why Jeff was killed?"

"Like I said, there's a lot more going on, and it'd be better if you didn't know."

"What does Bridget have to do with all of this?" Pete asked.

The leader took a deep breath. "I don't know."

"Can you at least tell me where she went?" Pete could sense the leader was an arrogant man who was proud of his superior knowledge. If Pete could play with that, maybe there would be a chance to escape.

"We saw her on the walkway by the palace, looking out over the moat with two of those shithead soldiers."

"Okay, Rob. Enough. Let's get the hell back to base," the second man yelled. "Don't forget the intercept, dude."

Pete felt the shift in attitude. "I'm warning all of you that the United States ambassador knows we are here. Anything goes wrong, you'll have to answer to him and the Marines."

A smiled crept across the leader's face. He shook his head. "Like I said, you don't know shit what's going on. The least of our worries are a couple of Marines. We outrank them. Besides, we're working closer with the embassy people than you are." He stepped forward and faced Moe. "Okay, Gunga Din, I want you to turn around with your girlfriend."

Moe hesitated, and Pete could see anger color his face.

"I know you can understand English. Now turn the fuck around before I smash your pumpkin face. We're trying to help you people since you can't seem to do it yourselves."

"I am lieutenant in Yangon People's Police Department. Moe Ma Kha can help if you talk with me."

"Talk with you?" the leader rolled his head back in a deep laugh. "You're part of the fucking problem here." He paused and must have given a thought to what Moe had said. "If I do talk with you, Gunga Din, tell me everything you know."

"Maybe working for same outcome. Please put down guns?"

"I doubt that. The rafts are really for—"

Moe glared at the leader and suddenly chopped his hand down hard against the leader's arm that held the gun. It bounced out of his hand and flew off to land with a soft thump under a tangle of broad green leaves.

Two of the other NGOs exploded into action. One of them slammed his fist across Moe's back, between his shoulder blades. Moe crumpled onto his knees and swayed while he fought for control of his body. His glasses dropped onto the ground and his head hung forward, exposing his neck to the man standing over him, poised to strike again.

Without thinking, Pete reacted to save his friend. As he had practiced hundreds of times in his Tae Kwon Do training, he raised his knee to the waist and pulled his toes back. In a linear move, he snapped his foot forward toward Moe's attacker. The front snap kick, called an *ap chagi*, was intended to stun or ward off an opponent; this time, Pete hoped it would incapacitate the man. Pete caught him high in the chest and sent him sprawling to the right. Pete raised his knee to the waist again and simultaneously rotated ninety degrees to the left. With the side thrusting kick, known as a *yeop chagi*, Pete landed his heel on another man's back. His head snapped backward, and Pete hoped the spinal cord had been severed from the blow. The next man came at Pete and swung his fist. When Pete leaned back, he could feel the rush of air across his face. As the man cocked his arm for another swing, Pete came in fast with a flurry of open and closed hand strikes. The idea was to not only confuse the opponent, but also to look for a vulnerable opening.

Pete saw it immediately and stiffened his open four fingers into a position called *chigi* and thrust them into the soft side of the man's neck. He stopped and choked with a deep cough before he rolled back onto the ground and lay curled in the fetal position.

Pete spun around in an effort to keep moving, to deny the opponent a stationary target. He saw the fourth man had disappeared.

Moe stood up with Mi Mi's help. He blinked several times and looked around at the damage Pete had done. He didn't say anything for a moment as he replaced his glasses. His eyes looked huge. "We cannot fight men. Please, we leave?"

Even though he trained regularly, Pete felt exhausted after the fight.

Moe led them up the winding mud path into an open part of the jungle and up into the last of the sun that dispersed through the floating dust to make it glow golden. In a few moments, several motor scooters buzzed into the clearing. Moe flagged them down and spoke in Burmese to the drivers, and they immediately shifted forward on the seats to give the three enough space to mount on the back ends. Mi Mi sat with both legs to one side and clung to the shoulders of a young boy who twisted the throttle. Leading the group, he churned through the dirt to get away.

In twenty minutes, they were back in the crush of traffic and people in Mandalay. Moe directed the group to the hotel he'd chosen earlier near the center of the city. Since tourism was only a few years old in the country, the hotels were either luxury or youth hostels. There was nothing in between yet.

The drivers dropped them off in front of the Royal Palace Hotel, where they had stored their luggage earlier.

The adrenaline drop had left Pete feeling tired and worn out. He'd never expected the search for Bridget would be this tough or last this long. Depression haunted him again and made Pete feel lifeless in spite of his physical survival in the jungle. When he was young and stupid, he'd gotten into endless fights. He'd justified them, back then, because he was defending a friend or helping the underdog. As he matured, he realized how futile and dangerous that practice was for him. Now, the country, the frustration, the threatening situation, and his own lack of control had put him right back into the behavior he wanted to avoid. Maybe he should just go home.

The country itself was a bigger mystery than the one he was trying to solve.

Mi Mi and Moe brushed off the dust of the road from their clothing and ignored Pete as they walked up three steps into the lobby of the hotel. Pete followed. Inside, flowers grew from every possible window, pot, trellis, and vase. They grew in yellow, lotus blue, red, pink, and orchid white. The smell was overpowering, and Pete had to stop to catch his breath. A young woman with shiny black hair, a wide smile, and thanaka painted on her cheeks met him inside the open-air lobby and bowed slightly. The tan cream on her face had a leaf pattern drawn into it. She welcomed him and offered a glass of fresh-squeezed mango juice. A porter told Pete he'd take care of everything. "*Mingalar par*," Pete said to him.

The change from the jungle where'd he just about killed three men to stand in a lobby and feel a soft breeze blow over the flowers and carry their scent caused Pete to stumble. It was surreal—just like the country.

After depositing their luggage in their rooms and washing up, the three gathered in the lobby again. Both Moe and Mi Mi were quiet, and Pete assumed the fight in the jungle had upset them more than he'd thought. Even for a cop, Moe probably didn't see much in the way of violence. The generals perpetrated plenty of violence toward the people, but most individuals were peaceful.

"Can we please get tea and talk about next move?" Moe finally said.

They walked outside and came down into the road. Across a four-lane street was a wide sidewalk with benches set at regular intervals, sheltered by tall mango trees with glossy red leaves. Beyond that, a huge body of water spread out for two city blocks. Across the surface, dotted with black cormorants and cranes, he saw an immense fortress set in the middle of the lake.

"The palace," Mi Mi said. "It is two miles square, and the water formed the original moat. The king and the court used to live there. Now it is occupied by the generals and the cronies. You can tell because they have removed all the decorative aspects to leave only the battlements." Mi Mi pointed to the tops of the walls.

They were creased at intervals with slots for firing weapons at invaders coming across the moat. Other than the dull red tops, the walls and doors of the old palace were strictly utilitarian. Two palm trees struggled to grow at one corner. Several concrete barriers were staggered across the four roads leading from each side of the moat into the fortress. Gates and guard houses stood in silence at the foot of the massive walls. It looked forbidding, and even in the heat, it seemed cold and lifeless. As if to warn Pete, several of the cormorants unhinged their necks and honked across the water in calls that sounded like sick cows.

Mi Mi paused on the sidewalk. "They have stolen everything. Even our history." The bitterness in her voice was obvious. "In Bangkok, the government has preserved the royal palace in splendid shape and open to the public. It is decorated in the original colors and designs. People come from all over the world to see it. And the Thais are proud of their heritage. To remember and understand your heritage is so important." She sighed and started to walk through the wave of heat from the sidewalk. "Here, we are like the Soviets and the Kremlin. The generals hiding behind walls of mystery."

Two dogs with tongues hanging out of their mouths loped past them.

The three walked slowly and came to a sheltered stand on the corner. Three large ceramic pots sat on a shelf with tin covers over each pot. A battered tin cup hung from a string off the wall behind the pots. Mi Mi stopped and lifted the cup. She opened a pot and dipped the cup inside for water, which she drank quickly. "Don't think I can wait until the tea shop," she said and covered the pot with the lid. She said to Pete, "Our version of the public drinking fountain. I know—when I got back from England, I couldn't imagine touching them. But you get used to the idea, and after a while, you participate with the culture. I haven't gotten sick yet." She smiled.

They reached a small open-air tea shop called The Golden Lion. Inside, it was slightly cooler in the shade. "Would you like to try some tea very sweet?" Mi Mi's eyes teased Pete.

"I miss Starbucks, but okay," he replied.

"Sugar was one of only luxuries we had during hard times," Moe added. He sat on the low stool and wrapped his legs underneath it. He ordered very sweet tea.

"Do you miss the gardens in England?" Pete asked Mi Mi. He waved his hand around the street. "Here, everything's green with lots of flowers, but it grows virtually wild."

Her expression, which had been flat, changed at the mention of gardens. "You're right. I do miss England. I studied in Kent, southeast of London, which is the garden heart of the country. Of course, an English garden is smashingly planned and organized. Here, we have gardens, but since nature is so powerful, we tend to let things go. It is enough work just to keep it trimmed back." She leaned back on her stool. "Winter is one of the nicest times here when my favorite plant blooms: the Thazin orchid. It grows wild and has tiny blossoms, paper-colored, with yellow stamens that curve over the green stems. It's the most exquisite and romantic flower in the country because even in spite of the cooler weather, it still insists on growing into something beautiful."

The tea came, and they all drank in silence for a long time. Pete could sense something had changed between him and the other two. He decided to ask them directly. "So, what's wrong? I can tell something's different."

Moe waited for a moment. "Yes, everything okay."

Pete had been in the country long enough to recognize the Burmese cultural tendency to pretend to agree with someone they thought was educated or in authority. It was one of many aspects of the country that frustrated Pete. Why couldn't they just say what they meant? "Tell me what you're really thinking," Pete demanded.

Moe stiffened and turned away.

Pete leaned closer to Mi Mi. Maybe her life in Western Europe would make a difference. "What's up?" he asked her.

She set down her small cup and looked at him. She cleared her throat. "This is difficult for me to say, but we are grateful for your help in the jungle. But we do not deal with things in that manner."

Pete jerked back and almost fell off the stool. ". . . *In that manner?* What the hell kind of 'manner' is it when some guy points a gun at you? And what about when they attacked Moe?"

Moe refused to turn around.

Mi Mi continued, "You are quick to use violence to settle everything. Moe could handle himself back there. But you seem to become just like the enemy."

"But he hit Moe first."

From over his shoulder, Moe said, "I pretend to be hurt, but it was not bad. Moe surprised at you often. For student of Tae Kwon Do, you know to turn enemy force against enemy."

Pete frowned but didn't say anything. What he'd first interpreted in Moe to be weakness and deference, Pete now realized masked deep convictions and inner strength. He'd come to respect Moe, but this was too much.

"That's an ancient Asian form of fighting," Mi Mi said. "Why did you study it?"

"Huh? I don't know. I guess I like the control and balance that you learn by practicing."

"Could it be a subconscious way of reaching back to your heritage?"

Pete hesitated for a moment. "I never thought about that. Maybe."

Moe glanced at Mi Mi, then said, "Please, we work apart? We appreciate help, but you are Brahma bull that cannot be controlled."

"If that's what you think, I'm all for splitting." He felt his face grow hot.

"Yes. Do not be offended. One practice of Buddhism is learn to accept things and life as they are. Moe cannot change you, and I must accept you but do not have to work with you." Moe drained the last of his tea and signaled for a refill. "Investigation of Jeffrey

Sumpter death is very risky for us. Your action make it more dangerous."

Pete stopped to think. It was tempting. He'd be happy to get out of this tangled country anyway. He could tell the congressman he'd tried to find Bridget but couldn't. Simple. It wasn't his problem. It was obvious that he couldn't accomplish much here anyway.

But then he looked at Mi Mi and realized that he wanted to keep going with her. She'd touched something in his lonely life that he didn't want to give up yet. "Hey, I'm sorry."

The other two looked at him but didn't say anything.

"I said I'm sorry. Let's start over. I'll do it your way."

Mi Mi shook her head. "That's not the problem, Pete. You do not respect us and our ways of working to accomplish our goals."

Pete's breath came harder, and the heat felt like a blanket had been dropped over his head. This speech sounded way too much like Martin Graves' speeches and Pete's problems back at the office. "Okay. Sometimes I act that way. But I fought those dudes because I was doing just what you're talking about. I was trying to help you."

Moe looked at Mi Mi for a long time. He said, "My sister want you to stay. Moe do it for her."

"But I have a condition—you have to come with me to a rally tomorrow," she interrupted.

"Oh?"

"Aung San Suu Kyi is in town and will hold a rally at the foot of the mountain across the river. I want to attend, and you will go with me."

Pete swiped his hands across the table. "I don't want to get mixed up in the politics, but I'll go with you."

"That would be a real clanger if you got involved. But you'll get an idea of what we're trying to do here, even in small steps."

"Sure. So, we're back on track with each other?" Pete looked from one to the other.

"To Westerners, all so simple. We understand things more complicated. Old Burmese saying: to live here is to unravel knots all the time," Moe said. He finished his second cup of tea.

They left and started to walk back to the hotel.

"I've got some ideas," Pete offered.

"Yes," Moe answered.

"Those guys in the jungle weren't like any NGO guys I've ever seen around the world. They looked total military to me," Pete said.

"So why are they looking at the same things we are?" Mi Mi asked.

"I don't know." Pete looked up at the puffy cumulus clouds rising high into the sky and was reminded of being on an ocean—this one composed of endless green waves of plants around him. He stopped walking. "Hey, what about Bridget? They spotted her here."

"With the soldiers. They must've kidnapped her," Mi Mi said.

"She could be anywhere now," Moe added. "But she know about rafts—and probably Jeffrey Sumpter also. If we find Bridget, we find answer to Mr. Sumpter death."

"I could tell the ambassador about the teak smuggling. They might be able to do something to stop it," Pete offered.

"Yes. Wait." Moe slashed the air with his hand. "Let me work on it first."

Pete didn't know what he meant, but in ten minutes, they were back at the Royal Palace Hotel. Moe found a secluded table in the back corner of the lobby, hidden by potted palm trees. He sat at the table and removed a thin book from his pocket. When he paged through it, frown lines creased his face.

Mi Mi must have seen the puzzled look on Pete's face. She explained, "Those books are offered at the pagodas and detail simple *yadaya* rituals for the answers to problems. Remember when Moe used the candles? That was directed by the book. Burmese and Shan subscribe to the belief that each letter of the alphabet is connected to a day of the week. That indicates a number. The correct combination of numbers can foretell the future."

Pete watched as Moe also brought out a pen and made numerology notes on the back of the book. He studied them for a long time, then raised his head to the other two. In a clear voice, he said, "You not tell ambassador yet. Not good time." He nodded at his notes. "Moe will handle it for now." He folded the notebook to indicate the issue was settled and that Pete shouldn't question him.

After the other two left for their rooms, Pete checked at the desk for messages. The Ex-Im Bank had provided him with an international phone, but it only worked in small sections of the country. Mi Mi had told him how thrilled she was that there was finally a way for her to buy pre-paid SIM cards for her phone. Prior to that, the government had sold them all at inflated prices—and then limited the access to tower coverage. Myanmar was slowly, slowly coming into the twenty-first century.

Pete found a wired message from Martin Graves. It was short: *Have you found her yet? The congressman is going crazy. If you can't get her out of there in the next two days, you will get pulled out yourself. He will send in the Marines. He's desperate.*

Pete took a deep breath. One thing he knew for sure in this convoluted country was that an "invasion" of a military force would destroy any chance they had of finding Bridget. He'd have to work faster.

The next message was from Carter Smith. It surprised Pete. She said: *I'm in Mandalay.* How long had she been here, and why hadn't she told Pete earlier? The message continued: *Meet me tomorrow at eleven at the Ciatti Hotel next to the palace. I've learned through sources about the Free the Oxygen group.* No big surprise, Pete thought. Her message concluded: *Be careful around them.*

He'd already discovered that.

Chapter Twelve

Pete walked around the old royal palace at eleven o'clock the next morning to find the Ciatti Hotel. The heat and humidity were already oppressive. He was anxious to get to the bottom of the raft business, where Pete hoped to find Bridget Holmes. He also remembered Moe's unusual reaction when Pete had saved them all by fighting with the soldiers in the jungle. Did Moe know something he wasn't telling Pete?

He came to the Ciatti Hotel. It was located on the opposite side of the central city from his hotel in an area sprinkled with a few high-end European and Chinese clothing stores and more hotels.

The Ciatti had an open air lobby with dozens of potted plants. Flower arrangements overflowed vases on every desk and counter. It was hard for Pete to sense the separation between the outdoors and indoors in this country. They flowed into one another seamlessly in a pleasant ignorance of their difference. Three men dressed in uniforms of the Myanmar royal court from the 1700s nodded a greeting to him. One offered help.

"I'm meeting Ms. Smith from the American embassy."

"Yes. She is here already." The man led Pete through the quiet lobby flanked by mirrors. Pete slowed to check out the new sunglasses. Looking good, he thought. At the end of the hall, two bamboo screen doors opened onto a small room with several tables set in front of a garden. Lotus flowers floated on still pools of water.

He saw Carter Smith sitting at a small iron table, her legs crossed and protruding to the side from under the table. She had half-rim glasses perched on her nose and was reading from a stack of papers. Next to her was a silver pot, and when he got closer, Pete saw she was drinking black coffee. The air felt cool.

Smith noticed him, pulled off the glasses, and stood. She didn't offer to shake his hand.

"Have a seat," she said. "Nice shades." She nodded at his sunglasses when he removed them.

"Thanks for the message." Pete sat in the opposite chair from her. Immediately, a waiter brought a second cup for him and started to pour coffee. Pete said, "I'd rather have tea. Sweet." Music came from somewhere in the ceiling, but Pete couldn't hear it well.

Carter chuckled at him. "You're going native, huh?" She looked around the room and said, "Beautiful place. And it's air conditioned. Some days, I can't wait to get back. To hell with the 'exotic' tropics."

"Why didn't you tell me you would be here when I said I was coming to Mandalay?" What was she hiding from him?

"Change of plans at the last minute." She put on her glasses, her eye ticked, and she dismissed Pete's concerns.

"The Ciatti Hotel. It's got an Italian name. Unusual," he said.

"Not really. The government has licensed several international companies from Italy, Spain, and China to build and manage hotels here. They want tourism but don't have any experience building or running hotels. So the generals charge exorbitant monthly fees like a franchise."

"What about Free the Oxygen?" he asked.

Smith shifted in the small chair. "We know they're a front for something and that Jeff Sumpter was part of it. I've got good sources," she insisted.

"I'm sure you do; I know how Washington works. So, what are they doing here?"

"I'm sorry to say, I don't know. But it's obvious that something serious is going on. You've got to understand there are many Washington agencies that come trolling around these third world, or should I say, *developing* countries. Maybe the NGO is really an agency of the US government," Smith added in a low voice.

"But how could that explain Jeff Sumpter's death?"

Smith shrugged and didn't answer.

"Do you know anything else that would help me?"

"No." The waiter came by to pour more coffee for Smith. "Not that you're willing to take my help, but maybe I should explain something to you."

"I've changed my mind. Tell me."

"The president's new Asian pivot policy has put many of these formerly backwater countries around the South China Sea into play, primarily as a counter-weight to the increasing power of China. The ambassador is a patriotic American, and it's his job to protect US interests here."

"What does that mean?"

"These people are wonderful and kind, but there's a personality split inherent in all of them. There's a potential for both charm and cruelty in each person in equal proportions. If you study their history, it becomes obvious that they need help. They've screwed up this country for a long time. The generals have finally realized it and are asking for help. It's either going to come from China or the United States. We're working hard to make sure we get in on the ground floor."

"With the natural resources and oil?"

"Of course, we would love to help them develop those resources, and it would be great for American business interests." Smith tilted back in her chair and honked a laugh. "For God's sake, that's what your bank is doing here."

"I know. We're working with a crooked timber-stealing company," he said with an edge to his voice. "After what they did to me, I'm gonna make them pay."

She pointed her finger at him. "If you go after the monster, often the monster becomes you. Be careful. I remember you were going to just do a surgical strike to find the Holmes girl and get out, eh?"

"Let's just say there are some things I want to get done here before I leave."

"Take my advice, Mr. Chandler: go back home. If the brutality of these dictators bothers you, get out. Let us deal with them in the only way they respect."

"Power and money?"

"Of course. In order to protect our interests, we have to deal with these tyrants. Remember when our government was 'friends' with Saddam Hussein? When we supported the brutal regime of the Shah in Iran or the military in Egypt? When Red China was our enemy until they weren't anymore? And here's the ironic thing—by getting control here, we can also help these stone-age people. Do you know there isn't even a motorized tractor in this country?"

Pete drank his tea and thought of Moe and Mi Mi. So powerless and so few in number. Maybe Smith was right. What was the use? "Where is Mr. Popham?"

"He's, uh, away on business at the capital." Her eye twitched, but she looked at him closely. "So, you haven't found the girl yet?"

"I want to talk about the ambassador. Why isn't he ever around? What does he do all the time?"

"That's none of your business, Mr. Chandler. Now, what about the Holmes girl?"

"She was seen here a few days ago with some Burmese soldiers." He was about to reveal the rafts on the river and the teak smuggling but thought of Moe's order. Crazy as it seemed, Pete decided to not tell Smith. Instead, he mentioned only the fight with the "soldiers."

"Hmm. Maybe Holmes was doing more than just looking at the books of the Yangon Timber Company, huh?"

"It looks suspicious. I'm still working with the cop from Yangon, and he seems pretty capable."

Smith blinked her eyes and looked at Pete again. "Sure." She shifted in her chair and smacked her lips in a kissing sound to get the waiter's attention. She looked embarrassed. "When in Rome, do as the Romans do. Look, Pete. I know you want to do a good job, but it's hopeless. The embassy has been in touch with the congressman, and we can take over the search for Bridget and investigate the timber company. Besides, you *don't* want to get mixed up with Free the Oxygen. I have a feeling they'd like to get even with you."

Pete took a deep breath. "I'm tempted to throw in the towel." He felt inert and colorless.

Smith nodded in agreement. "I'll even tell the congressman how hard you worked."

The waiter came over and took Smith's order for lunch. Pete declined. He thought of Karen and her boyfriend. Did Tim get the job as a sous chef at the restaurant? How were they doing? He missed her, but Pete's relationship with her was a hopeless mess. He didn't want to lose any more people from his life. After all, what the hell was he accomplishing here? A lonely guy getting in dangerous fights with strangers in remote jungles. Was he nuts? "Yeah, maybe you're right," he told Smith.

"I am right. And remember, the rainy season starts in about a week. Getting around the country will be difficult, to say the least."

"I can't leave without talking to the cop and his sister."

"Mi Mi?"

"How'd you know her name?"

Smith smiled. "It's my job to know everything that's going on."

"I'd like to talk with them. Mi Mi invited me to an Aung San Suu Kyi rally of the National League for Democracy tonight."

Smith's eyes squeezed tighter. "Be careful. For one thing, the Lon Htein will be thick in the crowds. The generals have also started using something called the *swan ah shin*. It means Masters of Force. They're an army of thugs recruited from the prisons to contain public demonstrations—any way they can. Because they don't wear uniforms, they can blend in with the people, and the government can deny responsibility for what happens. If you're caught again, I don't think I can rescue you."

"You said crowds?"

"Oh, yes. She'll draw thousands of people."

Pete was astonished. From the looks of the party headquarters in Yangon, he'd assumed it was a small shoestring movement of young people, unorganized and ineffective. "They really have some power?"

Smith leaned back in her chair. " 'The Lady,' as the people call her, has been elected to parliament, and her party may win the majority of seats in the upcoming elections. They will only have as much power as the generals allow them to have, of course. But it's a destabilizing force in this country."

"That's bad?"

"For the US and these people, in some ways, yes. I certainly don't condone the brutality and torture of the generals, but you need stability if you're going to economically develop the country.

That development will provide jobs and consumer goods to these poor people, which will improve the standard of living. In turn, that helps the US because we need a bulwark against the Chinese." Her face glowed, and it was obvious that she believed firmly in her words.

He thought of Mi Mi's words also—she wanted to destabilize the country. She was willing to sacrifice everything in the hope of a change for freedom. Pete looked behind Smith. Flowers bent over on slender stalks from vases on pedestals. He could smell the fragrance of cut lilacs. He saw a cluster of Thazin orchids and marveled how they could bloom so late in the spring. Pete looked back at Carter Smith. "Gotta run," he said. "Thanks for the information and help."

"Sure. I can help you get a plane out of here, too."

He shook her hand and left. Out on the street, the heat hit him like a big wave on a beach. Overwhelming. He stopped to take a breath. For a moment, he felt totally isolated as the light blinded him. Pete's eyes adjusted, and he was finally able to see people and motor scooters on the street. Buildings took their familiar shapes. Thank God he'd bought lighter clothing for the climate. He couldn't imagine how bad the rainy season would be. But he had read that not only did it rain constantly, but the temperature hit the highs for the year, often over one hundred degrees with ninety-five percent humidity. It must feel like you were drowning—above water.

On his way back to the hotel, he stopped at a small shop that sold bags. He decided to trade his cumbersome leather briefcase for a wool bag like Moe carried. In the shop, he saw dozens of bags hanging from the ceiling. He picked one that was square with a wide strap. The flat side was colored in blue, green, and purple stripes. Best of all, it was light and easy to carry. Pete bought it and put it over his shoulder. It fit perfectly.

Pete rested through the heat of the afternoon in the air-conditioned hotel and packed his bags in preparation to leave for Minnesota. He'd agreed to meet Mi Mi before the rally, eat some dinner, and walk on a wooden bridge that she had talked about. A wooden bridge didn't sound that exciting, but Pete was anxious to spend time with her. He hadn't been with a woman who interested him since Julie's death. Although he still had dreams of her and felt guilty, his loneliness was so palpable at times, it felt like hunger pangs.

Mi Mi was different from anyone he'd met before. She didn't care about having a new car, about shopping or the latest movies. Locally sourced food wasn't something she had to "find." It was all around her. It was her passion to achieve something larger than herself that drew Pete to her because it filled his vacant life.

In the late afternoon, he met Mi Mi in the lobby of the hotel. She'd arranged for a taxi to take them to the longest wooden bridge in the world. It spanned a branch of the Irrawaddy River. "We can watch the sunset from the bridge," she'd told him.

She turned out of the elevator into the lobby, and Pete saw that she wore a yellow *longyi* that hugged her hips tightly. The silk looked shiny and rustled around her legs while she walked toward him. As if to reinforce the Western influences in her, she wore a cotton t-shirt with short sleeves. In the design, dozens of lavender elephants wandered across the material. In consideration of the heat, she wore her hair back in a ponytail and carried an umbrella to hide from the sun, which even late in the afternoon shone with painful power.

For the first time, she allowed Pete to hug her. He tried to make it last, but she pulled away. "Do you ever get used to the heat?" he asked Mi Mi.

"Of course. Myanmar in the morning is especially beautiful. As you go up into the mountains, the air is soft and cool, and the mountains look purple. Along the fields, there are palm trees that take shape as the sun illuminates them and the sky turns from turquoise to blue." She lifted her face to him. "You should see it sometime."

"And I suppose there are always a dozen golden pagodas poking up over the trees."

"Yes. Over the centuries various kings were trying to get *merit*, or favor, so they built more blooming stupas."

The doorman waved to a taxi, which untangled from the traffic and slid to a halt in front of them. A smiling man wearing a brown *longyi* and flip flops jumped out and came around the back to hold open the door for Pete and Mi Mi. On the way to the bridge, Pete commented on how impressive the Ciatti Hotel had been.

Mi Mi reacted immediately. "These foreign investors cannot see the ugly symptoms of the generals' corruption that undermines the moral and personal fiber of our country. In the end, that will also affect their economic potential. For instance, the lack of an effective legal framework and all the corruption means these business people don't have any guarantees of fair treatment in transactions. They usually don't care that our health and education are deteriorating, but they should. If they don't have a healthy labor force, their projects will—"

"Okay. Let's wait for the rally tonight." He didn't want to get into the politics of the country.

"Sorry. You don't want to hear all our problems."

Pete thought of the work of the Ex-Im Bank. "I've never been too concerned about the business practices of the bank, but now that I'm here, I'm beginning to see things from your point of view."

"Don't get me wrong. We want foreign investment badly. But if the bank really wants to help us, they'll get more aggressive to force structural changes in the country. If they don't do something about the bloody high number of political prisoners in the country, they will face the same injustices when they are cheated in business or they cross the generals the wrong way."

Sometimes, her intensity overwhelmed Pete. He sat back into the corner of the taxi and watched the swarm of motor scooters pass them from all directions. He could hear the incessant buzzing of their small engines. For safety, some people wore helmets, but all of them wore flip-flops on their feet.

They came to a wide stretch of the river spanned by a new concrete bridge. The taxi moved into a line with other vehicles to cross it. Because of an accident, the traffic was backed up for blocks. A small truck that had been piled too high for its size had tipped over and scattered a load of steel bars across the road. Two police cars and various officers directed traffic around the pile. All the work of cleanup was done by hand. Finally, the taxi squeezed through the bottleneck and sped over the bridge. They turned left and followed a small road along the side of the river. Low trees hung far over the water, and they pulled into a dirt parking lot next to the river.

A few tourist buses were parked on the sloping river bank with other taxis and cars. Dozens of wooden boats were beached in the mud. They were long and narrow and painted bright colors of yellow and blue and pink. Some settled low in the water as if they were already water-logged. They looked handmade and cobbled together from scrap lumber, with gaps between the slats of wood. Pete could smell the damp odor of fish and water.

He followed Mi Mi around the edge of the bank to a set of steps that led up to a long wooden bridge. It ran high above the water all the way across the river. They climbed to the bridge and started to walk along it. Below, Pete saw the churning, muddy water flowing slowly underneath. The bridge looked rickety and on the verge of collapse. He thought it would never pass the American OSHA standards. There were no railings, no handicap access, and no safety features anywhere. People crowded onto the narrow walkway, threatening to push others off the edge. A few of the colorful boats from shore had filled with spectators and had paddled out around the pilings of the bridge. Halfway across the river, a low island had lounge chairs set into the sand. People mingled with coolers and drinks to watch the coming sunset. It looked like a daily party.

"What if someone falls off of the bridge?" Pete asked Mi Mi.

She laughed. "Are you worried? It's not too deep here."

He stopped on the bridge and looked downriver to see the blob of lemon sun flattening just above the purple mountains in the far distance. When the sunlight glanced off the water, it sparkled like precious gems in silver and blue colors. "It's beautiful," he said.

"For a moment, you can forget the muddy water below. That's what I like." She leaned against a crooked pole on the edge of the bridge. Her hand searched for his, found it, and fit into his palm.

"I didn't know colors existed until I came here. It's incredible." The decaying sun felt warm but not hot on his face. Around him, other people bathed in the saffron glow. Time slowed, and it felt peaceful, ageless. Far below, the river gurgled around the pilings. He looked at his watch. "Hey, we better get going to the rally."

Mi Mi closed her eyes for a moment. Then, opening them, she agreed, and they walked back to the taxi, which waited for them on shore. They stayed on the same side of the river and followed the narrow road to come back into a crowded area at the foot of a small mountain. It was the only one in the wide, flat river valley. Expensive houses, buildings, and pagodas poked out from the dense layer of trees that grew up the sides of the hill. At the crest, a monastery spread over the top. It gleamed in the setting sun—white and gold with green trim.

Mi Mi explained that the hill had always been a special place for centuries. "All our royalty has lived up there. Then the British came, and now the cronies and generals live there. Because it is often so bloody hot here in the valley, the elevation gives a respite from the heat and always has cool winds blowing at the top."

Pete could feel the breeze even at the bottom of the mountain.

The taxi dropped them off at the corner of a park. Trees bordered it on three sides, and there was dry dirt in the opening between the trees. Two stone elephants guarded the entrance. Several chairs had been set up in front of a small stage. Two speakers hung above the edge of the stage, and many people congregated on it already. As far as Pete could see, people of all descriptions crowded into the park. Along one side a row of food stands offered bowls of *mohinga*, deep-fried pastries, and tea. Pete could smell grilled meat and saw the wisps of white smoke rise from the kiosks. He could feel the excitement in the crowd and heard the loud continuous banter of Burmese voices. Most of them wore items of red clothing—the color of the NLD.

Mi Mi grabbed his hand and pulled him forward. "Hurry. We made it just in time. I've seats saved near the front."

He followed her through the people who parted and smiled at him. It seemed festive. Children, their faces painted with thanaka, peeked out at Pete from between their mothers' legs as he pushed through the group. He'd never been to a political rally before. This one was obviously organized, but looked amateur. There was nothing fancy or expensive about the stage, the sound system, or the banners that fluttered in the breeze.

In contrast to the middle of the crowd, around the edges Pete could see rows of soldiers in full uniform. Most had rifles resting along the sides of their legs. White helmets were pulled low over their eyes, and they remained motionless. Even for Pete, who had spent years in the military, they were still an intimidating presence. Probably Lon Htein, as Carter Smith had warned. Behind the men, Pete saw many camouflage army trucks parked under the acacia trees.

Mi Mi led him to two folding chairs. They sat and heard the ripple of applause followed by shouts and, finally, endless cheering. Pete looked around and saw a small procession heading for the stage. It was Aung San Suu Kyi.

She wore a red silk scarf tied around her neck, a dark blue *longyi,* and a pink blouse. A gardenia was pinned in her black hair, which was wrapped behind her head. She was sixty-eight years old, and Pete was astounded at how young and beautiful she looked in person. She moved slowly through a clump of people to reach the podium. He sensed something regal, yet without arrogance. At the podium, she turned to the large crowd, and while they cheered, she waved and smiled at them.

Because of her work for peace and freedom, she'd been awarded the Nobel Peace Prize in 1991—only to go back into house arrest for several years. Today, she was free and basked in the adoration of the people before her. Everywhere Pete had gone in the country so far, he'd seen photos of her in the shops, in hotels, in tea houses, in museums, and on the t-shirts and buttons of hundreds of young women. He glanced at Mi Mi and saw a glow on her face also.

In a few minutes, the crowd quieted and Suu Kyi began to speak. She talked in a low voice, quiet, but with passion. She thanked people, talked about the fight for election results, and moved into the issue of the prisons. Mi Mi translated for him.

"As many of you know, political prisoners must speak to their families through a double barrier of iron grating and wire netting so that no physical contact is possible. When I visited, I remember that children of the prisoners would make small holes in the netting and push their fingers through, trying to touch their fathers." Her hand went up over her face to shade it from the slanting evening sun. "When the holes became visibly larger, the authorities would patch them with thin sheets of tin, but the children would start all over again, trying to bore holes through to their fathers." She paused. "Is this the kind of activity our children should grow up learning how to do?"

The crowd roared back, "No."

"Why is it that the Red Cross left our country in 1991?" She waited for a moment, then answered. "Because of the refusal of the government to allow inspections by the Red Cross of the prisons. And how many of your loved ones spent time in *Ye-kyi-ain*, the intelligence interrogation center, before going to Insein Prison?" The crowd recalled their lost family members and moved with her every phrase.

As Pete listened to her, he also fell under her mesmerizing words. He began to see a glimmer of the terrible issues facing these people. It was so different from the United States, where people took simple freedoms and privileges for granted. The crowd around him seemed to be giving birth to democracy at its most fundamental level as they sat in the fading sun.

From beyond the river, dark clouds blew over, casting the park in shadows. The air temperature dropped, and Pete could smell rain on the wind.

An hour later, the meeting was over. The army had remained quiet at the edges of the park, and the people dispersed slowly. Mi Mi turned to Pete with an expectant look on her face.

He said, "I can't get over how brave these people are. I'm impressed how they can all come together here for a patriotic purpose, under such bad conditions."

"Yes. But remember, Asian democracy is different from Western democracy. Here, we emphasize piety, manners, humility, and the duties each of us has toward the community. In your country, individual rights are held up as the greatest freedom."

Pete thought about her words. "Your leader is certainly impressive."

"The movement has grown beyond a few people and Aung San Suu Kyi. She's a leader, of course, but there are many more of us. We must still be careful, but things are improving." She hummed a wordless tune.

"Slowly." He felt splats of rain hit him and saw puffs of dust where they landed on the ground. Out over the river, the rain slanted down in silver lines in front of the dying sun, a preview of the coming monsoons. Thunder rolled in from over the mountains. He started to run with Mi Mi to the taxi waiting for them. Then he stopped, looked up with his mouth open, and let the rain pour down.

"As a child, bathing in the rain was one of my greatest pleasures here." Mi Mi laughed as the tips of her ponytail dripped water. "The monsoons are difficult and our roofs all leak, but the season brings out explosive growth. The rains cause the plants and flowers to come up like thunder. New growth and new life."

In the taxi, they stuffed themselves into the seat to catch their breath. To ward off a chill, they leaned against each other. Pete smelled the fresh mineral odor of the rain in her hair. It was shiny black, and drops of water fell to mingle with those on his shoulder. For a moment, he felt better than he had in months. The rain drummed on the roof and they hugged each other, creating a bubble of warmth against nature outside.

Back at the hotel, the concierge gave him a small note with a handwritten message to call Carter Smith immediately. Pete used the land line at the hotel—one of the only phones to work in the area.

"Chandler, I thought you should know this." Smith talked fast. "The teak rafts you saw on the river—we're entirely wrong about the timber smuggling. The rafts are used as a cover for something a lot bigger and more illegal: gem smuggling. The teak logs are held together with hollow bamboo poles. Inside, gems are smuggled from further north up the Irrawaddy River. Ninety percent of the world's rubies come from Myanmar, so the dollar value of these thefts eclipses any value of the teak. The stolen gems are the real crime."

"At the hotel you told me there was nothing more to tell me."

"Uh . . . I just learned this." Her voice trailed off. "But we'll take action."

Pete remembered the soldier in the jungle who'd said the rafts were a cover for something else. And what about Moe? His behavior in the jungle was suspicious—he was so upset that Pete had fought with the soldiers. Did Moe know about the gems? And Pete wondered about the strange behavior of the ambassador. Where was he? Pete let all of that pass and said to Smith, "What about Bridget?"

She paused for a long time. "I hate to tell you this, but she probably became involved in the crime."

"I don't believe you."

"We have, uh, information about Bridget and Jeff Sumpter. Not only were they engaged, but they were both involved in this scheme. I'm telling you all this because now there's no need for you to do any more. We will handle everything. With the amount of money at stake in the gem smuggling, we're looking at a conspiracy in the highest levels of the Myanmar generals."

Now he really distrusted her. "Thanks for the warning, but I'm staying. I owe Congressman Holmes the effort to find his daughter and the truth about what's going on."

Chapter Thirteen

Pete hung up the phone slowly. He couldn't trust Carter Smith, the ambassador, Moe, and maybe even Mi Mi. The easy answer was to bail and get back to Minnesota. He worried about Karen. Pete wasn't an introspective person, especially in times of danger. He operated a lot on instinct. He let that take over now. And his instincts told him to go with Moe and Mi Mi. But what if Bridget Holmes was still in Mandalay? Maybe Pete should stay and search for her in the city.

Pete decided that if she were involved with the NGO or had been kidnapped, Bridget had probably left already. He'd follow that trail up the river.

At the Royal Palace Hotel, Pete met Moe and Mi Mi and told them about the gem smuggling. Moe became quiet and pulled all of them into a corner of the lobby. He looked over Pete's shoulder and finally said, "While you gone, many Tatmadaw arrive. They are watching us and NGO soldiers. If we go north, we will be in great danger."

"Maybe Mi Mi should stay—"

"No." She glared at Pete.

"It is Mr. Chandler who should be worried," Moe said. "The main area for gem mining is in Mogok Valley up river to northeast in mountains. It is primitive and has been closed to all foreigners." He glanced back and forth. "But it also near location of our people, the Shan. They will help if we need."

For a moment, Pete was tempted again to go back to the US. Get on a rickety plane in Mandalay and never stop until he reached Minneapolis. Then he looked at Mi Mi and saw small beads of water still clinging to her forehead. When she lifted her brown and damp eyes to him, his decision was easy. "I'll take my chances," he announced. "Will my presence endanger you?"

Moe shook his head. "My police identification take care of us."

"Do we fly up there?"

"There are no airports. It is remote, so we drive. Be prepared." Moe grinned for the first time since they'd moved into the corner.

Mi Mi added, "It's only seventy-eight miles, but the roads are so bad it could take us five to seven hours."

"We need good vehicle, and we must get 'tour guide.'" Moe's eyes rolled upward in the international expression of exasperation.

"I thought you knew the way to the valley?" Pete said.

"I do. But since generals close area years ago, everyone required to get military escort." He pulled off his glasses and clicked the bows together. He didn't look at Pete. "That will be first problem. Will escort allow you to travel there?"

They ate a quick dinner in the hotel restaurant. When the food was served, Mi Mi explained what she was eating. "Although we aren't Christian, this is often called the 'holy trinity' of food in Myanmar." She pointed to the orange fruit on the plate. "It's a combination of mango, pork, and lahpet leaves. Not quite the same as fish and chips in England." She laughed and finished eating everything on the plate.

Moe set up the appointment to meet their military escort first thing in the morning and suggested they get to bed early. At the top of the wide stairway that led to their rooms, Pete watched Moe walk down the hall in a rocking motion that made him look tired. He and Mi Mi stood beside each other. He reached for her hand and held it. She felt cool.

"I'm glad you're going with us," he confessed to Mi Mi.

"I am too."

"I want to find Bridget, but I also want to be with you."

"I've never been to the Mogok Valley. I'm a little collywobbles."

Pete let go of her hand and reached his arms out. He pulled her close to him in a tight hug. He could feel the softness of her breasts against his chest and smell the fragrance of her skin. The feelings that ran through him were crazy. He would go back to the US as soon as the mission was over. She would remain in Myanmar. Why was he letting his attraction for her grow? What could possibly come of their relationship? Then he understood. For a lonely man, this was the best he'd felt for a long time, and he couldn't let go.

But she pulled back and stood away from him. "Pete—it's not the right—not now."

"That's okay. I haven't since—" He couldn't finish.

Her eyes seemed to expand as she looked at him. Neither said another word. Mi Mi flashed a smile and turned to walk to her room. Pete watched her hips move underneath the *longyi* as she went all the way down the hall. Her bare legs peeked out from between the folds of silk. To hell with tight jeans on a woman, he thought. Watching her walk in a *longyi* was the sexiest thing he'd seen in years.

The next morning, Pete was in the dining room finishing a large bowl of *mohinga* washed down with two cups of very sweet tea. "*Mingalar par*," he said to Moe as he rushed into the room.

"Please, we go now." Moe's face was flushed. He carried a small overnight bag with him and a shoulder bag made out of blue wool.

"What's the rush?"

"There is old friend of mine at military escort office. He is Shan like me and may allow you through, but we must go now while he is on duty." He headed toward the front door of the hotel.

Mi Mi came down the staircase carrying a Styrofoam cup. She pulled a small suitcase behind her and carried a backpack strapped over her shoulders. She smiled at Pete and lifted the cup. "Tea is enough for now." She fell into step with him while their shoulders touched. They walked outside.

The fat salmon sun of the tropics crested the palm trees to the east of the square. The light seemed to have depth and weight and made all the colors more vibrant than normal. When Pete stepped into the street to catch a taxi, the thick heat hit him even this early in the morning.

They all squeezed into the small car, and it careened around the corner by the palace as the driver raced across the city. They passed the farmers coming in from the fields. Ox carts carried vegetables, fruits, cut wood, straw, and bags of rice. Some rode motor scooters piled high in the back with teetering loads of produce. The whine of the engines sounded like a swarm of bees. The taxi wasn't air conditioned, so the windows were wide open. Pete could smell incense burning somewhere.

Food kiosks cluttered the corners, and lines of people stood waiting for their breakfast. When they were served, the people would turn away carrying a plastic baggy filled with food.

At the tea shops, men squatted so low on the ground that their butts touched the dirt. They sipped from small China cups and watched the dust rise around them as the crowds passed by. Occasionally, they would spit into the dust.

Next to them was an open door with a sign that advertised a fortune teller. There were almost at many people waiting there as were drinking in the tea shops. Two of them in line held Natural dolls along the sides of their legs.

Horns honked. Pete heard chanting as they passed brick pagodas. Scrawny dogs wandered. Scooters dashed around them. Bells tinkled. Hundreds of people wearing colorful clothing reminded Pete of exploding fireworks as the people burst out of the small shops and narrow streets.

When the taxi turned the last corner, Pete saw a low, one-story cement block building. It had a red tin roof and open windows. On the roof, the yellow and green flag of Myanmar hung down like it was already exhausted from the heat. Burmese letters snaked across the sign above the door. A roll of razor wire curled around the front of the building, and two soldiers stood on either side of the door with rifles cradled in their arms. They wore uniforms and silver helmets that shone brightly in the sun.

"Here," Moe said. He looked to the left of Pete and continued, "Please, you allow me handle this?"

Pete raised his eyebrows but said, "Yes, sir."

They all got out of the taxi and followed Moe through the front door. Inside, Pete saw a large photo of the president, Thein Sein. Below that a sign read in both Burmese and English: *The Supreme Leader of the State Law and Order Restoration Council.* Before he had left for Myanmar, Pete had tried to learn something about the mysterious president—new since 2011. Even Wikipedia had few details.

Moe talked with the soldier at a low desk. He made several phone calls while the rest of them waited. Moe talked more, and the soldier made more phone calls. Everyone waited.

Pete noticed a newspaper stand in the corner of the office. He walked over and found the *New Light of Myanmar*. Mi Mi had warned him that it was a propaganda mouthpiece for the generals. The headline seemed to confirm that: *Protests Against the Democratic Government are no Longer Fashionable*.

After ten minutes, the door to an office in the back scraped open and a slight man came forward. He, too, was dressed in the green uniform of the army. When he noticed Moe, his face split open in a wide smile. His teeth were red.

They nodded toward one another and talked in Burmese. Moe occasionally waved his arm toward Pete and Mi Mi. After another ten minutes, Moe came over to them. In a low voice, he said, "I think it work. He allow you to go because Moe assure him I watch you. It is risk for him. Please remember."

Pete didn't like being told what to do, but he kept his mouth shut for once.

Moe went back to his friend, pressed his palms together in front of his chest, and bowed at the same time his friend bowed. He turned and nodded to Pete and Mi Mi to go outside and wait for the official vehicle.

Pete found shade under a lemon tree. He smelled the ripe fruit hanging inches above his head. "That guy's teeth were red," he said to Mi Mi.

"Betel juice. It's an old custom in my country for people to chew betel leaves and nuts. It's a mild stimulant, like nicotine. I'm surprised someone as young as Moe's friend chews. Usually, it's the older generation because the rest of us think it's so manky."

"And it looks damn weird."

"Yes."

Two Toyota Land Rovers came around the corner and stopped in a puff of dust next to them. By then, Moe was outside and met with the soldier who climbed out of the first SUV. They saluted each other, and Moe offered a stack of papers to him. The soldier studied each page for a long time. Pete could see a layer of dust on the side of his neck. The man looked up and studied both Pete and Mi Mi. Finally, he nodded and smiled briefly. His teeth were red also. The soldier got back into his seat.

A military jeep careened around the corner and skidded to a stop. From the back, Captain Thaung climbed over the seat and came forward. He saluted Moe and ignored the other two. "Luckily, I have found you," he said to Moe. "What are you doing?"

Pete could see Moe's face flush pink, but his expression remained passive. He talked for a long time to the captain, who stood motionless. Finally, the captain nodded and saluted Moe again. Moe marched to the Toyota. Pete had never seen him so upset.

Without speaking, Moe pointed toward the second SUV. Pete tossed his and Mi Mi's luggage into the back. Moe hesitated. He reached into his suitcase and removed something that looked like a doll. Pete saw that it was a Natural. It had long black hair surrounding a marble white face, and a black cape with red lining. Ignoring Pete's stare, Moe put the doll into his shoulder bag and said, "We get two drivers. One military escort, a tour guide, and"—he hesitated for an instant—"Captain Thaung."

When Pete started to smile, the look from Moe stopped him dead. They both climbed in, and Moe took the front seat. As the driver shifted into gear and moved forward, Moe added, "You experience one of lonely drives in Southeast Asia. If road is okay, we arrive at city of Mogok by late tonight."

The Toyotas squeezed through the streets of Mandalay. When people saw the government markings on the doors, they jumped out of the way.

Pete squeezed next to Mi Mi in the back seat. He asked about Moe. "I've never seen him so mad."

From the front seat a radio blared tinny music that Pete had difficulty hearing, and she whispered to Pete. "Moe hates him because he knows the captain is a stooge for the generals. Also, he has a history of recruiting children for the army. He, and others, go into the poor communities and offer the families about thirty American dollars and a bag of rice to turn over their boys to the army, some as young as twelve. They promise the family the boy will be fed and educated—all of which are lies."

"Twelve years old?"

"There are thousands of them even now in the Tatmadaw."

The caravan worked its way through the city along 63rd Street until they came to the north end, which opened onto broad, green fields of garlic and rice and flowers. The one-and-a-half lane tarmac road paralleled the Irrawaddy River. It had split into several smaller channels. In contrast with the broad, calm flow of the river south of Mandalay, the current here ran hard, and the turbulent water flashed in the morning sun. In the distance it looked blue, but up close the river ran with mud that had changed to the color of rotting vegetation.

In the back seat of the Toyota, Mi Mi bounced against Pete as the driver swerved to avoid the many potholes. He asked her about the Mogok Valley.

She leaned closer to Pete and lowered her voice to almost a whisper. "It's been the premier gem mining area of the country for over a thousand years. Even before the British came, the kings guarded it closely, and it's never been open to tourists. Ninety percent of the world's rubies come from there. The most famous one is called the Carmen Lucia Ruby, which is now in the Smithsonian museum in your country. It's more than twenty carats and has a color called 'pigeon blood red.'"

"Never heard of it. Are there other gems up there?"

"Blue sapphires and some of the best jade in the world come from Mogok. The color and quality are what people want so badly."

Pete asked, "I suppose the generals control it all?"

"The government nationalized all the gem mining in 1963. And in the last fourteen years, the generals have clamped down even tighter. The valley's legendary reputation has become even more mysterious."

"I think the US has a ban on Myanmar gems."

"It is still in effect because of the human rights abuses, like the use of child labor and no mechanization. It only serves to push up the auction prices in the rest of the world beyond belief, and the generals make a fortune."

"So that's why they're smuggling them out?"

"I don't know. It could be one group is stealing from another group and wants to hide that. There could be a secret war going on over the gems."

The SUV slowed, and Pete looked through the windshield. He saw a small house beside the road. Three armed soldiers milled in the road behind a red and white sawhorse. As the Toyotas approached, two more soldiers roused themselves from beside the house and stepped onto the road also.

"First military checkpoint," Mi Mi whispered.

The soldiers surrounded the vehicles while the driver and Moe showed their papers. They returned to look at Pete several times. Would the pass from Moe's friend work here? They waited in the SUV. Pete heard flies buzz in through the windows. Sweat rolled down the side of his face. The engine of the Toyota ticked as it cooled off. Ten minutes later, two of the soldiers lifted the sawhorse out of the way, and the vehicles proceeded forward.

Pete asked Moe, "Can you turn on the air conditioning?"

"Broken," he replied.

The road narrowed as they traveled north and became more rutted. The driver had to slow to avoid the worst holes. Dust from the first vehicle rolled out behind to choke Pete and the people with him.

Two hours later, Pete felt like he'd taken a huge step back in time—even in this country where he was already witnessing things from fifty years ago. There were more bicycles and oxcarts than cars. Dozens of people clad in bright, colorful *longyi* walked along a dirt path beside the road. Many of the women carried poles across their shoulders and balanced yellow cans of water, green bundles of sugar cane, and clumps of crooked sticks for cooking fires. They all wore flip flops. A young girl held a lamb over the back of her neck by gripping its tiny hooves near her ears. Her sister walked beside her, a black lacquer bowl balanced on her head that overflowed with gardenia petals.

They all smiled and waved as the vehicles passed within inches of them.

As time dragged by, the caravan passed along fields and past teak trees with gray, scaly bark. Royal palms swayed in the breeze as if they were waving the group onward. Occasionally, Pete saw farmers walking behind bulls that pulled wooden plows. Otherwise, the land was sparsely populated. Going up the river was like going back to the creation of the world, when plants ruled the earth and the colossal trees were heartless kings.

They drove through monotonous small villages. Low houses with red roofs dotted the sides of the road between long stretches of fields. Pete noticed several official-looking signs at the edge of some of the fields. He asked Mi Mi what they meant.

"Those are government-owned lands. They 'rent' them out to farmers for cultivation and pay them less than the market rates. At least they are guaranteed to sell their products."

The caravan slowed to allow a cart piled with straw and pulled by two humped Brahma bulls to make a wide turn in the road. The wooden wheels squealed as they made the corner. A man wearing a conical straw hat rode the cart and waved to them, looking as if he were one hundred years old. The Brahmas had been imported decades earlier because they could handle the heat better than other types of bulls.

The road twisted up toward the gray-green mountains in the distance. Above them, clouds gathered in dark bundles. The sun crawled over the sky to start its descent to the west, casting the valley into lengthening shadows.

Pete watched as they passed timber plantations of immense size. Other than the trucks used to transport the logs, he didn't see any mechanical means of harvesting the trees. He wondered how they were cut and carried to the trucks.

The air felt cooler and the humidity dropped as they went higher.

They traveled through a deep jungle of banana palms, pine trees, myrtle, and several brilliant flowering trees that Pete couldn't identify. The road narrowed to one lane. Luckily, there wasn't any other traffic. They came to a hill village, and Pete saw another checkpoint. It looked identical to the previous two: a small hut beside the road and a red and white sawhorse with flaking paint that prevented their passage.

While they all waited for the soldiers, he looked around the village. It clung to the side of a steep hill. Small tan houses stepped up the side, one piled on top of the other, to get lost in the misty belly of a cloud. Around them, flowers of all colors tumbled down in the opposite direction. A crooked bamboo pipe connected one house to the other. Pete assumed it was for water. He didn't see any electrical lines.

A woman squatted beside the road, her head wrapped in a bright orange cloth. She smoked a large cheroot while she held the string that ran to a spinning wheel. Two wooden poles held a blue awning above her, and stacks of colorful cloths stood in folded piles beside the wheel. Pete saw a lot of checked, tartan patterns. She ignored the vehicles that stood inches from her, their engines rumbling like large bulls.

On Mi Mi's side of the Toyota, a woman approached carrying a piece of wood. It held slices of orange fruit. The juice dripped over the edge to drop into the dust. She was selling mangos, and Mi Mi bought several, which the woman packaged in small baggies to hand through the open window.

Pete began to worry. The checkpoint was taking much longer than the previous ones.

Time ticked by, and he heard the swish of the wind in the trees high up on the mountain sides. From somewhere above him, children laughed.

He saw a stack of car batteries beyond the checkpoint. "What are those doing there?" he asked Mi Mi.

"There's no public electricity up here. People power everything on car batteries. Each morning, they're left out for pickup. A man charges them and returns them at night for a small fee."

Moe got out of the SUV and walked to the front of the line. He talked with the soldiers and the military escort. Finally, Moe came back and jumped into the front seat. The driver shifted, and they moved past the sawhorse. As they were leaving, Pete caught a flash of red color. He turned in the seat to see a row of silent monks walking barefoot along the road. Each held an umbrella against the mist, so their faces were hidden behind the line of red ovals.

The SUVs climbed higher into the mountains. The air felt damp. Shadows grew longer, and the clouds darkened in front of them. Pete saw a few mining operations, but they looked small and abandoned. One had a shack next to a rickety structure that looked like a child's homemade tower.

The driver struggled to get around some hairpin turns. On one side of the dirt road, steep drop-offs fell for hundreds of feet. On the other side, the Toyota scraped beside a sheer rock wall equally as tall as the drop on the opposite side.

At one sharp turn, Pete looked back and saw, far down the mountainside, two more SUVs struggling up the road. Mi Mi leaned next to him and saw the vehicles also. She asked Moe about them.

"Tatmadaw. They follow us."

Pete thought back to Carter Smith's words about the US using money, trade, or whatever was necessary to stabilize the country in order to improve the financial conditions here to raise the standard of living for everyone. A noble goal, certainly, and he agreed with it. But which moral choice to make? Should the US partner with the generals to impose stability—a short term, necessary evil that might lead to positive reforms? Or should the democracy movement be supported, which would lead to destabilization, possible chaos, and the deaths of thousands of people before freedom was achieved—if ever?

His attraction to Mi Mi would normally make up his mind. He'd support her movement. But over the years, he'd learned to temper his hasty decisions to fight for the underdog with a thoughtful assessment of things. The reality was that the generals had the power. Wasn't it better to accept a degree of their brutality in the hope of reforming the country at some point? But if you worked with the thugs, would you become like them?

It seemed overwhelming to Pete, and he remembered the limited reason he had come to Myanmar. Where was Bridget Holmes? He'd concentrate on finding her and getting back home.

Mi Mi nudged him. "Want some fruit?" She opened the baggy with the sliced mangos and held it out to him.

Pete selected one and ate it. Warm and fresh and bursting with juice, they were the best he'd ever eaten. He laughed with her. For a moment Pete forgot about Bridget Holmes, the generals, and the danger. After all, he was traveling through paradise with a woman who was the first one since Julie to make him feel so good and peaceful.

The driver slammed on the brakes.

Pete looked forward to see yet another checkpoint. He sighed with frustration. How many of these did the military need up here? While they waited, he and Mi Mi ate more of the mangos. Cool air penetrated the interior of the Toyota and brought the smell of pine trees. Pete could see the clouds still gathering across the mountains to the left. Ten minutes later, the soldiers had surrounded the two vehicles. They talked quickly to Moe. He turned around, and his face drained of color. He said to Pete, "They order you get out."

Pete felt like he'd been hit in the stomach.

"Moe do not know what happens. We stay in vehicle."

Three soldiers stood in a semi-circle by Pete's door, waiting for him. He looked from Mi Mi to Moe. No one spoke or moved. He left the unfinished bag of mangos on the seat, unhooked his seatbelt, and got out of the SUV. The soldier to the right slammed the door shut behind Pete. The other two were small as children. He recognized the Type 56 assault rifles made by the People's Republic of China and used in Vietnam. They were all pointed at him.

Chapter Fourteen

The smallest man prodded Pete with a rifle. Pete's chest pounded as they led him away from the Toyotas toward the forest behind the shack. This was not good.

He thought of Karen. What would she think if he disappeared? Then he thought of Mi Mi, and Pete realized how much he wanted to be with her. It had been so long since he'd felt this way about a woman, the need was powerful, like an ache. He glanced back and saw her blanched face watching him walk away.

The soldiers motioned him to the side of the road. He didn't think they'd try anything so long as he was out in the open. The third soldier walked away. That gave Pete a momentary sense of relief—the odds had improved slightly.

They stopped him at the edge of the road. He could hear the wind groan high above in the pine trees. The clouds had descended from the mountains so that it was as dark as dusk. He spotted an empty can of Tiger beer on the side of the road. It was crushed and bent in half.

When the two soldiers poked him with their rifles again, Pete's breathing became more difficult. They wanted him to walk around behind the small shack. That was where they'd finish the job. He hesitated, his feet stuck on the crumbling pieces of tarmac of the old road. One soldier shoved him. He stumbled forward.

Pete wouldn't accept his fate without a fight. At close range, a rifle is actually hard to maneuver. He could take advantage of that and try to disarm the first guy. By the time the second was able to get the rifle pointed at Pete, hopefully, he could take him out also. What would the military escort in the SUV do? Would they help the soldiers? Pete didn't have time to think about that.

As he rounded the corner of the bamboo shack, he calculated the angles and the distances between the three of them. He forced himself to take several deep breaths and prepare for the Tae Kwon Do moves he would execute. His muscles tensed.

"America, got passport?" the first soldier said. He looked like he was about fourteen years old.

"Huh?"

"Passport."

What was it about these guys that they all wanted passports? Pete lied, "It's back in my hotel."

"You come on road pay fine."

Pete let out his breath. It sounded just like the shakedown back in Yangon. Maybe he wouldn't die, after all. "A fine? How much?"

"Two thousand dollars. American."

Pete relaxed more. Good old corruption. He'd experienced this in other foreign places. He guessed they wouldn't really expect all that money. "I don't have much on me. How about fifty dollars? Brand new."

The soldiers' rifles dipped lower as they jabbered between themselves. The first one turned back to Pete. "Okay—this time."

Pete almost smiled with relief. He reached into the wool bag at his side and pulled out a fifty dollar bill. Before he let them take it, Pete insisted they put down the rifles and let him go back. The first soldier nodded. Pete stepped around the corner and dropped the bill on the ground. He scrambled back to the SUV and jumped in his seat. He yelled at Moe to get going. The driver revved the engine and shifted, and they sped forward as the soldiers fought over their ransom money.

The vehicle bumped up and down over the rough road. Pete was thrown into Mi Mi, and he gave her a hug. Tears leaked from her eyes while she grabbed his face in her hands. "You're okay."

He shook his head. "I've had too many close calls in this country."

"It's horrible. Now you have an idea what many of us experience all the time."

They bumped their way up the mountain and into thicker clouds.

In twenty minutes the driver made another hairpin turn, and the road leveled out. The narrow canyon opened up into a broad, green valley. On the far side, higher mountains rose to scrape the bottom of the purple clouds. The colors were intense: a hundred shades of green, the tan gravel of the road, and in the hollow of the valley, white homes with red and blue roofs spread out below them.

The driver slowed down. A woman walked by the vehicles carrying a hundred pounds of rice in a dirty gray sack on her head. She swayed from side to side but didn't drop the load. They drove under a tall arch of a sign that spanned the road. It must have been twenty feet high. In both English and Burmese letters, it read *Welcome to Rubyland.*

Pete laughed out loud until Moe twisted in the front seat and asked him to keep quiet. The road made a sharp turn as they passed under the sign. Pete could smell jasmine in the air and spotted dozens of bushes growing wild beside the narrow road.

As they descended into Mogok, Pete saw a city spread over the valley floor. On one side, a small lake reflected the clouds. Between it and the city, a green space like a park opened up. It was almost as large as the city itself.

Their caravan wound its way down into the town. The houses were small and jumbled closely together, as if for protection from the imposing mountains around them. Some had metal roofs that were maroon with rust. In the open valley, there were still a few hours of sunlight left.

It must have rained because there were puddles still standing in the road. Many of the roofs dripped water into wooden barrels.

They turned onto a crooked street that had one- and two-story shops lining it on either side. They all had wooden roofs that extended over the front to protect them from the sun and rain. Pete saw several taxi bikes with side cars attached to the front wheels. The side cars had cotton pads on the seats. Drivers in straw hats strained at the pedals as they transported passengers along the street. The few cars he saw were old and dented in many spots.

On the far side of town a temple complex commanded a view of the valley. Halfway up the mountain, it slumbered in a lush plateau. White stupas stood in a square around the main golden pagoda, which soared twice as high as the stupas. A low wall surrounded the complex. Inside, Pete counted over a dozen pagodas but didn't see many people. With its size and majesty, if it had been emerald in color, it could have been the City of Oz.

Moe turned around in the front seat and announced they were going to stop for food.

The driver poked his way between ox carts, bicyclists, motorbikes, running children, and women hurrying by with heavy loads on their heads. The sidewalks were so narrow that people spilled out onto the street to walk anywhere they could find room. The driver stopped for a robed monk who passed before the SUV, oblivious to its presence. He carried a shallow metal bowl and crossed the street. In front of an open air shop selling onions, he held out the bowl to the clerk. She reached into her bag and removed a few dirty *kyat*. After she deposited them in the monk's bowl, she took change back. He nodded and turned to come back across the street. Then the SUV moved forward.

They reached a small restaurant called Sein Thamadi. Pete unhinged his long legs to climb out of the back. With his loping stride, he was at the front of the restaurant in three steps. Next door stood yet another pagoda. This one was only two stories tall and was made of red brick without any gold ornamentation. Chimes rang from inside it.

Mi Mi stopped with him to look at the narrow door to the pagoda. "It is very old. Probably built in the 1600s. This ruler must not have been as rich—there's no gold on it."

Two small squatting statues guarded either side of the door. They were pink with grotesquely large heads, which were colored green and yellow. The eyes bulged with ferocity, and the lips were oversized and protruding. They were the ugliest things Pete had seen anywhere in the country. "What the hell are these?" he asked Mi Mi.

"Ogres. It's an ancient custom."

"In front of a Buddhist pagoda?"

"They protect the Buddha inside by scaring away evil spirits."

Pete shook his head. "I'm sure they'll do it."

A filthy dog walked up to the ogre and lifted its hind leg to pee on the statue. Pete laughed. "Maybe it doesn't work after all." Finished, the dog darted under a horse cart lumbering along the street. Pete walked into the open air restaurant.

At a table Pete saw a vase with cut flowers stuffed into it. There were bursts of every color imaginable. He thought of the juxtaposition of so many conflicting things in this country. Stunning beauty next to open sewers or trash. The sublime with the grime.

After a long drink of a cold Tiger beer, Pete surveyed the menu. It was written in Burmese and English. It offered appetizers: sticky rice crackers, tofu crisps, egg rolls. Below that, there were rice noodles with fish, prawns, chicken, and pork. Vermicelli could be substituted for the rice noodles. Two wooden ceiling fans revolved slowly. Pete could feel the tension drain out of him from the morning scare. The quiet restaurant provided a temporary oasis.

Captain Thaung arrived and sat with Moe and the "escorts." Within a few minutes, Moe left to sit with Pete and Mi Mi. "Moe worry about trouble at checkpoint."

Holding the bottle by the neck, Pete waved it in front of him. "Don't worry. It turned out okay." He tried to forget it.

Moe wouldn't. "My magic work."

When Pete looked at Mi Mi, he saw how serious they both were.

Their food came, and they ate without speaking. Pete watched Mi Mi as she lifted the porcelain bowl to her lips and scooped rice noodles from the soup into her mouth instead of using chopsticks. A carryover from her years in England, she'd explained. Mi Mi ate carefully but with gusto and occasionally slurped the liquid from the edge of the bowl. He had found himself studying her more often. Although she had pinned her long hair behind the ears, several thick strands fell forward, threatening to get caught in her lunch. Her delicate beauty that contrasted with her inner toughness impressed him.

After eating, they walked outside to the Toyotas. Shadows lengthened as the sun sank behind the mountains. Pete wondered if Bridget had come this way.

"Please," Moe called to him. "We look at gem sellers."

Followed by their military escort, Moe led Pete and Mi Mi down the street and across an intersection. Flags flew from sticks mounted on the roofs. Brightly colored curtains fluttered in and out of open windows. Buyers and sellers of products argued inside tiny shops, and food kiosks smoked from fires cooking dinners.

At the end of the street, Pete saw several tents set up along the sidewalks. All of them were colored in faded shades of red, brown, orange, and yellow. Moe stopped to shout above the noise of people. "*Panchan-htar-pwe* outdoor market. It largest gem market in country."

Hundreds of people mingled and moved slowly from one low table to the next. Some vendors were hidden by huge umbrellas. It looked like it could be a festive beach party without the water.

Moe continued, "I was child in Shan region near here, and Moe hear stories about market. See tables?" He pointed to a row of low wooden tables surrounded by wooden stools without backrests. Cloth covered each table, tacked along the edges. "This is reverse market. Here, buyer sit at tables. They wait for brokers and dealers and miners to come and offer gems for sale."

Pete watched two small men discussing something wrapped in a yellow piece of silk. The seller wore an American baseball cap that said *New York* on it. His fingertips unfolded one corner of the bundle at a time. The man sitting at the table scraped open a drawer on the back side and withdrew a wad of *kyat*. He started to separate the bills.

Moe smiled wickedly. "Sellers work in reverse because they have advantage. Buyer must be careful with bidding."

"What's the advantage?" Pete asked.

Moe pointed to one of the colored beach umbrellas. "Light filters through material makes rubies appear redder and sapphires look bluer than truth."

Pete looked down the street and across to the other sidewalks. He saw table after table with gems spread out on them. He'd never seen so many jewels in one place before. If this were the US there'd be more security people than buyers and sellers. Although the army presence was obvious, they didn't seem to be here to guard the gems.

Moe pulled Pete closer to a second table and pointed at the gems spread over silk squares. "Here are pink sapphires. This one yellow." He pointed at another table and Moe's voice grew in excitement. "There is amethyst and topaz. Maybe that one is green zircon and kornerupine over there."

The quantity and colors dazzled Pete. At the end of the row of tables, Moe stopped to show him the most important of Mogok's gems—the rubies. Table after table held red rubies. They were some of the largest he'd ever seen. Behind many of the tables were art pieces made of the gems.

One of the pieces drew Pete's attention. It was a tree carved from marble with delicate branches. The leaves had been made with tiny rubies—dozens of them. In turn, they were held in place with solid gold twigs that attached to the branches. Priceless.

An hour later, Mi Mi was tired and wanted to get to the hotel. They maneuvered through the crowds, always followed by their military escort and soldiers from the Tatmadaw who seemed to appear out of nowhere.

"You are one of the few Westerners to have seen this," Mi Mi told Pete. "When the gem mining was nationalized in 1963, travel here was severely restricted."

Pete looked behind him at all the military people following them and felt claustrophobic. He wasn't used to this kind of scrutiny. How could Bridget have managed to get by them—unless she had been kidnapped?

As if she'd read his mind, Mi Mi said, "We will secretly make contact with our people, the Shan. We will try to establish our own source of intelligence and help—separate from the army. Up here in the mountains, the generals have less control."

"Would the Shan be able to help me find Bridget?"

"Possibly. We can ask them. Do you still have the photos of her?"

Pete patted the side of the wool bag that hung from his shoulder. "Glossy and in full color."

Later that evening at the hotel, Moe said that he'd sneak out after dark to contact their people. "Tomorrow, we go to mining sites.

We follow trail to source. Try to discover truth. Our escort watch. It will be dangerous for us to ask many questions. Please to be careful."

The hotel was two stories tall—large for the surrounding buildings in town. It was made entirely of wood with polished teak floors. Each room had a balcony accessed through two French doors. When Pete stepped onto his balcony, he looked up to see the full range of dark mountains in the distance. At their base, the fading light had turned them gray. The night air cooled, and Pete felt good in spite of the danger around him.

In the tropics, the darkness came quickly. Within a half hour, a lopsided moon appeared through the clouds above the jagged mountains. As the moon rose higher, the glow of its light inched down the outer walls of the hotel. He could hear the hushed chiming of bells from below, tinkled by an evening breeze. Bats lofted silently into the darkness beyond as they hunted insects.

On the balcony next to his, Mi Mi opened one of the doors and stepped out. In the moonlight, her hair shone like it was wet, and her long robe shimmered like it was silver. She stretched her arms above her. Pete didn't say anything. After a while, Mi Mi turned and noticed him. She smiled. "Isn't it beautiful?" she whispered across the silent space between them.

"It's a perfect night."

They both waited. Finally, Mi Mi said, "Want to come over?"

At that point, Pete would've jumped over to her balcony. But he paused, then said, "Wait for me."

He walked back through his room, out into the hallway, and found Mi Mi at her door. She stood behind it with just her face exposed. She looked beautiful, her skin tan and flawless. She smiled up and him and opened the door, standing back to let him in.

"Reminds me of my dorm at Oxford when I'd sneak boys into my room." She giggled as he passed by her.

"Boys? You must have been busy."

"Well, one or two at the most."

He followed Mi Mi through the shadowed room and out into the silver light on the balcony. She turned to him, reached up with her arms, and hugged him closely. While her head nestled in the hollow under his chin, she said, "I was so worried today at the checkpoint. I thought those soldiers would kill you for sure."

"I thought it was all over."

"We never know when someone will 'disappear' and never come back," she murmured.

Pete could feel her pressing against him. Then she pulled back to study his face.

"Looking at all my lines?" He laughed. "It's not my fault; it's everything I've been through."

"Tell me about it. What did you do in Washington?"

Pete felt tightness in his chest. "I worked for a congressional committee that had oversight of the US banking industry. I did the majority of the investigative work."

"Did you like it?"

"At first, I did. I felt like I was exposing corruption and illegal activities. It made me feel like the work was worthwhile. But as I worked more, I realized the congressmen really didn't want to know too much about the problems."

"What do you mean?"

"It got to the point where I was covering up people's problems rather than exposing them." Pete lifted his head to look out across the valley. He heard monks chanting from far below the hotel. "I hated the job. My father always told me that a person should be proud of the work they do; otherwise it's not worth doing."

"Then why did you stay?"

"Uh, there was this female congressperson. Julie. I met her, and she had a problem that I, uh—" Pete couldn't finish. The depth of the pain still surprised him. Even now, it was difficult to talk about what had happened. He changed the subject. "So, it's almost a full moon, huh?"

"Why won't you tell me more?" Mi Mi's eyes softened.

He was tempted to let everything out with her. She was the first woman since Julie that he felt like he could trust. The loneliness that hung around him was tiring. He longed to be close to a woman again. Sex, friendship, soul mate—it didn't make a lot of difference at this point. He wanted to be with someone like Mi Mi, who seemed to fit so well with him. Like when they had eaten ripe mangos and shared the pleasure of the taste and laughed at each other as the juice ran down their chins. But he held back again. "I can't tell you any more now. It's too painful."

Mi Mi sighed and looked in the same direction he did across the valley. She said, "The full moon on the first of this month has passed. This is the second, 'black' moon that's coming." She pointed up into the sky.

Pete frowned. Moe might be taken in by this witchcraft, but Mi Mi too? After all, she was so educated and Westernized. "You don't—"

She turned on him quickly and stared into his eyes. "You don't know much of anything about this country. There are things that even Moe can't explain except to say it's magic. When I first returned, it was hard to accept these weird customs. I've got a doctorate in science, after all. But the longer I'm here, the more things I've experienced that can't be explained scientifically or with facts." As if to convince him, Mi Mi jabbed her finger at him.

"Okay, but in the meantime, how about a kiss?"

"Uh—" She turned away abruptly. From over her shoulder, Mi Mi said, "I like you immensely, but not in that way. We are too different and live in different worlds."

"I could change."

She sighed. "I don't know if you could. For instance, your Asian heritage means nothing to you. For me, it means everything."

"Why?"

Mi Mi said, "This is different than England or the US. There, each individual is given immense importance. Here, we are all part of a larger community. The individual is always sacrificed for the good of the village. It's part of the 'rice culture' that exists all over Asia."

"What's that mean?"

"Rice has been raised for thousands of years. But the process is difficult. It takes everyone in a village to work together to make sure the crop is successful. Otherwise, everyone will starve and die. It's created our culture."

Pete felt his face flush. "Maybe I could change."

"Maybe you could," Mi Mi whispered. "But in the meantime, we have a Buddhist saying: *If we become friends in this life, it's because of a connection from a previous life.*"

In the valley, bells chimed again, softened by the distance but overlapping each other's sound with urgency. At the end, they all rang in harmony until the ringing faded into the darkness. Pete and Mi Mi stepped back into her room. Pete knew it was over for the night, but he still felt a stirring for her. Could he ever recover from the memory of Julie?

Chapter Fifteen

The next morning the caravan of Toyotas crawled up the narrow and steep road that led to the mines. The sun had crested the mountains, causing the mist in the valley to glow like a cloud of gold dust. The people in the town had been up long before the sun, stocking the markets, getting water, taking kids to school, and praying at the pagodas. As always, several men sat on low stools in tea shops, drinking, talking, and smoking cheroots.

Something much more disturbing had also happened. As Pete was loading the luggage into the SUV, he glanced down the street. At the far end, he spotted the men from the jungle. The NGO—or whatever they really were. The leader, Rob, stood on a corner with his scraggly beard and a camouflage hat on his head. Rob didn't notice Pete, but Pete hurried the group along, and Moe persuaded the driver to leave quickly.

Pete was worried, but it also meant he was on the right trail. There must be a connection between Sumpter's death and something here that attracted the NGO soldiers. Even more disturbing was that the NGO didn't have a military tour guide. Why didn't they need one?

In the Toyota on the way up the mountain, Pete and Mi Mi squeezed next to each other in the back seat. They didn't say anything, but when he tried to hold her hand, she pulled it away. Mi Mi's palm felt damp. Was she as worried as he was about the NGO soldiers?

The gravel road had a series of switchbacks that turned 180 degrees on each other. Once around a turn, the driver shifted down and ground the engine, and the SUV strained up the incline.

Mi Mi leaned closer to Pete and whispered, "Moe met with Shan friends and family. I also have many female contacts. They will be a big help for us."

Pete thought back to what she'd told him yesterday. The country had over one hundred twenty ethnic minority groups, of which the Shan were one. They came from the highlands in the northeast corner of the country that bordered China. The generals were all from the Bama majority tribe, and they had been fighting a civil war for over sixty years with various ethnic groups. Right now, in the southern sections of the Shan region, there was still armed conflict.

The generals wanted the rich resources and control of the ethnic areas, such as the oil pipeline that had recently been completed. Built and financed by China, it stretched across Myanmar from the Chinese border to the Sea of Andaman. The generals had brutally suppressed all opposition from the many groups that were forced to give up their land for the project. The villagers that opposed them were simply killed or "removed."

"And beneath their insatiable need for money and resources," Mi Mi had told him, "the generals are racists. There's been a long campaign for the Burmese to have bigger families in order to 'purify' the country. The tourists and the outside world don't hear about that."

As Pete looked behind the caravan, he saw white and gold pagodas poking their steeples above the green top of the temperate rain forest. The wind blew harder and brought the smell of pine trees. He thought of how beautiful the country and its people were and, at the same time, how brutal and dangerous things were for them. When he first arrived, Pete hadn't even considered that issue. He had one mission—to find Bridget. But now, he saw what underdogs the people were, and that made him want to help in some way.

Within an hour, the road straightened out but still climbed upward. Occasionally, Pete could see rickety structures perched on the sides of the mountain. They looked like frames for flimsy houses.

Moe must have seen Pete staring at the contraptions because he said to Pete, "They used to wash down silt to spot gems hidden in dirt." He removed his glasses and pointed at the structure. "In past years over one thousand mines. Now, estimated to be about eight hundred. Many run by families who are poor and cannot pay for better structure." Moe turned forward in his seat, put on his glasses, and continued, "Wait. You see something most unusual."

The SUVs drove up onto a long ridge that was cleared of forest. Tall grasses swayed in the wind. The Toyota stopped.

"I show you something." Moe grinned as he lowered himself from the vehicle.

Although Mi Mi walked next to Pete, she seemed distant. Locked silently in her thoughts, she could have been across the valley without him. Pete wondered if he'd blown everything after last night. He was mad at himself. Why couldn't he toughen up and forget the past? He'd done that in so many other situations; why couldn't he do it now?

But surely, she'd have sympathy for him. Why didn't she show it? Maybe his earlier arrogance had turned her off. Maybe his blunt American ways had offended her more subtle Asian sensibilities.

The military escort remained with the caravan while Moe led Pete up the ridge. As they turned around the only stand of pine trees, Pete saw a long line of people. It looked like they were walking ahead of him. As he got closer, he realized they were statues. In single file, they curved over the ridge behind a low wall.

They were slightly larger than humans, and all wore golden robes. They had bare heads with painted faces. Each one was different, and they stood on pedestals. Some had long hair, some were balding, some were women, some had red lips, and some were smiling. The wind hummed around Pete as he stared at the lifeless procession. What were they doing up here? Where were they going? He turned to Moe, who shrugged and looked away.

"They are ancient. Moe does not know why they built here," Moe said.

It reminded Pete of the mystery of the oversized heads on Easter Island. He looked around as if he could find some clue about the statues. There was nothing else up here. It was bare of the dense vegetation found in the valley. Crows flew along the air currents the wind brought up from the valley. Occasionally, they would swerve around the line of statues. Then, as if they were confused, they would dart away to leave the statues to their silent procession.

It was a lonely place, and Pete was glad to get back into the SUV next to Mi Mi.

In twenty minutes, they had reached a large mining operation. Moe turned around in his seat and said, "Two types mining here. There is usual digging of rock out of ground, and there is panning in streams that flow out of mountains."

"Like your gold rush in California," Mi Mi said.

They all got out of the Toyota. Pete felt like he'd stepped into a moonscape. All the vegetation had either been removed, or nothing grew up here in these narrow mountain valleys. All he could see was tan and brown dirt. Huge boulders dotted the sides of the hills and seemed to be the only thing holding the ground back from a landslide.

They walked toward a building that looked like a warehouse. The military escort followed closely. Three banana palms growing around the door to the facility provided the only color in the drab landscape.

Moe said, "That is where we have lunch."

Pete laughed. "Oh? I thought we'd hit the gourmet restaurant on the other side of the mine."

"You Americans. So funny." Moe laughed quickly.

In spite of Pete's long loping stride, two of the men in the military escort moved up next to them. They shouldered Moe aside and took charge of the tour. Captain Thaung drifted along the side of the group, watching.

An explosion from behind the warehouse blew rocks, dirt, and dust high into the air around the group. Instinctively, they all ducked. The sound had been so close that it rang Pete's ears, and he felt the concussive force of the blast. He straightened up. "What the hell? Is this one of the war zones?" A cloud of dust floated over the spot of the explosion.

Moe shook his head. "Dynamite. They break rock open to find gems."

Mi Mi moved closer to Pete, and he could feel her body next to his as they walked ahead. He wanted to protect her, but the explosion had been so close they both could've been blown up. He thought of the safety precautions practiced in the US compared to this and began to worry.

To his right, about halfway up the side of the mountain, was another primitive wooden frame structure. Pete could see a long hose about nine inches in diameter snaking from the high side of the hill down through the frame itself. Two small men stood on top of the structure, and Pete wondered how it could support them. They smiled and waved at his group.

The "tour guide" barked at Moe, who turned to Pete and Mi Mi. "We have permission to look. We start at main tunnel."

From behind him, Pete heard vehicles crunch to a stop. He glanced back and saw several soldiers from the Tatmadaw get out of their trucks. They all carried automatic rifles and started up the hill toward Pete's group. That didn't look good. He glanced at Moe to catch his eyes. He'd come to know Moe well enough so that even when Moe's expression did not change, Pete could read the concern on his face. They moved forward.

Behind the warehouse, Pete saw the open hole of the mine entrance. Several shovels and picks leaned against a wooden frame around the opening. Three men stopped their work to turn to Pete's group and wave. The military escort fanned out in a semicircle. Two of them stopped and acted as "guards." The leader motioned to Moe that he could take the group inside.

Pete whispered to Moe, "What the hell are we doing here? What are we looking for?"

"Please quiet." Moe started into the mine. "This shows how successful government is with mining gems. We must act like we are interested. In meantime, we look for clues." He turned forward and moved deeper into the gloom of the tunnel.

Pete crouched at the waist and followed Moe through the low opening. Mi Mi hung onto Pete's shirt tail and walked behind him.

Inside, he could see the mine had been carved out of the rock. It expanded to about eight feet high and seven feet wide. Candles flickered with the movement of air and provided the only light as they penetrated the mine to about thirty-five feet. There were no supports inside the tunnel. The only timbers Pete had seen were those holding up the entrance. Sweat dribbled down the sides of his face, and he felt nervous. He could smell something damp and metallic. Several more miners appeared out of the dusty darkness as Pete's group came closer. They didn't wear any protective helmets or ear pieces. Several of them looked like children who wore tattered shirts and flip flops even on the rocky floor of the mine. Their faces were so blackened he could hardly recognize their features. When they smiled, their white teeth flashed momentarily and made them look like Halloween characters.

They talked fast and with enthusiasm as they pointed to the ceiling. They must have found gems there recently. Without warning, a small gas engine fired, and Pete could hear the rattle of the chugging motor echo off the walls. A jackhammer started and was so loud it hurt his ears. It seemed like the walls themselves shook with the pounding of the hammer.

Moe turned quickly and started for the entrance. They all followed, and when they got back outside the breeze cooled their faces. The sun lit up the front of the mine. Pete was relieved to be out of the deep hole in the ground. Even the desolate moonscape around him seemed welcoming. He also realized that if their military escort had wanted to end the tour permanently, it could have happened at the deep end of the mine. The outside world would never know about their bodies.

He looked down the hill and saw the Tatmadaw soldiers standing around the door of the warehouse. They didn't make any move to stop Pete's group.

Moe interrupted, "We see other types of mining. You may find a gem yourself." He smiled briefly. "But, of course, you cannot keep it."

The group followed the military escort as they walked at an angle further up the mountainside. In twenty minutes, they'd crested a rocky ridge to reach another rickety bamboo structure like those Pete had seen before. Once again, a long hose hung from the top and pointed down into a narrow gorge. As they approached, workers came out from under the rig. Two men and two children waved.

Someone shouted orders, and the hose twitched as a blast of muddy water shot out of it. It landed on the rough surface of the gorge underneath and worked like a high-pressure water cannon. Pete could see a top layer of dirt and mud tumble away to reveal a rough layer of rocks. When the cannon stopped blasting water, several other workers converged on the scoured ground. Most of them were women who all wore conical straw hats and walked barefoot. They squatted on their butts and, with busy hands, sifted through the remaining rocks.

Moe explained, "Water wash away lighter materials to leave heavy minerals and, maybe, gems exposed on ground. Women use more water to wash off rocks and search for gems."

"How long do they work?" Pete asked.

Moe shrugged. "Maybe twelve hours each day."

Even though Pete had learned not to judge the conditions in this country the same as those in the US, he still felt his anger rising. The few men in the workforce stood in the shade of the wooden rig while the women and children labored in the hot sun. With their backs bent over, many of the women also tended to babies and infants sitting next to them.

Moe lifted his arm and pointed across the gorge. "There is a stream from mountains. Many workers pan for gems. They dip flat basket into running water and pick up gravel from bottom at same time. They swirl basket and maybe they find more gems."

"The one advantage," Mi Mi added, "is that anyone can mine the streams. The government allows that, and if the women find anything, they get to keep it."

"Do they find many gems?" Pete said.

Mi Mi shook her head. "No. That's why the generals allow the people to search only the streams. Any other gems found belong to the government."

The investigator in Pete started to look for clues. If some of the generals were smuggling gems without the other generals' knowledge, how would it be done? And where would they hide the jewels until they could get them back to the rafts at Mandalay? If he could figure that out, it might also tell him where Bridget had gone.

Their small group walked over to the muddy stream and leaned over the shoulders of the women as they panned. The water was the color of clay, but as it swirled around in the basket, it dribbled out and left a layer of gravel. The women's brown fingers picked through it like insects looking for prey. If they didn't find anything, they tossed the gravel behind them and repeated the process.

As Pete approached, one girl stood up. She looked about thirteen years old. Her hands were cracked from all the exposure to water and the harsh sun. She held up something that looked like a mason jar. Inside was a pile of pink rubies about an inch high. She smiled proudly.

As Pete stepped back, he noticed this was the only woman who'd found anything. The others bent under their straw hats and sifted the waters. Their arms circled the outsides of their knees, pulled up close to their chins as they squatted over the water.

He turned to Mi Mi. She looked up at the bamboo scaffolding and remained silent. Was she as upset by the conditions as Pete was? Or was she upset with him?

A half hour later, they had come down from the rocky ridge. Next to the warehouse was a small shop that made paper umbrellas. To shield themselves from the tropical sun, the people of this region often used umbrellas.

Mi Mi pulled her brother to the side. "This is where she is." The military escort allowed Mi Mi to lead them to the shop.

Outside, Pete watched a woman bend over a large tank full of gray water. She used her hands to swish a sticky glob of gray mush back and forth in the water. She spoke to Moe, who translated. "She softens bark from thanaka tree. When it fully softened, she will pull out of water and spread it on frame beside her to dry in sun. While it dry, she flatten it many times until it is like thick paper. Then made into umbrella."

Mi Mi seemed impatient. "Come with me," she told Pete as she led him through the front door. The escort remained outside, some of them smoking Chinese cigarettes.

Once the door had closed, Mi Mi hurried to the back. A young woman stepped from behind a framed silk screen. Mi Mi reached for both her hands and held them. They talked quickly.

Moe pointed up to the walls. Brightly colored umbrellas hung upside down. In the corner on the floor, a man squatted and used a short knife to carve a piece of bamboo. Pete walked over to him. The man smiled up at Pete but continued to work. He cut a notch in the side of the bamboo and then attached several narrow strips of light wood to the end in the shape of a wheel. He applied a string of glue to each strip. Then he placed a round piece of lemon-colored paper on the wheel of strips, where it stuck to the glue. When he turned his work upside down, Pete saw a beautiful umbrella. The outside of the paper was covered with painted white flowers. The man handed it to Pete. It was made entirely by hand and completely of bamboo and paper.

Mi Mi came back and pulled them into the far corner. She looked behind Pete's back to see if the escort was coming inside. When Mi Mi decided it was safe, she talked fast. "The manager is Shan. I have information from her." Her face glistened in the light from the windows.

"Did they see Bridget?" Pete asked.

"I didn't ask yet. You show her the photos," Mi Mi continued. "But no one knows anything about smuggling of gems. It is possible, but would be dodgy for even general to sneak gems out. But there is something more mysterious."

The three of them leaned even closer to each other.

Mi Mi's eyes flashed. "Strange things are happening at Heho Airport near Inle Lake."

"What?" Moe's voice rose.

"No one knows for sure. The airport was suddenly closed to all travelers. The Tatmadaw surrounded it and has prohibited anyone from coming near it."

"I never hear of that happening before," Moe said. "Why is army there?"

"Where is this Inle Lake?" Pete interrupted.

Mi Mi waved her arm toward the east. "Up there in the high-lands in the Shan region. It is one of the largest inland lakes in the country. It is only accessible by boat or air since there are no roads anywhere."

Then the front door burst open. Two soldiers from the Tatmadaw entered and looked around. They wore tight-fitting uni-forms and dark green helmets. Both carried Chinese PPSh-41 sub-machine guns on slings over their shoulders.

Captain Thaung followed them inside. In a sharp voice, he called out to Moe, "By authority of Special Intelligence Department number four of the State and Divisional Police Force, I have new orders for you."

Moe's eyes swiveled from Pete to Mi Mi before he followed the soldiers outside. Pete looked at Mi Mi and saw the skin stretched tightly across her face. Her lips thinned, and she took a deep breath. He said to her, "Could we ask the manager about Bridget?"

Mi Mi blinked and regained her composure. "Sure." She led Pete toward the back, pushed aside the frame of silk, and said hello to the woman again. She placed her palms together and bowed to-ward Mi Mi as she did the same. The young woman's name was Ting Ting, and she talked with Mi Mi for a long time. Mi Mi said to Pete, "Do you have the photos?"

Pete reached into his wool bag and removed three large glossy photos of Bridget. He handed them to Ting Ting, who put on a pair of glasses and studied the pictures. She walked to a wooden desk that filled almost all of her office and phoned someone.

"Her aunt, Daw Kyaing, lives on Inle Lake and has been con-tacted. She is willing to help us when we get there. Our network of women is very extensive," Mi Mi said.

Pete was about to ask her about the women's network when the front door banged open. He and Mi Mi rushed back into the shop. Moe stood beside the door, propped against the frame with a stiff arm. His face was drained of color, and his glasses slid far down his nose as if they might fall off.

"What?" Mi Mi shouted as she ran to him.

At first, Moe couldn't talk. His head bobbed slightly forward a few times. Then he took a deep breath. "General Lo Win order me removed from investigation. Captain tell me."

Mi Mi gasped and fell back against Pete.

"I must return to Yangon immediately."

Pete said, "But you haven't found out anything about Sumpter's death."

"But I have found something." Moe looked up at Pete. "He involved with gem smuggling in some way. Otherwise, why would general pull me off case?" Moe's eyes dropped as he thought about something. Quickly, he continued, "Something else."

"What?"

"I found Nat doll under Sumpter body," Moe explained.

"Why didn't you tell me? And what the hell does it mean?"

Moe shrugged. "It means killer of Mr. Sumpter probably Burmese. The Nat was placed to scare off bad demons attracted by killing. It is thought people who die violent deaths come back as Nats."

Pete blew out some air. "Now you're saying that Jeffrey Sumpter will come back as a ghost?"

Mi Mi changed the subject. "We have a bigger problem. If the general thinks Moe has gone too far, it could be the end of his career. And considering our family history, it may mean he will be charged with a phony crime, one that could carry life imprisonment —or death."

Pete felt Mi Mi's body stiffen. He pulled her closer and wrapped his arms around her tightly.

Ting Ting ran into the shop from the back room. She waved the photos in front of her and stopped when she saw the distraught group. Ting Ting waited for a minute until Mi Mi nodded for her to talk. "Ting Ting has seen this woman."

Pete's head spun around to face Ting Ting. "Where? Is she here now?"

"No. But she was seen here few days ago. She was with soldiers, and we think she has gone deep into country. Up into highlands."

"Do you know where?" Mi Mi asked.

"Inle Lake."

Chapter Sixteen

Dinner with the miners, later in the afternoon, came as a relief to Pete. The tension between Moe, Mi Mi, and himself had risen to the breaking point. They hadn't solved the mystery of Jeffrey Sumpter's death. Moe's life was in jeopardy, as well as Pete's relationship with Mi Mi. Bridget was still missing, and Pete still didn't know anything for certain.

He sat on the hill while the tropical sun, reflecting off the rocks, blazed around him. At least the humidity was lower at this altitude. He hadn't seen Moe or Mi Mi for over an hour. Pete finished the third bottle of chilly Myanmar beer.

He thought of Karen, and even though he'd only been gone from the US for a few days, it seemed like years. He'd pretty much failed with the relationship up to now. Pete admitted it was his fault, and it seemed like he'd never be able to repair it.

What the hell was he doing here in Myanmar? At first, the search for Bridget had driven him on. Then it was the need to be with Mi Mi combined with finding Bridget. Both these reasons seemed as elusive as the search for the smuggled gems. What was the real reason he kept going?

Behind him, Pete heard another explosion. The rock he sat on shook as dust settled over him a few minutes later. Damn idiots!

By six o'clock, he heard Moe shouting for him. Pete turned around to see him at the door of the warehouse. The Tatmadaw had disappeared although the military escort remained. They lounged in the Toyotas with the doors flung open.

Pete stood and found the beer had hit him harder than he thought. Maybe it was the altitude and the heat. But what the hell, he'd have a few more anyway. Pete planted his feet carefully into the crumbling rock scree as he climbed up to the warehouse.

Although it wasn't air conditioned, the low building felt cool and dry. Pete found Mi Mi coming out of the one bathroom everyone shared. Inside, it had two stalls—one for men and one for women. Not that they were any different. Pete swerved to a kiosk in the corner that offered candy and beer and Pepsi Cola. He ordered another Myanmar beer.

When he reached Mi Mi, he tried to read her mood. Her eyes softened when she saw Pete. "Missed you this afternoon," Mi Mi said.

"Uh, I was thinking."

"If you should go on?"

"Yeah, how'd ya know?" He slurred his words slightly.

"I don't know what will happen with us, Pete." She dropped her head for a moment. "So many things are different between us."

"So what?" His voice came out louder than he had intended.

"I just don't know." She paused. "The other night—I like you, but I have so much work to do here. It seems obvious that we can't get together, ultimately."

Pete felt frustration building in him. His instinct was to argue with her. Fight. But he choked back the feelings. "Maybe we can still try."

Without saying anything, she walked toward a large open door at the back side of the warehouse. The square glowed brightly from the sun. When Mi Mi stepped into it, she became a black outline without any features. Pete sighed and followed her.

He came outside to a small dining area. Several poles held a tin roof over one section. Underneath it were two wooden tables. One tilted to the side. Next to that was another shelter of poles that supported a straw roof. The "dining room" was open air—how charming.

Moe was already seated at the table that didn't tip. He was surrounded by various workers, mostly boys. There were no women among the group. Some of the boys wore hats—straw conical hats, pith helmets, and American baseball hats. One young man wore his baseball hat backwards—probably what he'd seen on a pirated American film. Pete chuckled to himself and sat across from Moe.

Pete smelled dust on the men around him and the sweet odor of dried sweat. Meat sizzled on grills in the kitchen. Pete realized that he was starved.

Several pots of tea were served by two women who darted silently in and out of the tables. Mi Mi squeezed in next to Pete. She sat at the end of a long bench. Pete could feel her body pressed next to his and wondered what he could do to change her mind about him.

Pete looked across at Moe. When Moe went back to Yangon, would Mi Mi go with him? And if they went back to Yangon, where would Pete go? Without their help, how could he follow Bridget's trail? He'd failed in his mission already. The thoughts made him feel glum and defeated. He wasn't used to losing or giving up, especially when he thought the cause was a worthy one.

Beyond the table, Pete could see the opening to the mine tunnel about fifty feet away. He heard the rhythmic banging of the jack-hammer inside the mine and felt vibrations through the ground under his feet. A slight breeze blew up from the valley, cooling him as he sipped sweetened tea.

Moe finished talking with the man next to him and leaned forward to tell Pete, "This is *Palin Zing* mine. Very famous. It was reopened after rainy season last year. Eighty miners work here."

The number surprised Pete. "The generals make them work?"

"Yes. That is why so many. In past, number of gems discovered has been low, so generals push men to work hard and long to find more."

Pete looked back at the opening to the mine and saw several boys coming out carrying baskets on their heads. They were full of rubble and broken rocks. The boys marched in single file around the corner of the opening and, one by one, dumped their loads over a steep drop-off on the hill. The useless rocks clattered down the side of the mountain.

Four china platters were set on the table before Pete. Each one was mounded with stir-fried food, mostly vegetables with thin strips of various meats—chicken and pork since beef was rare here.

The wind stopped dead for the first time all day. Unusual. The talk around the table quieted as the men dug into the food using chopsticks and fingers. They ate very fast by lifting up their bowls and scraping the food into their mouths. Other than the clicking of the chopsticks, it was silent.

Pete decided that in spite of the heat, he was too hungry to turn down food. He shoveled a helping of vegetables into his bowl. He chose something leafy and green, the color of a Crenshaw melon. Mi Mi waited for him, and then she took her portion.

He looked up and saw boys streaming out of the mine. Dozens of them. They hurried around to the spot where the rocks had been dumped and sat on the ground. Some removed their hats and fanned themselves. Their bare legs stuck out in front of them like rolled cinnamon sticks. The noise of the jackhammer had stopped. It was so quiet Pete could hear the soft crunch of the boy's flip flops on the gravel as the last of them gathered on the side of the hill.

Pete squeezed his chopsticks around a piece of pork and bent forward to eat. Then a man came out of the opening of the mine and scrambled down the side of the hill while his straw hat flew off. He didn't stop to pick it up.

The cogs in Pete's mind ground together, slowed by the four beers he'd drunk. Something was wrong. As he put down his chopsticks, he tried to piece together the clues he'd just seen. What . . .?

At first, a dense cloud of dust burst from the opening of the mine, as if some giant had blown out the tunnel to clean it. Before his brain could work, the explosion followed, so loud that the pain in his ears caused him to scream. Dynamite. Some asshole had blown the mine shaft right next to the tables! Everything in front of Pete detonated toward him. The tin roof buckled, and two wooden beams holding it up cracked in submission to the blast.

The largest wooden support collapsed and fell toward him. With his legs trapped under the long bench he sat on, he couldn't escape. The dust choked him. Then the log struck him on his shoulder. He fell into the crumbling rubble and flying rock that threatened to crush the life out of everyone.

Chapter Seventeen

Pete's eyes didn't work. He couldn't see anything. He smelled dust—which he coughed out of his mouth—and he couldn't hear anything. As feeling returned to his arms, Pete tried to shove the weight off his chest. To his surprise, it felt soft and it moved.

He saw shafts of light and a shape above him. As his sight cleared, Pete recognized Mi Mi's face. Her body was covered with gray dirt. She pushed up with her arms while pieces of wood, gravel, and broken shards of china plates fell from her shoulders.

Pete realized that he'd fallen between two overturned benches, probably the one he'd been sitting on before the explosion. He propped himself on his elbows. Mi Mi sat next to him, her legs folded beneath her. Her face opened with a white smile.

Pete rolled to his side and reached for her. He hugged Mi Mi for a long time. He could hear her mumbling, but his ears still rang painfully. Around them, people struggled to shake off the debris and stand up. Objects that looked like gray mounds of dirt shuddered and moved to reveal surviving humans. Some of the other mounds remained lifeless.

Within a few minutes, Pete understood that Mi Mi had saved him. The pain in his ears receded, and Pete could hear sounds coming back. "What . . .?" he asked her.

"I saw you fall behind the table," she said. "And I just reacted and jumped on top of you. The table collapsed over both of us. Like a tent, it protected us from the falling rocks."

"Those idiots! Couldn't they see we were sitting here?"

Her forehead creased into several lines. She said, "This wasn't an accident."

Pete's first reaction was to look around as if to protect them from more attacks. Everyone else climbed out of the wreckage of the blast. Pete tried to stand, but his legs shook. He hung an arm around Mi Mi's shoulders. Together, they limped off toward the warehouse. He didn't see the Tatmadaw soldiers. Had Moe survived?

Inside the warehouse, they walked to the far wall and found a garden hose hanging from it. Pete reached through a hole in the wall to turn a red knob connected to a blue pipe. Mi Mi lifted the end of the hose and helped Pete rinse off his hands and face. Moe came up behind him, looking cleaner than the rest of the people.

Moe explained, "I go to bathroom. Moe left dining area when blast happened."

"Accident?" Pete asked him.

Moe scowled but didn't answer him. Instead, Moe offered a bottle of Alpine water to them.

"You picked the luckiest time to go to the loo," Mi Mi said to Moe as she drank.

"We have to get out right now," Moe said.

"So, you're going back to Yangon?" Pete asked. He looked from Moe to Mi MI.

Moe shook his head. Frustration showed when his eyes narrowed. "Moe does not want to give up, but I am ordered off investigation."

"Besides, someone doesn't want us here," Mi Mi said as she brushed dust off of Pete's back.

"I've come this far to find Bridget Holmes," Pete said, "and I'm going to find her." He dried his hands on a piece of cloth. "Ting Ting recognized her photo at the umbrella store. What did she mean by going 'deep' into the country?"

"Shan region," Moe mumbled. He turned and walked toward the door.

"What's that mean?" Pete asked Mi Mi.

Mi Mi explained, "You have to go over the mountains until you reach the central plateau." She waved her hand toward the northeast. "The British built a bloody railroad up there to reach one of their hill stations, or towns. They went up there to escape the heat during the monsoon season."

Pete studied her face. Even covered with dust and dark smudges, and with a small cut by her ear, she had never looked so beautiful. She'd saved his life. The frustration Pete had felt earlier about the relationship turned to dust. Now he had hope again. For her to risk her life for him must mean that Mi Mi's feelings for him went deep—whether she admitted it or not.

After all, he had denied his own feelings about her at first, had even fought against them. He had been certain no one could replace Julie, but then as Pete had gotten to know Mi Mi, he'd changed. Mi Mi was the first Asian woman that had attracted him. He discovered that Mi Mi touched something fundamental in him, something that made him feel good again and complete.

Pete asked, "Why do you think Bridget would've gone deeper into the country?"

Mi Mi shrugged. "Maybe the soldiers forced her to go."

"Why there?"

"It's isolated. There aren't any roads, so the only way to get around is by boat."

"I think we should keep going up there. After all, every step where we've followed Bridget has led us closer to what's really going on." Pete crossed his arms in front of his chest.

"Who are you going with?" Mi Mi grinned.

"What do you mean?"

"Moe has been ordered off investigation of Sumpter's death. We must go back to Mandalay. If he disobeys General Win's order, not only will his career end, but he will go to prison at the least—in spite of his excellent police work."

Pete shifted his weight to the other leg while his plan drifted away like the fading sunlight. "Well—" He didn't know how to follow Bridget's trail, where to go, or even how he would get there.

Besides, he was mad. This was the third time someone had tried to stop him. When Pete had first arrived in the country, he had been anxious to just do the job and get back home. But now things had changed. The search for Bridget was now more than a favor for a US congressman, or even an effort to find the young woman. Pete had always been motivated by a fight for a just cause.

Through Mi Mi, Pete had stumbled upon an underdog—the people he'd met with her. He'd seen the brutal oppression by a corrupt and dangerous government of generals. The ironic thing was that Pete's search for Bridget had also become a search for the truth about Jeffrey Sumpter's death and the underlying crimes of the generals. And he thought of his father, making good steel, who'd always told Pete that a job isn't worth doing if you can't produce an excellent product. Pete wasn't proud of the "product" he had produced with his life so far.

"I'm going to find Moe," Mi Mi said. She walked out of the warehouse.

Pete went to the wooden counter and bought a bottle of water. He followed Mi Mi outside. Dust still hung in the air. Through it, the setting sun glowed in rainbow shades. For a moment it looked magical until Pete saw the wreckage of the kitchen and a row of still bodies in the dirt.

Three other people also lay on the ground. The women who had been servers tended to their injuries, because there certainly wasn't any medical help up here. Pete felt sorry for them, but at least they had survived.

Moe ran up from the Toyotas below the warehouse and said, "We go immediately. Our escort very upset."

"Are we going back to Mogok?"

Moe panted from his run up the hill. "Mandalay."

That surprised Pete. "All the way back? It'll be dark on the way down."

"I know. Very dangerous, but explosion scared escort. They must know something we don't know. They want to get rid of us."

Pete hesitated. "But what about following the trail of the gems?"

"You come now or we leave you alone." Just as he spoke, Moe's eyes turned away, but Pete caught the dark anger in them. "You have no idea how dangerous situation is now." Moe spun on his foot. He started to walk away, stopped, and shouted over his shoulder, "Moe take risk of driving down mountain over risk of getting killed." Moe ran down the hill to the SUVs. Mi Mi waited by the back door to one of them. She held it open for Moe.

The sun dipped below the mountains on the far side of the valley. Long shadows climbed the hill toward Pete. Like dark fingers, they closed around his feet. He heard the engines of the Toyotas start, and he ran down the hill.

Before the sun rose, the Toyotas approached Mandalay. The fields of rice and garlic and flowering niger slumbered in the dusk. A fuzzy glow of light curved over the ancient city. They crossed the Irrawaddy River and headed into town. The caravan turned onto 35th Street. Unlike during the day, when vehicles, animals, carts, people, and dogs crowded the streets, nothing moved now. The sound of the SUVs echoed back from the walls along the street, waking a few dogs that started barking.

As they approached the old royal palace in the center of the city, Pete saw army units patrolling in small groups. A few rode in open jeeps. Pete's vehicle stopped before the Royal Palace Hotel. After the three of them tumbled out and retrieved their luggage, the Toyotas sped off, leaving a cloud of sweet-smelling exhaust.

Pete was worried about what Moe and Mi Mi would do now. He tried to talk with them. Moe waved him off with a tired expression and plodded up the immaculate steps of the hotel. Pete climbed up to his own room and fell into bed.

After a few hours of sleep, Pete sat in the restaurant and ate his breakfast alone. The other two hadn't come down yet. Pete ordered fruit and toast. "*Kyay zu bar be,* thank you," Pete said to the waiter. He took a drink of hot sweetened tea. After he'd finished half of his breakfast, Pete paused and picked up the *New Light of Myanmar* paper. The propaganda amused him as it was such a pathetic effort by the government. A banner across the front page read: *Support Government Policies and You Will Be Healthy.* He turned the page. There were two color photos of a general laying a circular wreath of gardenias before a fat golden Buddha. The general looked serious.

Someone hooked a finger over the top edge of the newspaper and tugged it down.

Mi Mi's face appeared. Her brown eyes searched over him. She smiled and sat down next to him. "You look like you survived yesterday," she said.

Pete loved the tone of her voice, and this morning it carried a rough edge from her sleep. He said, "One more time and I may not make it out of this country alive."

"Do you still want to leave?"

Pete hesitated. Did she want to know, or was she really asking about his feelings toward her? "I've uh, grown accustomed to this place. The people, and especially you." He took her hand in his. It felt warm and slightly damp. "At first, I couldn't wait to get out of here. The heat, the oppression, and the corruption. But then I met you. I don't know if I can leave without you now."

Mi Mi took a deep breath. Her lips tightened. "I'm sorry, Pete. But I've given up so much to come back here. The dreams I had for my own life—marriage, kids—you know. All the normal things people want in Great Britain and America. But my country isn't normal."

Pete started to chuckle until he saw how serious she had become.

"If we can reduce the power of the generals, we may be able to create a form of democracy here. As an American, I don't think you can even imagine what this means. I could use my education to help food production and help my people out of poverty."

Although Pete had felt devotion to Julie and his daughter, he'd always stood alone. The individual struggle. With her life and devotion, Mi Mi had introduced him to something different. The community came first. It made him think of his Asian mother.

Pete grasped her hand. "Can't you think about marriage, a husband, or a family sometime in the future?"

She didn't respond to him. She dropped her head and sipped from a cup of tea.

Pete persisted. "Don't you understand that I've changed? Of course, I still want to find Bridget, but now I'm beginning to understand your struggle. You're amazing."

"I'm knackered. What's the use?" she whispered. "We went all the way up to Mogok and the minute we got close to solving this, someone tried to kill us. They won't fail with their next attempt." She sighed and picked up the menu, but it was obvious by her vacant expression that she really wasn't hungry. "And now Moe is in serious trouble. They will hold our family's history against him. I'm worried."

Pete could also see dampness in her eyes. She was about to cry. Pete shifted closer to her and wrapped his arm around her shoulder. He felt her shudder. Public displays of affection were not common in the country, so although he felt like kissing her, he didn't. Her head pressed against his face, and Pete could smell her perfume. Today it was jasmine. "What can I do to help?"

Mi Mi sniffed back the tears and lifted her head. "I don't know. Maybe I should go back to Great Britain."

"No. Don't give up the fight."

She smiled slightly. "I'm thinking of a song called 'Red Dragon.' It's a song of patriotism. We used to sing it when I was a child. I can remember every word and how my mother could never sing it in tune. But she was the loudest." Mi Mi hummed a few phrases of the song.

Pete sat back in his chair. He couldn't imagine how difficult the struggle must be for Mi Mi and the others like her. Even with national leaders like Aung San Suu Kyi, most of the battles were small and quiet and dangerous ones like Mi Mi and Moe were fighting now. There were no rallies or adoring crowds to support them. Pete would support her. "What can I do to help?" he said.

Moe came toward them. He shuffled his feet as if he were still exhausted. When the waiter noticed, he brought tea for Moe, who slumped into the cane chair next to Mi Mi. He didn't speak. Mi Mi leaned toward Moe and spoke softly to him.

Pete didn't want to intrude. He bit into a piece of toast. When the waiter came by, he ordered more sweet tea and wondered what the hell he was going to do. He glanced at the mirrored wall and put his sunglasses on. They definitely made him look good.

The waiter came back unexpectedly. He handed Pete a note. When he opened the thin paper, he saw it was from Carter Smith. Both the ambassador and Smith were in Mandalay now. They wanted to meet with Pete. He noted the date, looked at his watch, and saw he had made it back to Mandalay just in time. He would meet them later this morning at the Ciatti Hotel. Pete looked forward to it. If Moe and Mi Mi were going back to Yangon, maybe the ambassador could help in the search for Bridget Holmes.

He perked up and felt a sliver of hope. But what about Mi Mi and the cause she fought for? Pete was torn between going home and helping her in some way. Would the ambassador be interested in exposing the general's crimes? Would the embassy help in any way?

He turned to Moe and asked him, "What will happen now?"

Moe shrugged and responded, "There is old saying: *It is impossible to predict shape of clouds.*"

Pete finished his tea. Moe and Mi Mi ate bites of fresh mango and cantaloupe. The color had returned to Moe's face. He said, "We must go to Yangon. The investigation of Jeffrey Sumpter taken over by others. Moe will never know who kill young man."

Mi Mi agreed. "There are so many people who disappear or die and we never know what has happened to them. It is the ultimate mystery of my country."

Pete looked from one to the other. He'd come to trust and admire both of them. He told them about his meeting with Smith and Ambassador Popham. Pete focused on Mi Mi and held her eyes for a long time. Her eyebrows slanted to the sides, and her eyes seemed lifeless. Could he really leave her? For good? "I'd like to say goodbye and thank you before you go," Pete said.

Mi Mi didn't speak, but Moe said, "Yes. But in Buddhism there is no goodbye. Since we are friends, we always meet in future place and future lives."

That didn't provide Pete with much comfort. He didn't want to meet Mi Mi in a future life when they both came back as caterpillars. He wanted to be with her now. For the immediate future, they all agreed to meet at the hotel in the late afternoon.

They stood while Moe and Pete placed their hands together in front of their chests and bowed toward one another. Pete checked the wool bag on his shoulder to make sure he had all the evidence about Bridget he'd accumulated to show the ambassador. He turned from the other two and walked quickly through the lobby.

The fragrance of the jasmine bushes lingered with him even as he stepped out of the lobby and into the street.

Thick, gray clouds blanketed the sky. The heat clutched him with damp fingers, and he heard the rumble of thunder from off to the west. Pete had planned to get out of the country before the monsoons began. He didn't think that was possible now and dreaded what the conditions would be like when the rains started.

The presence of the military was more prevalent than ever. He hurried down the sidewalk and around the royal palace. Pete glanced behind him to see if he was being followed. He didn't spot anyone.

Sweat seeped out across his forehead. Still, he hurried to the meeting. A block from the Ciatti Hotel, he stopped. Two men from the NGO Free the Oxygen were seated at a sidewalk café. Pete recognized the leader, Rob. He spotted Pete. Without hesitation, Rob shoved back, his chair clattered over, and he charged toward Pete. The second guy ran behind Rob.

Pete looked around. Three soldiers stood next to a parked jeep. They noticed the men running but were slow to react. Pete couldn't depend on them for help anyway. He backpedaled until he came to a narrow alley on his left. It was crowded with market shops and open air stalls of products. Between high walls, it offered shadows and hopefully, protection. Pete dived into the crowd of people at the entrance.

To the right, several shelves held woven straw baskets. To the left, sprawled across the floor, were plastic buckets and straw containers that held vegetables. Light green asparagus, lettuce, bok choy, dirty brown bulbs of garlic, yellow corn, and red peppers were all offered for sale. Behind the food, several people squatted on the floor. An older woman wore a straw hat and smiled with a toothless grin as Pete ran by. Grandmothers, kids, women, and men all sat on the floor, weighing the food and preparing it for display. Behind them, items of colorful clothing hung from pegs in the wall. For Pete the best part was the far end, which shaded into darkness. The aisle he ran along was only wide enough for one person at a time. He tried to weave through the crowd, but when he heard Rob shout and realized how close he was, Pete used his size to bully people out of the way.

He stumbled on a basket of green beans and heard it tip onto the floor. He grabbed a small man who blocked his path. Pete jerked him to the side and ran past him. Deep into the darkness of the market, Pete slowed enough to glance behind him. All he could see were the bobbing heads of shoppers who closed in behind him. It was as if he'd never even left a wake. The NGO soldiers had disappeared.

Three blocks later, he came out into the open street again. He panted and leaned forward to rest his hands on his knees. He had to get to the safety of the Ciatti. Pete took three deep breaths and ran to the right. He covered two blocks and turned right again. His sense of direction was perfect because he came out in front of the Ciatti Hotel. Without pausing, he ran into the lobby. He doubted the NGO men would do anything there, even if they caught up to Pete. He rested until he could breathe normally again. When he peeked out into the street, he didn't see the men.

He wiped his sleeve across his face, looked at his watch, and saw that he was late for the meeting by ten minutes. He walked into the restaurant.

Carter Smith stood up from the wrought iron table. She smiled and waved at him. When Pete walked over, Ambassador Popham looked up at him and nodded. He dropped his head quickly and studied a pile of papers in front of him.

Smith said, "Did you get lost?"

"Sorry I'm late. You won't believe this, but those two guys from the NGO Free the Oxygen were out there and chased me."

Popham's head jerked up for a moment before he went back to reading. Smith frowned and said, "That's not good. I thought we'd taken care of them."

"What do you mean?" Pete asked.

She waved her hand between them. "Never mind. We have more important things to discuss. Have a seat." She stepped back to let Pete settle into the vacant chair next to the ambassador. "How have you been?" she said.

Pete exploded, "How have I been? Just fucking . . . er," he glanced at the ambassador. "Uh, just great. I've almost been killed a few times, these thugs from the NGO are after me, and I still can't find Bridget. Other than that, I'm fine." He glared at Smith as if it were her fault.

Carter nodded and tried to smile. "Well, I think it's time we took over this mission."

"Huh?"

"You're in a screwed-up country where your limited resources are of no use. It's time you went home and let us handle every-thing." She set her chin on an upraised palm. "After all, that's what you told me originally—that you wanted to get the hell out of here as soon as possible. We can get you an expedited plane ticket back to Minnesota."

Pete took a deep breath. She was correct, but that had been days ago. He'd changed, and how could he tell her that he didn't want to give up? That he didn't want to leave without Mi Mi? That he might be in love. "You're right, but I think—"

Popham cleared his throat and spoke in a deep voice. "Pete, you're a good investigator, but this is out of your league."

"I've got help," he lied.

Popham looked around the restaurant. "Where are they? And where is Bridget Holmes?" His pale green eyes studied Pete like a snake.

Pete felt flustered. "Well, I'm still—"

"Bullshit. As we say in Texas, you can't rope cattle if you can't find 'em. Take my advice and get out of here." A tuft of hair stood up at the back of his head.

"Wait a minute. Maybe you don't know what I've found out." He told them the entire story, starting from Mandalay, the rafts, the gems, and the expedition up to Mogok and the attempt on his life. He noticed both of them glance at each other while he spoke. Their expressions didn't change, but they leaned forward over the table. "You've offered to help in the past. Here's what I need. I'm certain Bridget has gone up into the Shan region, and the trail of the gems goes there too. I need to get to Inle Lake and find her."

Carter Smith said, "Inle Lake, huh? You have to fly up there."

"I know."

After a long wait, Popham shoved back his chair. He said, "I've got something to show you. It proves how dangerous this operation has become. And it's no place for you. I'm ordering you back to the States. Immediately."

Pete felt his gut tighten. That was the wrong thing to say to him. He felt like fighting. "You don't have any authority to order me to do anything."

"Oh? We'll see about that. In the meantime, take a look at this. Our operatives took it at a hotel here in Mandalay." Popham nodded at Smith, who held up a wrinkled photo that was almost torn in half.

She handed it to Pete.

Pete looked at it and saw Bridget Holmes beside a soldier. Rob, from the NGO, walked on the other side of her.

Chapter Eighteen

A jolt of excitement flared inside Pete. He tried to keep his face neutral in front of the two. Bridget was still alive, and his suspicion that she'd been kidnapped was true. But was she in the Shan region, as Moe's friend had suggested, and how could Pete possibly find her? "When did you get this?" he asked Smith.

"Two days ago."

"Where is she?"

Popham added, "We don't know."

"I'm going to find her. That's what I came here for."

"You're not going anywhere. In fact, I've already had a conversation with her father, the congressman. I have a special relationship with him." Popham held out his hand to Smith, who passed him another piece of paper. "I've studied your file, and I didn't expect that you'd take my advice. Therefore, I had to act on my own to, uh, protect you." He took the paper from Carter Smith.

"What do you know about me?" Pete felt the first twinge of anger inside.

"I know all about your trouble in Washington. You couldn't save—"

"Shut up!" Pete screamed. "You don't know shit about what happened then." His face blazed hot, and he wanted to hit Popham.

But Popham didn't back down. His cheeks quivered with his own anger. "I've had it with you, Chandler. Carter has tried to warn you previously, but you don't take advice. You're way over your head, and if you keep pushing this, you're going to get killed." He slid the paper across the table to Pete. "And I don't want the responsibility for your death hanging on me. I'm sure you know how that feels."

That twist of the knife caused Pete to rise up out of his chair. The only death here would be Popham's. Pete took a deep breath to calm himself. He picked up the paper. It was a copy on the Ex-Im Bank stationery, dated four days ago. "How'd you get this?"

"We're one of the few institutions that can get Internet communications, although it's unreliable most of the time. Go ahead, read it," Popham insisted.

Pete looked at the memo. It was from his boss, Martin Graves. It said: *Pete, I've been advised from several sources that the conditions in Myanmar have deteriorated to the point it's too dangerous for you to remain in the country. I conferred with Congressman Holmes, who has engaged other resources to find his daughter. You've done a great job, but it's time for you to get out. I'm ordering you back to the US. Ambassador Popham will get you a flight immediately. Come home—the snow is finally melting here!*

Pete set the paper on the table and looked at both of them. This reminded him of the time he'd met Moe and Mi Mi and wondered if he could trust them. Could he trust the two who sat before him now? In order to buy a little time to think, Pete called for the waiter.

When he hurried over, Pete said, "*Tea lah?*" and ordered sweet tea. "*Kyay zu bar be.*" He thanked the waiter after he set down the pot of hot tea. He sipped and looked over the rim of the cup at Carter Smith. She glared at him, angry and impatient. "When is the next plane?" Pete asked finally.

Smith let out her breath. "Well, you've missed the one to Taiwan today. Tomorrow at eleven in the morning you have to catch the puddle jumper back to Yangon in order to get the Air China flight out."

"Okay. I have to say goodbye to a couple of people."

"The cop and his sister?" Popham spoke up. "They're part of the problem."

Pete's anger rose again to tighten his chest. "What do you mean?"

"The United States' interests can only be advanced with a stable government. Those two are part of the movement to destabilize things."

"Destabilize things like torture, murder, corruption, and loss of freedom?" Pete said. "Is that why you are against the movement?"

Of course not." Popham spat out the words. "The United States always supports democracy movements. But for them to take root, there has to be stable ground." He relaxed his shoulders and, for the first time, smiled at Pete. "And we have to help these people. They are far behind in the self-government business. They need all the help we can give them. Remember, both of us," he waved toward Carter Smith, "came out of the education industry."

For a moment, Pete could almost believe what the ambassador said.

"I know we disagree about your role here," Popham continued, "but I suspect we agree on the course for this country."

"We do?"

"Sure. We both want progress, we both want to help these poor people, and we both want their standard of living to rise. Health care, education, food quality, and basic freedoms."

Before he'd arrived, Pete hadn't cared what happened here—halfway around the globe from America. He'd assumed this developing country would be like so many he'd worked in before: brutal, feudalistic, and backward. But now, he'd met the people, fallen in love with one of them, and had changed his mind completely. And when he thought about the ambassador's words, Pete didn't disagree. He sighed, not sure what to do next.

"Besides, you don't see the bigger picture."

"Oh?"

Popham settled back in his chair as if he was lecturing students in Texas. "The Chinese are taking over everything around the South China Sea. Even here, we're only about two hundred miles from the Chinese border."

Pete protested, "I don't see any Chinese troops around here. All I see are the thugs the generals use to get their way, like the Lon-Htein."

"It's more complicated than that. At the embassy, we keep the statistics. The Chinese have infiltrated almost every business in the country. Sometimes they even own them with the generals. Like the oil pipeline just completed from China to the Sea of Andaman. Built by Chinese, financed by them, operated by them—all to pump Chinese oil to the sea. The generals collect a fee for the use. Look around at all the manufactured products in this country. There's one main small engine used all over the country—Chinese made.

The majority of motor scooters are Chinese. These developments threaten the United States' interests here. We must make sure the existing regime is strong enough to stand up to the Chinese."

"How about freedom? Don't you think people like Aung San Suu Kyi could stand up to them? She's one hell of a tough lady."

Popham shrugged and looked over at Smith. They both shook their heads. "We aren't putting any money on her or her movement —at least not now. Maybe in the future, they'll be stronger." His voice softened into a Texas burr.

Pete realized that it was a waste of time to argue with these two.

"Okay, it's settled." Ambassador Popham stood up from the table. He shot his arm across and shook Pete's hand firmly. "You've done a hell of a job, Chandler. I appreciate all the information you've obtained and the details of the widespread crimes the generals are involved in."

"You're going to follow up on the teak and gem smuggling?" Pete looked from one to the other.

"Absolutely." Anderson Popham bowed slightly as if to seal the promise.

Pete didn't trust him, but before he could ask more, Carter Smith had grabbed his elbow and ushered him toward the entrance to the restaurant. "Get your things ready." She grinned broadly. "You're gonna get the deluxe embassy treatment on your plane ride back. All the best the taxpayers can afford." She honked a quick laugh.

He was back out on the street. Pete looked around and studied the shops across the road. Were the NGO thugs still here? He didn't see anyone but decided to take a cab back to his hotel. He waved for one, got in, and sped to the Royal Palace Hotel.

In his room, he flopped onto the firm bed. Pete was still angry, and thoughts tangled his mind. He looked up at the ceiling fan, the wooden blades cutting through the humidity. From the open windows thunder rumbled and echoed in the narrow street outside. Soon, rain pattered on a hundred tin roofs around the hotel. Wind puffed through the open window, making the curtains dance and bringing in a metallic smell.

The rain drummed harder. The breeze picked up. He got out of bed and went to the window. Moisture spattered over him. The rain came straight down as if it were so heavy it couldn't even be blown at an angle. Soon Pete couldn't see anything across the street because of the wall of falling water. The air weighed heavily on his skin, and he heard the steady hiss of the downpour. Orange mud flowed through the gutters in the street below.

Within an hour it had stopped, the sun flooded the street, and the air smelled fresh but still hot. The palms and frangipani trees seemed to have swollen in size from all the extra water.

Pete was tempted to escape from the country and go home. He would be welcomed by Martin Graves, thanked by Congressman Holmes for the work he'd done, would probably keep his job, and maybe he could patch up his relationship with Karen. All that tugged on him.

But he hadn't really been successful here. He still hadn't found Bridget Holmes. There were still issues about helping Moe and Mi Mi that challenged him. The mission wasn't over, and Pete didn't like to leave things undone that he'd committed to accomplish. And finally, he didn't want to leave Mi Mi.

He put on a white cotton shirt that fastened with wooden buttons and walked across the hallway to Mi Mi's room. Pete knocked softly. She came to the door, her eyes puffy as if she'd been napping. She looked up at him, smiled, and yawned to confirm the nap. "Hey, how did you like the rain?"

"I've never seen so much of it. I think of all those years I worked in the Middle East. We would have given anything for even a cup of rain."

"We'll get more when the monsoons really come in. Most of the roads will be impassable."

Pete stepped inside her door, shut it, and told her about his meeting with the ambassador and Carter Smith.

"Well, at least they're going to do something about the teak and gem smuggling," Mi Mi said.

"I'm not so sure about that. I told them everything we've discovered. Maybe they'll do something that helps you and Moe and the movement."

Mi Mi frowned. "Doesn't surprise me. All foreign occupiers, the British, the Chinese, and now the Americans who come and offer 'help,' really don't have our best interests in mind."

"I understand, but don't be stupid. If they're willing to help you expose the crimes and corruption, why not use it?"

"Of course. But I'll believe it when I see it. Isn't that the expression you Americans use?"

Pete laughed. "That's right."

Mi Mi tugged on his arm as she opened the door. "Come. We're meeting Moe outside."

They walked down the quiet hallway, descended the curved staircase, and went out through the fragrant lobby. In the street, the rain had left a layer of humidity worse than ever. The thought of getting on a plane back to Minnesota seemed pretty good to Pete. Moe came out from the shadows of the hotel. Sweat stains spotted his shirt where it clung to his skin. Moe didn't make eye contact but nodded to follow him.

The three of them started to walk toward the shade of the tamarind trees across the street. Pete looked around to see if the NGO soldiers were following. He didn't see anyone. When they'd moved far away from the hotel and were alone, Moe walked next to Pete and said, "Mi Mi and I have made decision. We go to Shan region to follow investigation." Moe's sandals splashed through puddles on the sidewalk.

Pete stopped. He peered at Moe. "But your general said to get off the case."

"I know, but there are ways—"

"What are you going to do?"

Moe looked from left to right. "Moe say I am taking holiday to visit family at Inle Lake."

Pete looked at Mi Mi. "You're going along with him?"

"Yes."

"Won't it be dangerous if the general finds out what you're really doing? How about Captain Thaung?"

Moe nodded and removed his glasses. He clicked the bows together.

Mi Mi said, "Yes, but we'll be very careful. Besides, the female network will hide us well."

Pete struggled to understand what motivated them. "But why?"

"Moe is not dreamer, but one dream I have is to see corruption reduced," Moe said. "To solve murder of Jeffrey Sumpter and expose generals' crimes will be big step to help. Our parents resisted, and Moe must honor the memory. Not like you Americans. In Myanmar, individual not king. My needs are second to needs of community. So what happens to me is of little care."

Bells tinkled from a pagoda down the street. Doves chirped in the branches above them and flittered back and forth freely. Pete said, "I wish you good luck. I've been relieved of my investigation also. I leave at eleven o'clock tomorrow morning."

Mi Mi slid next to him and looped her arm through his. "Come with us. We can get you to Inle Lake, and you can still look for Bridget. We will help you."

Pete thought about the offer for a few minutes. If he snuck out of Mandalay, what could the ambassador do to him anyway? He was like Moe—Pete wanted to finish it. This was an opportunity for the three of them, renegades now, to help each other against some powerful forces. But then he realized how stupid it all sounded.

"Tonight we fly to airport, Heho, and sneak into Inle Lake region," Moe assured him.

"I thought the generals had shut down the airport?" Pete asked.

"They have, but there is one last flight going there. Probably to transport more soldiers. We may be able to get on it," Mi Mi said.

Back at the Royal Palace Hotel, Pete went up to his room and found his small suitcase. On the end table next to the bed was another note Carter Smith had handed to Pete earlier. It read *Pick-up at 10:00 sharp!* The embassy Mercedes would take him to the airport. He held it in his hand for a long time, then returned it to the nightstand and started to pack his suitcase.

From his luggage, Pete pulled out his hiking boots. He'd need them tonight. Mi Mi had said there weren't any roads at Inle Lake —should be interesting. In ten minutes, he was ready. He decided to eat in the hotel in the late afternoon with the others, waiting for dark.

Within a couple hours, they all sat in the restaurant. Pete ate a chicken stir fry. No one talked.

When dusk came, they left the hotel with their bags. They hugged the shadows along the side of the Royal Palace Hotel as they crept toward the back and the gardens. Leaves sagged over them and dripped evening dew on Pete's face. It was one of the only things that felt cool.

Mi Mi had changed from her usual *longyi* to a pair of loose jeans. She'd tied a wool sweater around her neck that caused rivulets of sweat to streak down the sides of her neck.

Moe, in the front, dropped down to squat on his butt. Mi Mi leaned forward and Pete joined them. In a corner of the garden, bushes had been cut back to leave a patch of short grass. A Chinese car with rusty side panels turned into the grassy section. It idled there for a few moments. The inside of the car was too dark to see anyone, but then a cigarette flared, something unusual in this country of few smokers.

Moe stood and ran to the car. The back door opened, and Moe ducked inside. Pete and Mi Mi followed. When the engine revved, it sounded like a lawn mower. The driver shifted into gear and drove onto a rutted dirt road.

An hour later, after bumping over every hole and crack in the road, they reached the Mandalay airport. Pete had thought the potholes in Minnesota were the worst—nothing compared to the dozens he'd just bounced over.

The sky to the west colored in turquoise and tangerine and yellow as the sun flattened on the horizon.

Shadows smothered the palms and bougainvillea that draped over walls and tumbled from every window. A few lights shone from inside the new terminal. As they drove closer, Pete could see only two men working the gate. A woman dressed in a faded blue *longyi* carried a bucket of water and a cotton mop. The driver turned off the engine. Mist hung above the runway, and it smelled swampy.

The driver walked inside, and Pete watched him approach the gate and talk to the man there. The clerk pointed to the wall clock. The driver held up three fingers. The clerk shook his head. The driver reached into his wool bag and drew out a small packet. He handed it to the clerk, who glanced at it and raised his head to look around. The driver hurried back to the car. He yelled something in the Shan dialect through the open window to Moe.

"Hurry," Moe said and crawled out of the tiny back seat. "They have only three tickets for last flight."

That didn't make Pete feel good at all, especially when he thought about the plane that had almost crashed. He went through the gate with a short line of other passengers. Most of them were military. Both Moe and Mi Mi peeled out of the line and clung to the far wall. Pete followed their example.

After scanning the line of soldiers, Moe said, "Moe does not recognize anyone. We go now."

They walked out onto the tarmac. An airplane idled at the far end of the runway. Its propellers roared to life, and the plane taxied over to stop one hundred feet from the passengers. Everyone walked over to climb the wooden steps into the plane. Pete checked around the area to make sure no one tampered with the cargo hold. Even after he'd been seated, he looked out the window to watch for last-minute bundles to go in the hold. No one added anything.

The plane lumbered down the runway to lift into the setting sun. Then it banked northeast toward the mountains and the darkness.

The fight took a little more than an hour. The pilot spoke in English and instructed people to refasten their seat belts. The plane dropped, and Pete could feel the humidity seep through the fuselage in spite of the air conditioning inside. The wheels bumped on contact, and within a few minutes, they had climbed down the steps and started toward the small terminal. The plane taxied away.

The lights around the runway blazed over the tarmac in a glare the color of gray tombstones. But the edges of the runway were concealed in shadows that led off into total darkness.

As the last of the soldiers entered the terminal, the lights on the runway shut down one by one until only security lights remained at the four corners. Moe led the way. "My cousin waiting for us outside," he told the others. Pete and Mi Mi leaned close to each other and followed Moe. The terminal was the smallest one Pete had been in so far—one large room with two open bathrooms on the left side. The one concession stand was closed and dark.

Two men in one-piece blue suits pushed a flat wooden cart on wheels out to the plane. By hand, they unloaded the hold and strained to push the wagon back into the terminal.

More soldiers flooded into the terminal with guard dogs and machine guns. Pete looked at Moe. The color had drained from his face. Was this a trap? Pete's instincts caused him to look for a weapon. His body stiffened while they moved to a quiet corner.

The soldiers marched forward to assemble at the doors to the runway. Pete was sure it was all over. He edged in front of Mi Mi and could hear her heavy breathing. Moe's face was slick with sweat, and his glasses had slipped down on his small nose. He took them off.

After ten minutes, when no one approached the three, Pete began to relax a little. It didn't appear they were a target for the army. Like soldiers the world over who are forced to wait, these soldiers became bored. They leaned against the door frames and talked with one another. Pete could hear murmuring that became louder as soldiers passed on orders. The few civilian passengers were told to leave immediately and that the airport was closed until further notice.

"What's going on?" he whispered to Moe, who raised his eyes to the ceiling. He didn't know.

The passengers formed a snaking line and started to walk out the front door. Bushes grew in a semicircle before them, and several buses huddled at the far end of the parking lot. It was dark and hard to see.

From behind him, Pete heard a commotion. He turned and saw the runway lights all blaze on at once. He tried to stop and see what was going on. A soldier jammed Pete's arm with the muzzle of a rifle. Pete turned back to follow the crowd.

Then he heard the rumble of an incoming plane. Pete thought theirs had been the last flight. What was happening? Pete looked backward and took advantage of the soldier when he also turned to watch. Pete darted behind him and, concealed by the bushes, worked his way back to the terminal. He knew Moe would wait for him.

The open-air bathrooms stank. Pete decided that was the way to go since no soldier would be interested in guarding them. He was right. Pete slipped through the women's bathroom and peeked out into the lobby. It was filled with soldiers and a few civilians in suits. Three of the men from the NGO Free the Oxygen mingled with the troops. Pete recognized Rob. His beard had been shaved, but he wore the same dirty hat. Was Bridget Holmes here? Pete didn't see her.

Everyone waited, shifting from one leg to the other. The roar of an incoming plane grew louder. Then the pilot cut back on the speed for landing. The crowd of soldiers surged forward toward the tarmac. The plane's tires squealed when it touched down, and the engines whined in reverse.

All the soldiers were looking outside, so Pete felt confident they wouldn't turn around and spot him. He stepped out from the corner and looked out to the tarmac. A bulky silver plane rolled by, immense in comparison to the small prop plane he'd flown in on. The terminal lights bounced off the fuselage in bright explosions. It slowed down near the doors but kept rolling. More lights from the ground flashed on. Whoever was on that plane must be pretty damn important.

The plane taxied in a tight circle, and as the tail came under the lights from the terminal, Pete tried to read it. He didn't recognize the name.

He ducked back through the bathroom and with his long strides, loped back to tell Moe and Mi Mi. He found them out in the parking lot. They had heard the plane landing but couldn't see it. Pete told them what he'd discovered.

"What is it?" Mi Mi whispered.

Pete studied her face, which was creased with lines. In the dark they looked like cuts. He looked at Moe, who hissed, "We leave and get help." A horse cart clopped in a circle to stop before them. Moe's cousin urged them to get inside. Pete held back. He almost laughed—a horse cart as the get-away vehicle? As they hesitated to make a decision, two troop transports churned along the road and turned into the airport parking lot. Dozens of soldiers jumped out to run into the terminal, ignoring the horse cart.

"Please to come. We leave," Moe said.

Pete had to see what was happening in the terminal. He turned to go back. With a loud sigh, Moe turned to follow. His cousin jumped down from the wooden seat and handed Moe and Pete each an old American .45 caliber pistol.

"From Vietnam war," Moe explained. Mi Mi refused to wait, and she followed a few steps behind.

When Pete got closer, he shrank down behind a row of bushes. Except for the lights from the airport, everything else disappeared into the darkness. Pete looked back to search for Mi Mi and noticed a pale glow the color of marble in the sky behind him. He looked up and saw the second full moon of the month rising.

Chapter Nineteen

Pete argued with Moe. "We've got to get closer. Find out what's in that plane. And why did it land here?"

"It is dangerous. If caught with pistols, we will be arrested," Moe warned.

"All right. Let's have a get-away plan."

"What?" Moe's face screwed up.

"A plan to get the hell out of here if anyone finds us," Pete explained.

Moe nodded. "Moe get cousin to have cart close to terminal." Moe scuttled back to the parking lot. In the dark he was invisible, but his sandals scraped over the loose gravel.

Pete shook his head at the thought of depending on a horse to escape. He waited for Moe to return.

"Something big is going on here," Mi Mi whispered. "It came in from the east."

Pete could imagine the gleam of the South China Sea under the moon and the ghost airplane slipping through the clouds to fly toward this secret destination. Clearly, it had the generals' permission to land at Heho Airport. But why?

Moe came back out of breath. "Okay. We have plan." He smiled briefly with both excitement and anxiety. "Moe click cigarette lighter, he come to rescue."

Pete fell back on the training from his work with the CID in Iraq. For the first time, although nervous, he felt like he could handle the situation—even here in Myanmar. The only thing that worried him was the presence of Mi Mi. She wasn't trained for anything like this. Pete waved to the group and started to cross the front of the terminal, moving to the left. The plane had stopped at the far corner of the tarmac. He wanted to get close enough to see what was going on.

Pete decided to use the cover of the stinking bathrooms again. He slid between a bush and the wall of the terminal. He took one step, waited, then took another step. It was so dark that Moe bumped into Pete. When he turned around a corner, the bathrooms glowed yellow and Pete smelled them. He led the other two through the loose wooden door into the first bathroom. Pete worried that the squish of his boots on the damp floor might attract attention. He stopped to listen for the soldiers while he raised the pistol in front of him. He hoped not to have to use it here. The echo of a shot on the tiled walls of the bathroom would be enormous, drawing every soldier in the place to them. In spite of Moe's "plan," they'd never make it out alive.

The sounds of people talking and shouted orders came through to the bathroom. Hugging the wall, Pete peeked around the corner. No one looked back at him. He eased out farther into the empty lobby. Everyone had gone outside to stand around the huge plane. Pete signaled the other two to follow. They crept along a low railing to reach two desks that had been used earlier for checking in passengers. Pete squatted down behind one while Moe and Mi Mi did the same behind the second desk. There was a gap between them from which they could see the plane clearly.

"Okay. Now we wait," Pete said.

The men in one-piece blue jumpsuits with wooden wagons had been replaced by mechanized tractors with front loaders attached to them. They chugged out from the jungle around the airport and came into the blaze of light to stop by the cargo bays of the plane. They waited while two men opened the silver sides of the body.

It took four men to unload the wooden boxes from inside the plane. They weren't lifting luggage. Pete watched as the first set of boxes came out. The men heaved them on to the front loader of the tractor. Stamped on the side of the box was *M203 Grenade Launcher.* The tractor driver shifted gears, the engine belched diesel smoke, and he drove back into the jungle. A second tractor came forward and stopped before the plane. This time the men hefted another wooden box labeled *M40 A1 Sniper Rifle* onto the tractor. That was followed by boxes that read *FIM 92 Stinger SAM.* The tractors ground back and forth between the plane and the jungle as they offloaded the crates.

"God damn," Pete whispered. "Those are surface to air missiles." He couldn't believe the crates would be labeled with the contents. It meant the generals were even more brazen than Pete had thought.

The next box out said *BGM-71 TOW*. Another read *FGM-148 Javelin*.

Pete rocked to the side and sat with his back against the desk. He wiped sweat from his forehead. "I can't believe it. The first is an anti-tank missile, and the next one is a self-guided missile to knock aircraft down. What the hell is going on?"

"The generals supervise unloading," Moe said.

"What shocks me is that it's all American weaponry. Our government forbids any sale of this kind of shit. Where is this coming from?" Pete said.

"Oh, no," Moe hissed as he fell back to rest beside Pete. His dark face had turned pale. "It is boss, General Win. He is here."

Pete peeked through the gap and saw the man who been part of his beating the day he'd been grabbed at the Shwedagon Pagoda in Yangon. It proved one thing: the plot that had started with stolen teak and led to smuggled gems had now come to this—illegal and heavy firepower. How was it all connected?

Mi Mi crawled up to them. "We must get evidence." She squeezed between them and raised her cell phone in the gap between the desks. She held it steady and started to shoot. Her flash exploded in a white burst.

Pete grabbed her shoulder and wrenched her back behind the desk. He reached for the automatic pistol and waited for the worst.

"Sorry, sorry," she whispered. "I bloody forgot."

They waited five minutes. Nothing happened. The soldiers had probably been so intent on the unloading, they hadn't noticed the flash. Mi Mi pushed the camera between the desks and took dozens of photos without the flash, including several different people in each image. When she finished, she sat beside Pete and showed him a few. He gasped when he saw Rob, the leader of the NGO, standing beside General Win. He recognized Win—the bull shoulders, small eyes, and pockmarked face. They were in this together. And on top of that, Jeffrey Sumpter—who was maybe an innocent bystander—had been killed.

For a moment, that brought back memories of Pete's work in Washington, of how hard he'd struggled to discover the problems facing the members of the banking committee and then to cover up the same problems to follow orders. Pete thought of the scumbags on the committee, other congressmen, who didn't deserve to be protected. He felt disgusted.

And he thought of how he'd failed to protect the person that meant the most to him—Julie.

Moe begged, "We leave now. Moe afraid we be discovered."

Mi Mi agreed. "I've got a lot of pictures with all of the generals and the NGO thugs in there also."

Pete delayed. He asked Mi Mi, "Did you get some clear shots of the packing cases with the American stamps on them, identifying the weaponry?" When she nodded, he continued, "All right. Let's get the hell out. I've got to get back to the ambassador and show him this stuff. That should blow the lid off of everything."

The group crawled back along the floor toward the bathrooms. Behind them, Pete heard the distinctive clop of boots on the linoleum floor. They came closer. He glanced over the railing and saw two soldiers coming at them. Probably wanted to use the bathroom. Mi Mi was in front, and Pete brought up the rear. He shoved Moe in the butt and hissed to get moving. Moe scrambled on his hands and knees.

At the bathroom, they all stood and darted through the wooden door to the outside. It flew open easily, and they stepped into the darkness. Pete was the last one out. Before he could close the door, Pete glimpsed a form in the shadows just beyond the glow from the bathroom. The man stepped into the slice of light. It was Rob from the NGO.

He carried a small pistol in his right hand, pointed at the group. He still wore the same stupid and dirty hat that Pete had first seen in the jungle by the river. Rob smiled to show crooked teeth. "I come back here to take a piss, and look who I find wandering in the wilderness," he said.

No one responded to him, but Pete pushed Mi Mi behind him.

"I warned you assholes to stay out of this, and you obviously didn't listen. Chandler, I told you to go home, and I think several others have said the same."

"What's going on with the weapons?" Pete asked.

"None of your business. Besides, where you three are going, you won't care anyway." Rob flicked the gun to the left, indicating the group should follow him back inside the airport.

"You do not need me or sister," Moe said. "I am police lieutenant from Yangon. This is not part of job."

"Too late, Gunga Din. If it's not part of your job, what the hell are you doing here?" Rob peered closely at Moe. He chuckled. "Truth is, I figure you're toast already. These generals don't fuck around." He flicked the gun again. "Come on."

He stood just far enough away from Pete that he couldn't reach Rob with any jabs or kicks. The anger that had boiled in Pete's stomach flooded over him. Hanging in his hand, hidden behind his leg, Pete still had the .45 pistol. He clicked off the safety and waited for a chance to take out all his rage on the man who stood before them.

Moe walked forward, and he passed Rob. Mi Mi followed. Pete waited until they were beyond him. Then Pete stared at Rob to fix his exact position in his mind. Pete started to walk forward but suddenly slammed the bathroom door shut. Darkness surrounded them all. Pete's eyes couldn't adjust fast enough, and he knew Rob would be in the same situation—blind for now. Pete raised his pistol, pointed it at the spot he'd fixed earlier for Rob's location, and fired.

In the flash of the muzzle, Pete could see the bullet strike Rob high in the chest and he cartwheeled over onto his back as he crushed the bush behind him. The shot was loud although the foliage had absorbed some of the sound. Pete called to Moe and Mi Mi. He worried the soldiers in the bathroom might have heard the shot. "Get your cousin!" Pete yelled to Moe.

The three of them stumbled in the dark. Their hands groped the side of the terminal wall to find the way back to the front. When they finally reached it, Moe pulled out his lighter. He flicked twice, and nothing happened. Pete danced from one foot to the other, scared that the sound of the shot would bring the entire army after them.

Moe flicked again, and the lighter only sparked. Pete tried to grab it, but Moe jerked to the side, flicked it again, and a flame burned blue and yellow. The sound of a horse neighing came from the darkness of the parking lot.

From out of the gloom, a horse cart swayed into the light from the airport. It turned a circle and stopped. The driver had a conical straw hat pulled low over his face. He turned toward the three. Moe urged the others to climb into the back end.

Pete hesitated. "This is our escape vehicle? A God damn horse cart?" Soldiers shouted from behind him, and Pete lurched toward the cart. Then he saw three other carts turn into the parking lot. They looked identical. He put his foot onto a metal step and crawled into the cart with Moe and Mi Mi. Two wooden seats filled the sides of the carriage, and a canvas surrey stretched over the top. The sides were open.

Mi Mi helped Pete lie on the floor of the carriage. Moe tugged a brightly colored blanket over them, and his cousin snicked at the horse, who took off with a jerk. The other carts followed behind them.

A group of soldiers burst out of the airport into the parking lot. They waved guns in the air and shouted. One by one the other carts trotted between the soldiers.

Finally Pete understood. All the carts confused the soldiers. Moe's plan might work. Onto the paved road, their cart swayed from side to side, and the horse clopped along without concern. For now, no one followed.

In a half hour, Moe's cousin stopped at his truck. It tilted to one side on the shoulder of the road. The three left the horse cart, and Pete helped Mi Mi transfer into the bed of the truck. Moe followed.

The tires spit gravel, and they lurched forward. The three crawled to the front end of the box and sat with their backs toward the cab, facing the rear of the truck. Moe was about to lean back when he looked down at the floor. He reached for something that had dropped out of his jacket.

Pete watched as Moe picked up the Nat that he'd been carrying. It had a face the color of the moon and was wrapped in a black cape with red lining. He stared at Moe.

"I found under Jeffrey Sumpter's body." Moe must have seen the look of surprise on Pete's face because he continued, "Mr. Chandler, many things about this country you will never understand. Also, we go up into mountains to ancient culture. Things different there."

"But you're educated. You don't really believe in all this magic stuff, do you?"

He stared into Pete's eyes. "I tell you. I am Buddhist, but I also rely on help from other sources. To show example, general did not see me. That was not luck. Something protecting me now. In Moe's world, you can never have enough help." Moe's face relaxed in a round shape, and his skin gleamed.

Pete tried to wedge closer to Mi Mi. She stiffened and didn't respond. He tried to talk with her. "Very clever to use the horse carts," he said. He felt proud that he'd saved her and Moe. It was kind of like repaying the favor she'd done for him when the mine blew up. Pete turned to Moe on the other side and asked him, "Now what do we do?"

"We go up into Shan country to Inle Lake. My cousin tell me shipment go there. He saw trucks go north." Moe looked toward the end of the truck bed.

"Why there instead of Yangon?"

"It's more remote and hidden," Mi Mi said.

"But aren't the Shan hostile to the generals?" Pete said.

"Of course, but the generals have the power and military to do whatever they want, even in our region," she told him.

"And maybe Bridget is there also." Pete turned back to Mi Mi. "What do you think?"

She wouldn't answer.

Pete watched the jungles pass by them and thought of the incomprehensible country he rode through now. With all the darkness and twists and mysteries, it rivaled the work he'd done in

Washington. And Mi Mi seemed just as incomprehensible now. He asked her, "What's wrong?"

She jerked her head to face him. "You have really gone over to the bad side now."

"Huh?"

"You killed a man."

"I don't think I did. It looked like a flesh wound to the shoulder. But it sure as hell stopped him and saved you," he grunted.

"I don't care. It is the same thing you have done before. You resort to violence for everything."

"Sometimes that's the only thing that works."

"Maybe, but if we use violence, then we are no better than all the generals and thugs they employ to use violence against us. I don't want to be a part of anything you do."

"I can't believe this," he said. "You're naïve if you think you can simply march in parades to oppose these thugs."

"Pete, this is why I don't think it will work between us. I am very sad about that, but it is the truth. You have not learned anything. You are still a broken man who doesn't believe in hope or the goodness of people."

He felt anger rising and he shouted, "You don't know what's changed in me. Give me a chance. I can show you." He rubbed his hands together. "You're the reason I have changed. I want you to succeed."

She turned her head, and the wind blew strands of hair across her face. Pete couldn't make out her features. When she looked back at him, her cheeks were wet. "I have so many feelings for you, Pete. But I can't go on with someone who is so angry that he will use violence so easily."

Moe, who sat next to Mi Mi, interrupted and said, "Mr. Chandler, we have saying in Myanmar. *Most difficult tiger to tame is tiger within person.*"

These people were simply naïve. When he'd worked in the Middle East, violence was a daily event. Washington wasn't physically violent, but it was in every other aspect of combat. It was a fact of human existence. That had been his life for so long, maybe

Mi Mi was right. She'd always said his violence came from being American. But she held a double standard. He'd seen just as much violence in Southeast Asia. And how about the generals in Myanmar who were notoriously violent?

She was right about something else, too. His anger and pain were temporarily relieved by the use of violence. He had to admit how great it had felt to shoot that asshole Rob. It solved the problem easily. "Maybe—" he began.

"And you won't tell me what happened to you in Washington. We cannot have secrets from each other if you want to be with me."

He felt a lump in his throat. In an effort to get over it, he'd buried the pain deeply, so at times he could almost forget it. Not now. Should he finally tell her? "Okay." The truck lurched to the left around a sharp twist in the road. He leaned against Mi Mi until the truck righted and sped on into the dark.

"I worked in Washington for many years as an investigator for a congressional committee. Bridget Holmes' father was chairman of the committee. He trusted me with everything. I was supposed to be investigating issues the committee wanted to look at in preparation for new legislation.

"But as I got into things, the job changed. I began to find all kinds of dirt, corruption, crimes, and behind-the-scenes problems the congresspeople on the committee were involved in. I started to spend more time protecting those people from exposure than actually investigating other legitimate issues. My job was to cover up for all of them, to protect them from scandal."

"Is that why you quit?" The wind tore off Mi Mi's words as the truck bumped over the dirt road.

"No." Pete felt himself choking. He took a deep breath. "No. I got to know one of the congresspeople. A young woman from Wisconsin named Julie Critelli. She was newly elected in a swing district. That made her vulnerable to defeat. Her mother had been the first woman elected to the state legislature, so politics ran in the family. About halfway through her term, her opponents found some serious dirt on her and threatened to expose her."

"What was that?"

"In college, she'd gotten pregnant and had a secret abortion. It was no one's business, but the voters in her district were very conservative, and it would have been disastrous to her career if it got out. I was assigned to help cover it up. I tried. And as I worked on the case, I fell in love with her. It became more than a job for me. I had to save her." He pictured Julie in his mind, a small, blond woman who looked Scandinavian although she was almost entirely Italian. She smiled often and was a born politician. Contact with people actually energized her. But he'd really fallen in love with her intensity and her passion.

"What happened?"

Pete said, "I failed. The stuff came out, Julie's career was ruined, and she committed suicide." He couldn't talk for a moment. "I feel totally responsible because I wasn't able to hide it like I did for everyone else on that committee." He lifted his head and took a deep breath, smelling the damp odor from the rice fields. "She was the only woman I'd ever really loved, other than my daughter, and I couldn't save her."

Mi Mi moved her hand to Pete's forearm and rested it there for a long time. No one spoke.

Tears moistened Pete's eyes, and he barked out the words. "Can't you see why I shot that jerk back there? I can't fail again."

They drove on for several hours. Moe's cousin tapped on the window of the cab. He waved his hand frantically toward the back of the truck. Pete roused himself. In the light from the full moon, he saw two military jeeps following far behind them.

"Someone saw us leave airport," Moe shouted. He put on his glasses and studied the pursuers again. "Moe cannot have cousin caught with us. They kill him—then us."

Pete felt Mi Mi stiffen beside him. He reached for her chilly hand and gripped it.

"As soon as it gets light enough, they'll start shooting to stop us," she said.

Pete thought of the pistols both he and Moe had. Not much firepower against soldiers who had just unloaded assault rifles and rocket launchers. Besides, what cover did they have in the open bed of a truck? The back gate was missing, and the three of them were totally exposed. His legs had been spread and, without thinking, he crossed his legs, one over the other.

Moe's cousin shouted out the open window, and Moe leaned forward to talk with him. In a few minutes, Moe crabbed back to them. "He will speed engine to get ahead of soldiers. Next we stop and get out to hide."

"Where?" Pete looked around them at the level fields and lakes of rice paddies. It was flat for as far as he could see. How could a tall guy and two other people run through that without detection?

"I have an idea," Mi Mi said. She leaned toward Moe and talked into his ear. Pete couldn't hear them.

"Yes, maybe work," Moe agreed.

At the next curve in the narrow road, the cousin stepped on the gas, and the truck lurched forward. They rocked from side to side. In ten minutes, they'd lost the jeeps. Moe's cousin braked to a stop, tires screeching on the asphalt. Moe yelled, "Please get off here." He leaped from the back end of the truck. Pete jumped out, turned around, and helped Mi Mi climb down onto the road.

"Hurry," Moe shouted. He led them over a small embankment along the side of the road and out toward a rice paddy.

Pete had no idea what Moe was going to do. As far as he could see, water stretched out across the field. Walking paths of raised earth bordered the lake to allow people access to the interior of the paddy. When the sky brightened, they'd be spotted easily if they tried to run along the dikes.

Moe skidded down the side of the embankment and approached a long, narrow black boat. He splashed into the water to retrieve the rope at the bow. Quickly, he tugged at the rope, and the boat responded. A sleeping crane uncurled its head and flapped its wings to lift off from the shallow water nearby. The boat floated toward the three.

When Pete reached it, he could see the shallow boat carried a thick bundle of long, dried grass. Moe urged them all into the boat. Pete gripped the two sides at the same time to balance it and placed his legs into the bottom. It was wooden, dark from years of use, and smelled like oil. It floated only two inches above the surface of the water, and both ends of the boat flattened into worn platforms where fishermen could squat. Mi Mi slid to the stern of the boat. When they were in it, Moe splashed through the water, pushed the boat out toward the middle of the paddy, and, at the last minute, jumped onto the bow. He balanced with both legs and dropped into the bottom.

Sunlight peeked out from between crevices in the mountains. Long shafts of salmon color reflected off the water. "Hope it work," Moe said while pulling the straw over them all. In a few minutes, they floated on the quiet pool.

Chapter Twenty

From across the water, Pete heard the jeep's tires sing along the road as they chased Moe's cousin. Ten minutes later, the jeeps returned. Tires screeched on the pavement not far from where the boat floated. Someone shouted orders. Boots clumped onto the asphalt. A rattle of leaves meant they'd scared the birds out of the trees. A few of them cawed as they lifted off, and their sounds faded into the distance.

Pete could almost laugh at the circumstances: he had come here determined to find Bridget Holmes and was now hiding in a damp boat in a lost rice field—hoping to stay alive. What a screw-up! And the weapons? How crazy was he to think he could fight the power of these generals?

Pete's sense of hearing piqued. Boots scraped over gravel and then went silent. The soldiers must have moved off the road and onto the grass by the edge of the lake. A commander barked more orders, his voice carrying easily across the water.

Pete and the others didn't fit well in the small boat, but they knew not to shift their positions. The sun warmed the air and made the space under the grass hot and claustrophobic. Pete felt like sneezing.

He thought about his daughter, Karen. If Pete died out here, he'd disappear forever. She'd never know what had happened, and worse, she'd never know how much he'd loved her. A sense of hopelessness and depression crowded into the boat with him. Not a religious person, Pete still tried to negotiate a deal—if he survived Myanmar, he promised to patch up the relationship any way he could.

Then the soldiers went silent. Mosquitoes, probably carrying malaria, buzzed at the edges of the boat. Some had flown in under the grass and circled Pete's face. He could envision the soldiers scanning the countryside, searching for them. Ten minutes passed. His leg cramped, but he didn't dare move. He smelled cigarette smoke. Was the boat drifting that close to shore? The grass hid the three out on the lake, but at close range the soldiers would spot them easily. A burst of gunfire cracked over the lake, and the rice behind them rustled when hit by the bullets.

Someone barked an order. Boots scuffled onto the pavement again, engines revved, and the springs of the vehicles squeaked as they filled with men. Then the jeep engines groaned into low gear, rose in pitch, and faded away. Pete thought the shots had probably come from a frustrated young soldier, anxious to fire his weapon.

Moe said to wait. Fifteen minutes later, the sound of another vehicle echoed across the lake. It stopped, and its engine ticked as it idled. Moe lifted his head to peer through the grass. "Okay. Safe to go," he said.

He pushed the grass aside as the others sat up. Pete stretched his legs and hoped the feeling would return to his feet someday. Mi Mi's face had a coat of tan dust. Pete helped her wipe it clean. He looked to the shore and saw the cousin's truck. Moe instructed them to paddle. Since the water line was only a couple inches below the side of the boat, it was easy to use their hands to get back to shore. Once there, they sloshed through shallow water, ran up the slight incline to the road, and jumped into the box of the truck.

Moe stood by the door, talking quickly to his cousin. He came around the back end and climbed up. "We hurry to catch trucks at Nyaung Shwe. If we miss, they are able to get away onto lake and can hide weapons. Then never find them."

"How big is this lake?" Pete asked.

"Inle Lake is one of the largest in the country," Mi Mi said.

"Anyone live there?"

"Of course. But since there aren't any roads, all the towns are 'floating' villages. You'll see," Mi Mi assured him.

"You told me the Shan army has been fighting the generals. Why would they hide the weapons here?" he asked.

"The army fights them in the south. Up here, we have only the secret networks that try to undermine the generals' power. This area is so remote, it's easy to hide something, even as large as all these weapons," Mi Mi said.

The truck chugged up the winding road into the mountains and within an hour had come out onto a broad plain. Set in a green valley like children's toys were small clumps of houses along with pagodas that resembled golden tulip bulbs. A narrow river wound its way through the towns. The mountains looked soft and furry from their covering of vegetation.

"This is the Shan plateau," Mi Mi told him. "To the northeast, we border China. Only a hundred miles away."

The truck passed beside a long railroad trestle. Mi Mi explained, "Built by the British for their mountain stations. Wait until you see the first village."

They descended into the valley along straight roads that bordered more fields. A lone man in a red shirt swung a scythe into stands of grain. Hitched to a wooden cart, a Brahma bull waited in the shade. As the houses multiplied, Pete noticed the architecture resembled houses found in England, made of brick with peaked roofs and formal gardens.

They came into a small, one-story town with an open-air market along the road. Colorful bags, shirts, and *longyi* hung from hooks on the market stalls. A large billboard advertised Grand Royal rum. There were more restaurants: the Kipling, the Golden Lion, and the Jasmine. There was a fortune teller who sat in the shade under a bright green tree. There was something odd about her until Pete realized that she sat on a chair instead of on the ground.

People crowded everywhere. Moe's cousin drove fast, and Pete was worried they'd strike one of the pedestrians, but everyone seemed to get out of the way at the last moment. They turned over a small bridge that spanned the narrow river. A sugar mill perched on the edge of the far bank. The dirty white building leaned to one side and was covered by a rusted tin roof.

The sun rose to heat up the air, and it smelled fresh. Pete threw his head back and, for a moment, imagined he was simply vacationing here. How beautiful the country was and how peaceful it looked to a tourist. He thought of taking a slow trip with Mi Mi as she pointed out all the historical sights. It seemed so "normal" in comparison to their real purpose. He put on his sunglasses and felt great if even for a short time.

The truck jerked to a stop. Pete leaned around the cab to see a herd of goats stroll across the road. The driver honked, but the goats ignored him and took their time crossing the road. They seemed alone; there wasn't a shepherd anywhere. Bells tinkled, and the goats brayed at the interference.

In a half hour, they'd reached the edge of the town of Nyaung Shwe. It was the gateway to Inle Lake. Mi Mi had explained to Pete that the lake spread between two mountain ranges in a narrow but long body of water. Recently, there had been some economic development for the first time in centuries as local people built almost forty hotels around the lake. The generals, in business with Italian and German companies, now planned at least sixty more in the coming years to attract tourists—something rare in this high, remote plateau.

"The environmental degradation is unimaginable," Mi Mi had said. "It's so bad, the lake is shrinking for the first time ever. It's another example of them raping the land for their own financial advantage."

Moe's cousin slowed as they came into the outskirts of the town. Pete saw wooden stands built along the side of the road. A rough horizontal plank held several plastic bottles filled with liquid the color of egg yolks. It was a "gas station." The bottles held gas for scooters, and payment for a fill was on the honor system. A dented metal box to hold the cash nestled between the bottles on the plank.

Fields of buckwheat and yellow niger seed petered out as they came into the town. More markets spilled over the streets. Blankets lay on the ground to display vegetables, fruits, baked goods, lettuce, and carved wooden items. The people sitting on the blankets were shorter than those in Yangon and their skin darker. Many of the women wore colorful wool wraps on their heads—apple red, blue, and corn yellow. Men stood behind braziers that heated pots of oil to deep-fry pastries.

Because of the crush of people, Moe's cousin had to stop often. Young boys crowded around the truck and offered items to Pete and Mi Mi. The most popular one was a colorful paper bird on a string that looked like origami artwork. The boys thrust them into Pete's hands and spoke Burmese. He didn't understand the words but certainly understood the salesmanship. Then the boys yelled, "Lucky money, lucky money," in English. Pete understood that. He bought two for fifty cents. Maybe the delicate birds would bring them all good luck—like Moe's dolls and number games.

In ten minutes, they stopped before a two-story house. This one had glass in the windows and shutters on either side. The three walked to the front, and Mi Mi knocked on the ornately carved door.

A middle aged woman opened it, and her round face split into a broad smile. She gave Mi Mi and Moe each a loose hug and stood back to shake Pete's hand. Mi Mi introduced her as Daw Kyaing, an old friend of the family. She had dark skin and long hair wrapped in a glossy pile on her head. She stepped back to invite them all inside.

"We cannot stay long. You know what we are here for?"

Kyaing nodded without smiling. "It is most serious. I have talked to all our friends. We are ready to help in any way." She led them to the simple kitchen and started to prepare tea.

Mi Mi turned to Pete. "The term 'daw' is used for respect. Kyaing became very rich by trading illegal dollars years ago. She has used her money to buy things for the local schools since the government doesn't pay for much. Kyaing also is part of a network of educated women who are trying to make our country more progressive." Mi Mi scowled. "It would be a clanger to depend on the men here, so we depend on each woman in the network instead."

After a short break for tea, the three left Kyaing's house. The original driver had returned with the truck, and they climbed in again. As the truck dodged people and animals through the markets, it seemed like a slalom race to get to the port on the lake. The street narrowed, and Pete knew they couldn't go much further. Finally, Moe's cousin halted. They got out of the back end and grabbed their packs.

"We will get bike from here to port," Moe said as he hurried off.

Next to Pete and Mi Mi was a flower market. Other than in a nursery, he'd never seen so many flowers—in all colors and shapes.

"This is an orchid market," Mi Mi said. "We grow hundreds of them all over the country."

"I remember how difficult it is to grow these in Minnesota. This is amazing."

"Oh, look here." Mi Mi skipped ahead. "This is the Thazin orchid I was telling you about." She pointed at the slim stalk that rose into the air until it drooped over with a long row of white flowers. New buds resembled green artichoke hearts. "It's also called the Royal Orchid," Mi Mi added. When they stepped back, the stalks looked like the poised wings of dozens of delicate birds. "I'm surprised to see them. The season's almost over, but these are still growing against all odds."

They moved back into the street to wait for Moe. Behind them, small shops and houses squeezed next to each other like strangers in a commuter train, different colors, sizes, shapes, and designs. Many had open windows with only a straw curtain to cover them. Horns honked and scooters whined around them. Pete saw dogs wander among the stalls of food, their heads hung low.

"I was impressed with Daw Kyaing," Pete said to Mi Mi.

"Yes. She's one of the few smart women who are independently rich without being a part of the cronies."

Sweat dribbled down the sides of his chest underneath his shirt. Dust curled up behind mopeds as they raced along the street. He glanced at his watch. Where was Moe? They hadn't seen any of the generals' trucks with the weapons since they'd reached Nyaung Shwe. Were they already too late?

Pete saw Moe running toward them. He was followed by three strangely-shaped bicycles, each with a driver. The bikes had small reclining seats attached to the sides with a third wheel supporting the seat. Pete's driver stopped. He wore a yellow and green shirt advertising Royal Club rum. Moisture glistened across his brown face and flat nose, and he smiled to show white but crooked teeth. He dismounted from the bike and brushed dust off the thin cushion on the seat. He invited Pete to climb in.

Moe and Mi Mi got on their bikes and propped their bags behind them, and the three started up the crowded street.

Pete heard his driver grunt as he stood on the pedals to move forward. Once they gained speed, the boy sat and could maintain the pace easily. Some of the roads were dirt and some were paved. They rolled by a series of restaurants, and Pete could smell the wonderful cooking: saffron oil, cilantro, and pungent onions. With his fingers, he tented his shirt away from his skin to cool off. They passed seven monks with dusty feet walking in a row.

Then he could smell water. They must be getting closer to the lake. People carrying bundles on their heads walked on worn flip-flops alongside them. Wooden carts pulled by bulls creaked by, and an occasional small truck passed them, all loaded with produce, stalks of sugar cane, dirty bags of rice, long pieces of cut wood, and five-gallon cans of oil.

The shops and restaurants gave way to one-story warehouses. Rickety wooden fences guarded their entrances. Men squatted on the corners in small groups and looked up as the three bikes passed them. Most were smoking, and Pete smelled the sweet odor of cheroots, made by rolling the leaves of cheroot trees around tobacco and honey.

His driver looked back to smile and, with a free arm, pointed ahead.

The crowds thickened and reminded Pete of a busy airport. People and packages, animals and produce dodged each other as they hurried for the port. The bikes wound their way through the tangle to turn onto a long street. On either side, cars and trucks were parked in a jumbled pattern.

On their left side, the street bordered a churning river. Several wooden docks perched over the water. Some of the docks were covered by unpainted old roofs that sagged in the middle. In contrast, the hundreds of people all wore colorful clothing. They bunched together at the docks.

The three got off the bikes and grabbed their bags, and Moe led them toward a small shack on the dock. It had windows with cloudy panes of glass on two sides. Moe led them inside and talked rapidly. A man in a t-shirt, shorts, and flip flops kept pointing at a clock on the wall. It was missing three numbers. Moe must be trying to buy tickets. Finally, he showed them his official police badge, and the man by the clock quieted.

Mi Mi listened and turned to Pete. "They insist it is too late to go onto the lake."

"Is that true?"

"Of course not. The boats run until it is dark."

"What's going on?"

"They want more money."

"Can't we go to another port?" Pete asked.

"This is the gateway to the lake. There is no other way to go onto it."

Pete took two steps to reach the window that faced the river. He saw a narrow channel and the opposite bank, similar to the one he was on. It, too, had concrete walls along the river and wooden docks that leaned over the water. If he had a rock, Pete could have easily hit the workers unloading a boat on the other side.

They lifted straw baskets of fish from the bottom of the narrow boats. The fish glistened in the fat lemon sun, and Pete was close enough to smell their tangy odor. The boats were all made of wood and were long and narrow, with bows that curved up into points. Inside, wooden planks covered the bottom. This boat was designed for cargo since there was nothing else inside. Some boats were obviously used to carry passengers. Those had four to five Adirondack chairs set on the floorboards. The outsides of the boats were all painted in garish colors like circus rides.

Mi Mi came to stand beside him and watch. She said, "The men are afraid and won't tell Moe what's going on. Something's wrong."

He glanced back and saw the clerk frowning. Pete turned to face the river again. "All the boat motors look alike," he said to Mi Mi.

"They're from China. Years ago, the boats all used Johnson outboard motors made in the US."

Pete interrupted, "Johnson outboards? Those were made in Minnesota." He laughed.

"But as the lake has shrunk, it's become shallower, and the outboard motors can hit bottom. So the owners adapted the cheap Chinese engine. See how the shaft of the motor sticks out behind the boat for twenty feet?" She pointed at the boat on the other side of the river. "It can be raised or lowered depending on the depth of the lake."

Pete nodded. He looked up the river and saw dozens of boats tied to each other along the quay, sometimes four boats deep. He watched men step from the outer boats over each other boat until they reached the dock. To load them, the men retraced their steps while carrying heavy baskets on their heads. It was hard because the current and waves jostled the boats against each other.

Meanwhile, boats of all sizes roared up and down the river, snaking through tight openings between the traffic. The water churned into waves that looked the color of a latte drink.

Moe came over to them. He said, "Men afraid to help Moe."

"Why?" Pete asked. He looked at the clock on the wall.

"An hour ago, trucks with weapons came from airport on only road and stop near here. Soldiers order everyone to clear out dock while weapons loaded onto many boats. Men saw it happen and do not want to have anything to do with Moe or soldiers."

Pete's shoulders collapsed. "Are we too late?"

"We missed first shipment. Remember, many trucks full of weapons. We may find the rest." He looked closely at Pete while reaching into his wool bag. Moe removed the Nat and held it up to Pete. "Maybe we get lucky." He grinned at Pete.

The three stepped out of the shack and waited on the dock. Along the river, wooden steps the length of the dock descended to the level of the water. Other passengers got on and off the boats. They carried so many baskets and bags that Pete worried the boats would capsize. When the boat was loaded, the driver would pull the starter rope on the engine, adjust the throttle, and dip the shaft with the propeller into the dirty water. With a roar, the boat lurched into the choppy channel to move toward the lake.

Pete didn't want to wait. He'd come so far, and the frustration at this point overwhelmed him. He looked around at the surging crowds and the dirty water, felt the heat, and smelled the dust from the road next to the docks. With all his efforts, would he be stopped here?

His stomach growled, and he remembered none of them had eaten for hours. At the opposite end of the dock from the shack was a small counter that sold fruit drinks and something that resembled potato chips. He walked over and bought four bags along with drinks. When he offered them to Moe and Mi Mi, they all gobbled everything quickly. Then they waited again.

Pete paced along the dock while dodging clumps of passengers who also waited. They squatted next to plastic crates full of their possessions. Many had brought food in straw baskets that they ate. Some of the people saw Pete and offered him fruit and rice. At first, he declined. His hunger came back, and he accepted a mango. A woman handed him several slices of the orange fruit. Juice ran down her uplifted arm. "*Kyay su bar be,*" he thanked her.

He went back to pacing. All his training had taught him to act and not wait. Americans weren't used to waiting for anything. You lost opportunities when you failed to take action. In the US there was quick coffee service, fast food, communications that traveled faster than ever over the Internet, and beating the competition— these were the hallmarks of life in America. And Pete had succeeded, like so many others, by not delaying, by taking charge and bending circumstances to what he wanted.

It was different here in Myanmar. Although Pete fumed and paced, there was nothing he could possibly do to speed up the process, nothing that would bend the world around him to his needs.

He remembered Mi Mi telling him about Buddhist philosophy. Buddha had taught that frustration and anxiety were a product of humans wanting things. If a person could eliminate wanting, the negative aspects would disappear. Mi Mi had told him, "None of us can really change our environment. In the West, people think they can and have had some success in doing so. But it comes at a big cost. All that we can change is *our response* to events in our lives."

A half hour later, his resolve was fraying along with Buddhist philosophy. People and boats had come and gone throughout the morning. Still no trucks or shipments of weapons. Maybe they had missed them, after all.

From up the narrow river to the right, a rumble of noise unrolled toward Pete. The sound echoed off the walls of warehouses that lined the waterway. Then the sounds became more distinct—shouted orders, outboard motors, the sound of waves smacking against wooden hulls, and the throbbing whoosh of the propellers as they churned in the water. He saw the first two boats come toward him, bows up in the air to expose the painted wooden hulls the color of celery and corn and the blue sky. They sliced through the channel and looked like they were cutting the dirty water into two halves.

Several boats followed as if they were in a parade. But no one was smiling in the boats. Most were filled with military people who sat in tight rows on the bottom of the boats, their rifles sticking up in the air like stalks of rotted sugar cane. The drivers stood in the sterns and maneuvered the boats. Their skin was dark from constant exposure to the sun on the expanse of the lake.

Then came more boats with Adirondack chairs. Each one held a general. Pete could tell by the number of medals and golden braids hanging from the shoulders of their uniforms. Pete stepped back into the shadow under the roof before anyone could spot him. Moe and Mi Mi did also. It was good they had moved since General Lo Win rode with his adjutant in the next boat. His chair spanned the width of the interior, and his shoulders overlapped the backrest. The general had his head up, motionless, while he stared at the crowded docks. He looked bored, but his small eyes moved constantly.

While Moe jerked on Pete's arm, he hissed, "Get back. If they spot us, we are killed right here."

"I don't see any boxes of weapons," Pete said.

Moe peeked around the wooden column that supported the roof. He ducked back into the shade and removed his glasses. He folded the bows and said, "They come."

After the generals had passed, armed soldiers rode in more boats that were loaded with wooden crates carrying the weapons. The weight caused the boats to ride low and wallow through the waves. Each soldier balanced an automatic rifle in the crook of his arm. They were pointed toward the crowds, oblivious to the danger of an accidental shot hitting someone. The soldiers didn't care.

"How can we stop them?" Pete said. He shifted his weight from one side to the other.

The three hid behind a group of men waiting to load cases of bottled water onto boats. No one else dared to shove off until the military had passed. People watched in silence. Pete tried to count the transports. It seemed to him that all of the weapons had been moved. They were too late.

Pete wouldn't give up. He'd try to call the ambassador. Maybe there was something he could do, some investigation Popham could start to expose the illegal weapons sales. Maybe Mi Mi's idea of exposing the weapons to the media would help in some way.

Pete's shoulders relaxed. He had hoped for more and didn't like to lose. But unlike America, where you either won first place or lost everything, here in Southeast Asia, victories were measured in steps over a long time.

The number of boats carrying weapons decreased. A final boat brought up the end like a caboose. Pete sucked in his breath when he saw members of the NGO, Free the Oxygen, riding in it. He didn't see Rob, but Pete saw the other thugs who had tried to kill him in Mandalay. It was obvious they were still working with the generals. The ambassador would certainly be interested in the American connection, and it might motivate him to really dig into the case. There were several US prohibitions about arms dealing with Myanmar. The NGO was probably guilty of violating every one of the laws.

The boat chugged toward Pete. Some of the passengers had popped open blue umbrellas to shade themselves from the sun. Near the stern of the boat one of the umbrellas hid the entire person. The boat came closer. Around the edge of the umbrella, Pete saw a long curve of black hair rise on the wind. It danced for a moment to reveal a red barrette that held the hair in a ponytail.

The boat passed, and underneath the umbrella he stared at Bridget Holmes.

Chapter Twenty-one

Bridget's head swiveled in Pete's direction. Her face was expressionless, but her cobalt-colored eyes searched among the people on the dock. Hundreds of Burmese lined the side of the river, and Bridget scanned them until she spotted Pete—from the Ex-Im Bank in Minneapolis.

Pete started forward. He stumbled over the first step. He almost fell into the water until two men grabbed him. Bridget's boat pulled away. Pete yelled, "Bridget!"

She jerked around to stare at him; her eyes grew large and round. Her hand moved up tentatively until one of the NGO soldiers shouted at her. Bridget resumed her original position and the boat churned into the sun, casting a glow around her head until the umbrella hid her face again.

Pete jumped up to the top level of the dock. "Come on," he shouted at Moe. "We've got to catch her." He breathed hard with excitement. After all the trouble, work, and false starts, he'd finally found Bridget Holmes. And now she had disappeared into the big expanse of the lake.

Pete charged back to the small shack with the two men and the broken clock. He burst in the door and started yelling at them. He wanted a boat right away. The man in the t-shirt didn't understand Pete's words. Moe arrived shortly and translated for Pete. The clerk still refused to get a boat. Pete's chest tightened. He shook with anger. Finally, he reached into his money belt and removed a crisp, new American $100 bill. He shoved it into the clerk's face. His head jerked back, but he saw the bill and grabbed it. He yelled at the assistant. Within a few minutes, a boat was tied up at the dock, ready for Pete.

Moe and Mi Mi ran down the steps and clambered into the boat after Pete. Moe ordered the driver to get moving, and before they were even seated, they lurched away from the dock. Two other boats converged in front of them to block the path. Pete's driver split the space between the boats with only a slight bump on either side. He twisted the throttle, and their boat leaped forward.

For ten minutes they hummed along a narrow passage of water that led to the open lake. The buildings disappeared behind them. Tall grass and flat banks of mud bracketed the river. An occasional restaurant balanced on stilts at the edge of the grass. A billboard leaned to one side on old cypress poles. It read *Inn Shwe Pyi, the best food on Inle Lake.* Boats coming off the lake passed by them within a few feet. Pete thought the wake from the boats would swamp everyone. But the old wooden boats were so heavy, they didn't even jiggle.

Most of the incoming boats were empty. Small men in bare feet squatted on the back ends, which were flat pieces of wood that hung out over the water, sometimes only a few inches above the water. The men were burned so darkly from the sun, Pete could hardly make out their faces.

Behind Pete, a parade of boats followed them. They were loaded with goods of all kinds: cases of bottled water, dirty Styrofoam coolers, furniture, and straw baskets filled with clothing.

The sun glared off of the water and the yellow grass to the sides. Pete found an umbrella on the floorboards beneath the Adirondack chair. He propped it open above his face. As the boat picked up speed, the wind pressed against the umbrella, threatening to collapse it.

He strained to see the general's boats, but they had disappeared far ahead. The river widened and became calmer. Cranes with pencil legs hunted along the shoreline. Their snow-white feathers contrasted against the backdrop of green and yellow grass.

The boat roared past a bamboo frame structure that rose two stories into the air. Ropes hung down from metal cylinders on the top and were attached to large buckets with tangled knots. Pete guessed it was some kind of rudimentary dredging system. On the back side, he spotted the identical Chinese engine that powered their boat.

A crow had perched on the roof. It watched them like a spy until the boat got closer. With two flaps of its wings, it lifted off the structure and headed out over the lake. Pete heard its warning caw repeated until it became a black speck against the dark blue of the sky.

The sun burned his bare arms, and hunger gnawed at his stomach. He ignored both, anxious to catch up with the other boats.

In twenty minutes, the driver slowed down. Ahead stretched the silver blue expanse of the lake for as far as Pete could see. To the right a mountain range sheltered the lake in a long series of green and lavender humps. A similar range lumbered off to the left, rising abruptly from the shore of the lake. Several boats floated in place like they were waiting in a harbor.

"Fishing for the bloody tourists." Mi Mi leaned forward from her chair and shouted over the noise of the wind into Pete's ear.

As they came closer, Pete saw a few boats filled with tourists. They were dressed in tropical, safari-style shirts and large sun hats. Everyone had a smart phone out and was filming. Each of the fishermen stood on one leg. The other was wrapped around a shaft of wood that he used to pole the boat forward. With his free hand, he tossed a conical framed net into the water and pulled it back by a rope.

"Fake fishermen," Mi Mi said. "It's an ancient way of fishing, but now they only do it to get money from the few tourists up here."

She was right. After a short "show," the tourist boats came close, and money was passed to the "fishermen."

Pete's driver cruised past the entertainment, then opened the throttle again. They headed out into the open lake.

Pete took a deep breath in response to what he saw. The lake was flat like glass, and only a few other boats moved silently across the surface, far in the distance. Pete's boat was alone and skimming faster than ever over the water. The wind smelled fresh and dry, washed clean by the intense sun that burst in thousands of sparkles over the water to the east. From the other side, Pete could see a reflection of the green and purple mountains lying across the surface as if they'd been painted there.

Although bundles of cumulus clouds piled up in the western sky, he could see darker clouds far off to the east, carrying monsoon rain. In spite of the danger ahead, Pete felt wonderful. He had a hard time remembering when he'd been in such a naturally beautiful place before.

They raced across the lake for another forty-five minutes. Their driver pushed the old engine hard.

"There they are," Pete yelled when he spotted a line of dark shapes in the distance.

"Faster."

The driver adjusted the rudder, and the boat angled closer to the shapes on the water. In another ten minutes, Pete could make out individuals in the boats and see the soldiers with their guns. They had slowed in front of a long clump of low land. It looked like they were lined up.

The driver shouted something to Moe, who relayed it to Mi Mi, who spoke over Pete's shoulder. "They're heading for the floating farms."

Pete could see a low-lying stretch of ground rising about two feet above the surface of the water. At regular intervals, tall bamboo poles rose from the land. He saw bright red dots of tomatoes and their vines tangled around wooden frames. Mi Mi had told him earlier that because of the shortage of land for growing, farmers cut thick swatches of land from upriver and floated them down into the lake. They were anchored by bamboo poles jammed into the shallow bottom.

As they raced closer, the driver of Pete's boat slowed down. He raised the long shaft from the engine higher in the water. The propeller churned near the surface, sending a geyser of water in a high spout behind them. Then the driver stopped the engine while the boat drifted.

"We not want to get close yet," Moe said in the sudden silence.

Pete was amazed at the ingenuity of the floating farms. He asked, "Why would the generals go there?"

"For protection. The floating islands create a labyrinth that's difficult to penetrate. Some of the routes through there are known only to the farmers," Mi Mi said.

"Do you think they'll anchor the boats?"

Mi Mi shook her head. "Can you see the large red building?"

Pete stood up in the boat so he could look over the floating is-land next to them. He saw a one-story building with a silver metal roof. It seemed to float on the horizon just like the farms. "What is it?"

"A monastery. It's also a school and has a warehouse beside it. It's the largest structure out here. I'm sure they'll store the weapons inside of it."

"Don't the people care?"

"Of course. They hate the generals and the cronies, but what can they do in the face of guns? They will cooperate," Mi Mi said. Her face darkened with anger.

"What can we do now?"

"We can try to sneak in there and get more photos. I will add those to the ones I have from the airport."

Pete sat down and crossed his legs. Suddenly, her fight seemed small. And hopeless. What were photos against guns and power?

As if she'd read his thoughts, Mi Mi said, "I'll get them back to the party and Aung San Suu Kyi. She will take them public and spread it around to the world's media."

Pete thought of the ambassador and the illegal arms trade with the NGO. He asked if Mi Mi had her cell phone. "Will it work way out here?"

She pulled it from the wool bag on her shoulder. "There is one tower back in Nyaung Shwe. Maybe, if we're lucky—" She swiped it, and her face brightened. She was able to get reception. "What should I do?"

Pete gave her a number. "Call Ambassador Popham. I want to tell him all about Free the Oxygen and how they're dealing in weapons illegally. That will push him into action. He can bring some big help for us."

Mi Mi dialed and waited. She spoke into the phone. "Is this Ambassador Popham? Oh, Ms. Smith. I have Pete Chandler with me, and he wants to talk to you." She moved next to Pete and handed him the phone.

"Carter, you won't believe this. Free the Oxygen is dealing heavy weapons in violation of several US laws." He explained quickly what he'd seen in the past twenty-four hours and what had happened. "I thought you'd like to know. We need help. Right now, we've followed them to a floating farm on Inle Lake. And the best part is, I've found Bridget Holmes."

Smith yelled, "What the hell are you doing? I waited for you to go to the airport."

"Uh, changed my mind," Pete said. "When can you get up here?"

Smith paused and said, "We're here already."

"What?"

"We're way ahead of you, Chandler. We knew about this days ago. The ambassador and I are here and on the lake as we speak. We've got two boats and a contingent of Marines with us."

Startled, Pete didn't know what to say. How did they know all about the smuggling of weapons and the race out onto the lake? Why didn't Smith tell him earlier? He asked her about it.

"Because we told you to go home. This is way too big for someone at your pay grade, Chandler."

"But you knew I was looking for Bridget."

"Of course, but I'm sorry to say she's only a minor distraction for us at this point."

"Well, she's not a 'minor distraction' for me," Pete insisted.

"Don't be foolish. The ambassador has ordered you to stay out of this. Besides, you'll get hurt—or killed—and we can't promise you any help."

When someone ordered Pete to do anything, that was when the skin on his neck crinkled and he wanted to fight. "Where are you right now?"

"We're just entering the lake."

Pete clicked off the phone. He wanted to throw it overboard but handed it back to Mi Mi. He told Moe and her what Smith had said. "We're not leaving. It's great the ambassador is here; they'll deal with the generals and get those weapons back. But I want to rescue Bridget. Can we get closer?"

Moe conferred with the driver. He shook his head. Moe talked some more, but the man looked scared and refused to budge. Pete climbed around the chairs and stood before the driver. Pete offered crisp American bills to him. His eyes darted from one side to the other, but he took the money. He started the engine and spoke fast to Moe.

"He says there is secret way into center of monastery, but it is hard to find it. He will try."

"Good. Let's get the hell going," Pete shouted and scrambled back to his chair. The engine hummed and the driver maneuvered the boat in a tight circle to head into the labyrinth from a different spot. Within a few minutes, they were lost between clumps of floating land. They all looked identical: black soil at the water line, lush green vegetation supported by a wooden framework, bamboo poles sticking up into the sky, and between the islands, silver channels of water. The driver poked his way through the openings.

"Faster," Pete urged.

The driver opened the throttle but ran aground in a narrow channel. He had to stop, back up, and get a run for it. As the engine whined with the strain, the bow of the boat leaped up over a low stretch of dry land. The boat balanced for a moment like a teeter-totter and then splashed down on the far side. At the last minute, the driver pushed down on the shaft, and the engine roared as it popped out of the water and crested the dry land.

They passed several houses on stilts between the endless clumps of land. They were constructed of wood and painted in bright colors: turquoise, blue, green, and yellow. All the windows were open. Each one had a small wooden boat tied to a flight of stairs that led up to the house. Sometimes, children sat on the boats or swam in the still water underneath the houses. Pete didn't see any electric lines, gas lines, or telephone lines into the houses.

In an open stretch, the driver made good time. Pete didn't know how he was going to rescue Bridget, but he hoped a plan would develop when he reached her. They turned around a sharp bend in the channel, and the driver stopped abruptly.

Before them, two farmers squatted in the bottom of a small, shallow boat. One held a rope attached to the nostrils of a huge black bull that swam through the channel behind the boat. They moved slowly as the bull sometimes walked when it could touch the bottom. It looked surprisingly agile in the water.

"Come on," Pete yelled. "Can we get around them?"

The driver waited for the procession. The farmers paddled their boat slowly, heading for a house on stilts at the end of the channel. Two white egrets hopped over the hump on the bull's back. They pecked at his hide, which didn't seem to bother him in the least.

Pete could smell the damp vegetation, so pungent it almost smelled like it was rotting. "Come on," he said again. He rapped his fists on the armrests of the chair.

When the farmers and the bull had passed, the driver revved the engine and their boat shot forward. In ten minutes they broke out of the islands and turned onto a "street" of water. It could be the Venice of Southeast Asia. Houses fronted the open stretch of water on both sides. They were all on stilts that raised them to a second-story level. Underneath, the families had boats, floating storage boxes, and narrow stairs that led to small balconies by the front doors.

Women and children sat on the porches, surrounded by colorful clothing that waved in the wind. These were small and dark people compared to the Burmese in Yangon. Everyone smiled and waved. The floating houses were arranged in squares to create corners for the watery streets. Several boats passed Pete going in the opposite direction. One long boat rode low in the water and carried about twenty young boys. All their heads were shaved, and they all wore maroon robes. Like a row of dominoes, when they noticed Pete and his boat, they all smiled right down the line.

"Young monks going to the monastery for class," Mi Mi explained. "Daw Kyaing's network has contributed money to buy the boats. They're like school buses. Otherwise, these boys would never get any education."

Pete could hear neighbors chatting with one another, some called to children in the water, and many men worked on boats that bobbed in the water. The men bent over tangled piles of fishing nets, stretching them out to repair holes. Everything floated. There were no roads and no vehicles anywhere. A few of the floating farms had walking paths down the middle, but otherwise there weren't even sidewalks. He couldn't imagine what it must be like to grow up without dry ground to walk on. How did kids play? How did they ride bikes or throw Frisbees or play soccer?

When the water changed to a pewter color, he looked up to see monsoon clouds tumbling in from the east. They crested over the mountains and now bore down onto the open lake. They were gray on top with bulging black bellies underneath—as if they were pregnant with rain.

Pete thought back to the shower he'd experienced in Mandalay earlier. If they had a deluge like that on the lake, he worried the boat would fill with water and swamp. How could he find Bridget? He turned to face the driver and yelled, "Come on, move your ass!"

The driver nodded but didn't go faster. Maybe there were speed limits on these streets.

Mi Mi leaned forward and said, "We have to sneak up on the monastery. Be patient. With all this open water, the generals will be able to spot us easily. The driver knows what he's doing."

"We can't wait," Pete insisted.

When they had passed through the center of the town, Pete saw a huge red structure rise out of the green expanse of the floating fields. It had a steel roof that sloped up to a peak crowned with an ornamental pagoda. The four corners also had ornamental gold and red decorations. There were several doors, each with an overhanging porch. Dozens of boats were anchored near the doors. It was too far away from Pete for him to make out what activity was happening. The generals were probably unloading the weapons to hide them safely inside. They could also turn the monastery into a fort and defend it easily.

The boat slowed to a crawl while the driver twisted the throttle down to a quiet burbling sound. Plans flitted through Pete's head. Should they wait until dark to try and get Bridget? But what if the monsoons started before then? And in the dark, how could they find their way back to Nyaung Shwe? After all, there were no street lights out here, and Pete could imagine the lake was perfectly black at night.

They should probably wait until dusk, at least, and hopefully the rain would hold off.

The driver inched closer, and Pete could see the boats lined up, riding low in the water with heavy crates. They were waiting for their turn to unload. Then, near the end of the line, Pete saw Bridget's boat. He turned quickly to Moe. "We have to go there. Maybe we could pick her off before the generals saw us."

Moe removed his glasses and clicked the bows together as he thought. His face clouded over like the sky. "Mi Mi and Moe must be very, very careful. We cannot be seen, or our entire family will be in danger—besides us."

Pete glanced at the bottom of the boat. He found more umbrellas. "Here. You could lie in the bottom and cover yourselves with these. I'll do the work." He lifted his shirt to reveal the pistol he had used at the airport. "It's certainly not enough firepower against those rifles, but if we can surprise the men in Bridget's boat, this might be enough to convince them to release her."

Moe frowned and looked at Mi Mi. She didn't say anything. "I do not agree," said Moe.

Mi Mi interrupted, "If we can get closer, I will be able to get more pictures. Once you get Bridget, we can get out and back to Nyaung Shwe with the evidence."

Pete thought over their idea. If he had to fire the pistol, it would certainly attract attention—something he didn't want. Surprise was his only chance. He agreed. "And we'll have proof for the ambassador to take action." He waited for Moe to come around to the plan. Moe dropped his head while he thought. Meanwhile, the line of boats crept closer to the monastery.

He said, "Moe does not agree. It is month of black moons. The only thing will happen is disaster."

"That's crazy," Pete said. "Take your Nat and talk to him. Do anything you need to do, but we're going in there to get Bridget."

Moe glared at Pete and wouldn't respond. Mi Mi took Moe's hand. Together, they knelt in the bottom of the boat and spread umbrellas above them.

Luckily, there was a long mound of floating land in front of them. The driver cruised behind it in order to screen their movement from the people at the monastery. If they ran up to Bridget's boat fast, they might be able to board it, grab her, and get away. But at the far end of the floating island, there was open water. They'd be fully exposed at that point.

They all ducked down as low as they could in the boat. They moved along the island. Pete pulled out his gun.

They came closer, and he could see into the last boat. The umbrellas were down, and Pete saw Bridget. She had moved toward the stern. That would make it easier to get her off. Once she recognized Pete, she'd jump at the chance to escape.

As they approached the end of the floating field, large waves lapped along the edges. There must be some movement on the lake that created them. The driver reached for the throttle. At Pete's signal, he would shoot full blast toward the last boat. Pete was ready to give the command.

The bow of their boat came around into the open, and Pete looked back at the driver. He yelled, "Hit it!" But the driver didn't respond. He stood still while his face turned even darker.

Pete whipped around to see four boats come from behind the mound of earth on the right. They surrounded his boat quickly. Each boat had six soldiers in it, each with machine guns pointed at Pete.

The commanding officer shouted. Pete didn't understand the words but could guess at what the officer meant.

Finally, from under his umbrella, Moe said, "They will board and arrest us."

Chapter Twenty-two

Before anyone moved, Pete heard a loud splash from the back of his boat. He peeked around to see the driver dive off the boat. He slapped the water with both arms as he swam for the last island they'd passed. His hair was shiny black like the fur of an otter. The next moment, Pete heard a burst from a machine gun, and the driver's head exploded like a melon to expose the pink interior of his brain. Then blood streamed out behind him from the forward momentum of his body. He sank quickly.

The officer yelled in English at Pete, "Do not move."

Pete didn't plan to move.

"Hold hands up," the officer ordered as his boat angled alongside Pete's boat. The officer climbed across the gunwales and boarded Pete's boat. He held an automatic pistol to Pete's head while he patted along Pete's body. When he found Pete's gun, the officer pulled it out and threw it overboard. He said something to Moe in Burmese. When Moe answered, the officer's eyes opened wide.

The officer nodded toward two more soldiers, who boarded the boat. One pointed his gun at the three while the officer relaxed and told the second man to drive the boat. They all sat down while the boat crossed the short space between the island and the line of military boats.

They motored up to the boat with Bridget Holmes. Pete could hardly sit still. He'd come this far and worked so hard to find her. This wasn't how he had expected it to end. The wooden sides bumped, and the NGO soldier in the front threw a rope to the man in Pete's boat. Pete sat across from Bridget.

She glanced at him with dry eyes. "You're the last person I ever thought to see up here."

Pete glanced around. The others were busy getting the boats tied together. He told her about his mission and that her father was worried. "Are you okay?"

Bridget shrugged. "Yeah, I'm fine."

Pete didn't want to waste time on details now. "I don't know how, but I'll get us out of here." Did she know about Jeffrey? Pete decided to let her know right away. "I'm sorry, but Jeffrey was killed in Yangon."

Her eyes dampened but no tears fell. She nodded. "I tried to get him to see it our way."

"I'll do something," Pete tried to reassure her. He felt the boat tip to one side. He looked up to see one of the NGO soldiers climb across from the opposite boat. He balanced with his arms outstretched for a moment and then walked over to Pete. The soldier stared down at Pete.

"Like a bad penny, you keep turning up," the man said. He wore a red bandanna over his head, tied in a knot at the back of his neck. Without warning, he slammed a bunched fist into Pete's head. Pete almost fell out of the boat. "God damn. That's for Rob. You nearly killed him. And when you fuck with the team, the team fucks with you." His breath smelled of cigarettes. "This'll be a pleasure."

"What'll be a pleasure?" Pete said.

"We got permission from these generals to take care of you personally. The rest of your friends will go to the military. I don't expect any of you will get back to land." He leaned back and laughed.

Pete thought of the vast expanse of the lake. The guy had a point. Just like the driver—a quick bullet to the head, dump the body overboard, and no one would ever know where Pete Chandler had gone. "You can do whatever you want with me. Just release Bridget Holmes."

His face twisted.

"Why do you need her?" Pete asked.

"You don't know, do you?" He sniffed to clear his nose.

"Her father's a congressman. When the US ambassador finds her here, you'll have to fight the Marines. Give her up and get out now."

The man leaned forward and came close to Pete's face. "Don't you remember what Rob told you by the river?"

"What?"

"This is a hell of a lot bigger than you can imagine."

Pete sensed a crack in the situation that might work for him. "I don't care about what you're really doing. My mission is to get Holmes back home. Let me do that and I'll be gone."

The soldier shook his head. "Problem with your plan's that we don't fuckin' need you."

"What about my friends here? They're Burmese citizens, and they have nothing to do with Bridget Holmes."

The man stood back and started to walk to the end of the boat. "They're not my problem. I'll tell one of the generals, and they'll be his problem. I don't think their lives are worth even as much as yours—which ain't much." He reached over the side of the boat to catch a rifle tossed from another soldier. He clicked back the magazine to check that it was loaded and rested it upside down over his shoulder. "Okay, smart boy. Stand up."

Pete hesitated.

"I said get the fuck up," he shouted. Everyone else around them became silent. Perched on top of the monastery, a crow called once.

Pete's eyes darted back and forth. He'd been in a situation like this once before in the Middle East. If he didn't act, the rifle would be lifted off the shoulder, aimed, and shot in the next few seconds.

A shout from the far boat caused the man to glance away. Pete grabbed an umbrella, popped it open, and jammed it into him. He stumbled backward. Pete took the chance to dive into the water. The lake wasn't deep, but it stopped the bullets from reaching him. Pete stayed near the bottom and pulled with all his strength. He heard more bullets thud into the water above him. They must all be shooting at him.

How far was the island? Could he manage to swim behind it and hide?

When Pete's lungs started burning, he had to come up. He darted sharply to the right. He tipped his head back to minimize the exposure and gulped air as deeply as he could three times. He dove again. He heard more bullets strike where his head had gone under.

Pete zig-zagged toward the island. Would they follow him in the boats? If so, this would all be over quickly—and he'd lose.

At the last moment, he came up again. This time he looked around and was surprised the island was less than twenty feet away. The sounds of guns forced him under, and he swam harder. He crossed to the left in an effort to get behind the island. After a few minutes, he had to come up again. He found himself at the end of the island. A couple breaths, a glance behind to see two boats bearing down on him, and he submerged like a rock.

He turned and stroked through the water. His left hand in front, pull back to the side. Next the right hand out front. Back and forth. Keep going. Keep swimming.

He tried to come up slowly, but his head bobbed out of the water. He saw that he'd made it to the back side of the floating island. He could hear the chop-chop of the boats' propellers but couldn't see any of them. Pete lowered his body and inched his head under some overhanging grasses whose ends touched the water. It wasn't much of a hiding spot, but maybe they wouldn't follow him. Or maybe they'd miss him even if they cruised by.

Pete could hear the men shouting. The propellers grew louder. They were coming for him. He couldn't out-swim the boats. He thought about trying to hide in the tomato plants on the island but decided he had a better chance in the water.

Two boats rounded the end of the island and chugged straight for him. The bows held two snipers who lay on the flat wood at the bows of the boat. Their rifles, which were only a foot off the surface, swung back and forth as the boat rolled in the water. Pete could see a dark face with black eyes squinting down the barrel and through the V-shaped sight.

One rifle opened up on automatic fire. The shooter raked the side of the island with bullets just above the water line. The loud bursts from the guns contrasted with the slapping thuds the bullets made as they struck the mud.

Pete heard the thuds coming closer. He took a deep breath and slipped under water. He turned around and tried to see what was in front of him. Although the water was murky under the floating farm, Pete could see a few things. It was a strange world. Pale hyacinth roots hung into the water. They swayed as if they were breathing. Small fish darted away from Pete when he came closer. He heard bubbles pop and faint grunts as the island shifted in the water. Above him, clods of mud and black earth pressed down.

He couldn't stay underneath much longer. The soldiers probably had the island surrounded. He heard zinging as more bullets were fired directly into the water. These remained lethal at deeper depths. Soon Pete would be forced to come up with the boats.

Besides a lack of oxygen, he started to overdose on carbon dioxide. He felt a little high and colors splashed in front of him; some he'd never seen before. He fought the urge to gulp for air. Faces traveled across his vision—Karen, Mi Mi, and floating in front of him was Julie. She looked concerned, and her eyes widened when she saw him struggling. He knew she'd help. He wiggled his body, trying to escape while his weak arms dog-paddled toward her. He wanted to live. Then his vision darkened. He quit swimming and sank down.

He rolled onto his back and spotted a straight pole sticking down from underneath the island. A hallucination? Pete wondered and, with a last burst of effort, reached up. It was solid, and he gripped it with his palm. He pulled and his body floated up. He saw joints like arthritic knuckles along the pole. Bamboo. It must be one of the anchoring bamboo poles that had popped out of the bottom. He pulled his face to the end of it. Could it work? Pete clamped his mouth onto the end, waited one second, and gulped with his lungs. He'd either get mud or air, and that would decide the end.

Sweet, warm air filled him. It tasted like green onions. He hung there for a while until he'd recovered. If he waited long enough, the soldiers might assume they'd killed him and his body had sunk.

He didn't know how much time had passed, but it was getting creepy under the island. The long, white roots waved in the water. Some curled around his legs and arms. The soft tentacles urged him to stay.

He gulped several deep breaths to oxygenate himself. He pushed off and swam under the island to rise slowly along the edge. He burped up above the water line and saw that the boats had gone.

He was too exhausted to swim further. And where would he go, anyway? If he swam back to Bridget's boat, he'd be caught for certain. Instead, Pete gripped the grasses that hung down from the island vegetation and into the water. He heaved once and fell back into the water. He ducked under the grass and looked around. He didn't see any boats. Again, he grabbed on, and this time he used his knees to scramble up the slippery side of the island. Over the top, he flopped onto the tomato vines, which smelled faintly like onions. He rested.

He got up on all fours and hid behind the frames that held the vines off the ground. Bridget and Mi Mi and Moe remained at the end of the line of boats where Pete had left them. The procession seemed to be stopped.

He looked up at the sky. To the west, puffy clouds reflected the setting sun in tangerine, salmon, and lavender colors. The mountains rose up in jagged peaks to almost touch the clouds. From the opposite direction, low, black clouds carried in monsoon rain. Pete felt like giving up. A deep core of him fought the idea, but reality asserted itself—the situation was hopeless. He'd worked so hard, but he'd failed at everything. Bridget, Mi Mi, Karen, and Julie—the list was a long one. For all his self-sufficiency, independence, and cockiness, all he'd accomplished was to wallow in mud and squashed tomatoes.

Maybe if it poured rain, he could swim undetected back to the boats and figure out something. But the ache in his arms and legs told him to forget the idea.

From the opposite end of the island, he heard the roar of boat motors. More military? But it couldn't be—they'd all left Nyaung Shwe earlier. Pete crawled behind the tomato plants to the other side of the island. He laughed out loud at what he saw.

Four boats crashed through the waves. They rode beside each other in a formation. And the funniest, sweetest, most hopeful thing he saw were American flags flapping from the stern of each boat.

Pete stood up and waved and screamed at them. He could see Carter Smith and Ambassador Popham surrounded by dozens of US Marines. They were all armed. He yelled at them again.

Someone noticed him, and the flotilla swerved toward the island. In five minutes, the boat with Smith and Popham bumped up against the muddy edge of the island.

"What the hell are you doing here?" the ambassador demanded.

"Long story. We've got to get around the island. Bridget and the weapons are over there. Trying to hide. Hurry." The words tumbled out faster than he could speak.

"Slow down." Carter Smith came forward in the boat as they shoved off with Pete aboard. "Tell us what happened."

"Be careful. The Burmese army is around that end of the island." Pete took a deep breath and told them the entire story about leaving Nyaung Shwe.

Popham leaned forward from a wooden chair. He wore a tan safari vest and carried a large pistol in a holster on his hip. When he saw Pete look at it, Popham said, "Use it all the time in Texas. Never know when a rattler will come out on your trail." His eyes focused on Pete. "It's too bad you're still here. I warned you to leave."

"I know, but I finally found Bridget—"

Smith interrupted, "We'll handle things from here. Stand down," she ordered. She glanced at the ambassador, and something passed silently between them.

Popham shrugged and said, "We'll just finish everything here. It'll be more efficient, anyway." He looked around at the other American boats, revolved his finger in the air, and they all surged forward at full speed.

A metallic smell crossed the water from the monsoon clouds that bore down on the lake. The wind turned chilly. Pete sat back and rode with the boats as they leaped over the waves. Pete expected shooting to start. They were all exposed; what could they do?

But when they reached the line of boats, no one fired a shot. The army must've seen the flags. Pete's boat stopped, and the stern bobbed up as the wake came forward to lift it. He started to wave at Mi Mi. Smith grabbed his arm and jerked it down.

"I told you we'll settle things from here," she told him.

The NGO soldier stood in the other boat. He looked over at them and waved. Carter Smith signaled back.

Pete looked around. What the hell was happening?

"They've just started off-loading," the soldier shouted to Smith. "See you found a water rat." He pointed at Pete.

"No problem," the ambassador called back. He smiled.

"I want his ass."

"No way. He's in my charge," the ambassador replied.

Pete whispered to Smith, "Why don't you get to the front of the line? That's where all the weapons are. You won't believe it."

"Oh, I believe it. I just hope they're all there," she said.

"Sure. I suppose it's better to catch them with all the incriminating evidence, right?"

A frown passed across Smith's face, and she shook her head slightly. The ambassador stood beside her and said to Pete, "You're about as dumb as a longhorn. You've got everything wrong."

Pete looked back and forth between them and felt like he'd been punched in the gut. They weren't here to rescue him or Bridget or Mi Mi or to stop anything. They were part of the plot. "You son of a bitch," he said to Popham.

"Oh, come on, Chandler. The world isn't a neat, tidy place like a shopping mall in America, where kids play on rides and laws are followed. This is war out here. Look around." He swung his arm toward the lake and the mountains on the other side. "You think the Chinese are going to ask for permission to take over this country?" His face reddened as he talked faster. "They're less than one hundred miles from here. We need to prop up the Myanmar generals. God knows they're not Boy Scouts, but it's the hand we've been dealt. They're the lesser of two evils."

"That's ridiculous," Pete shouted. "You could support the democracy movement here and change the government to a better one that America could work with."

"When we first met, you were lost. Now your two friends from here have changed you into an idealist. But I operate in the real world."

"And what about these illegal weapon sales? What will happen when I get back and tell the congressman? How long do you think you'll remain the ambassador here? You could go to jail yourself."

It was a weak threat. He felt a sting of fear in his chest, but he figured the ambassador wouldn't kill him in front of all the Marines as witnesses. Pete stalled for time. "How could you afford to pay for them?"

"You should know that already." Popham grinned.

"Huh?"

"With the generals' help, we've sold teak and precious gems. Especially now, the price of rubies is way up." The ambassador stood back. Behind him, Pete could see people transferring from boat to boat. Bridget sat in the end of the same boat, but now only one NGO soldier remained with her. Next to them, an empty boat bobbed in the water.

"What about Bridget?"

Popham frowned. "It won't hurt to tell you now."

"Tell me what?"

"She's one of us."

"And I suppose you're going to deny involvement and blame the NGO for everything?" Pete said.

Popham moved to the back of the boat.

"What about Jeffrey Sumpter?"

"An unfortunate casualty of international politics. The NGO knew he was getting too close to figuring out everything. Unlike Bridget, he wouldn't join us, so they lured him to the Shwedagon Pagoda with the promise of a secret meeting. High level Myanmar military personnel. Instead, Sumpter was eliminated. But it's been covered up nicely." Carter Smith walked up to the ambassador.

Popham turned back to Pete. "And now, we have to keep you quiet."

Pete's chest tightened again. His eyes darted around the boats, trying to assess the full threat. Mi Mi and Moe sat alone in a boat, almost forgotten. The generals probably hadn't noticed them yet. Could they get away in time to save themselves?

Carter Smith called to the ambassador, "Do you want to get up front?"

Popham looked back at her for a moment. Pete took the opportunity to dive into the water once again. He swam under two boats and popped up on the far side. It wasn't much cover, but maybe he could buy some time. He peeked over the wooden edge of the boat.

"God damn," the ambassador yelled. "Kill him!"

"We haven't got time, sir," Smith said. "We've got to get to the monastery right now and take charge."

Pete heard the engine start and Smith shout, "I've got a better idea." He heard boats clunking together and then heard Mi Mi scream. He lifted his head above the gunwale to see two Marines force her into the boat with Popham and Smith. They turned back to Moe and threw him overboard into the water. He sputtered and swam away. One Marine stayed in the ambassador's boat to drive it, leaving the other three in the middle. The stern dug down into the water as the engine roared. They headed for the monastery.

Pete swam to the empty boat, climbed into it, and flopped across the floorboards. He was wet and more exhausted than he could ever remember. It took him a long time to get up and look around. Bridget remained in a boat with one NGO soldier guarding her.

Should he go get her? After all, that was why he'd come here in the first place. That was all he was expected to accomplish. He could grab Bridget and turn the boat out to the lake. Even the ambassador might let him go with her if Pete assured him of silence. Maybe Popham was right—this was a lot bigger than Pete had ever imagined. Pete could go back to his job, assured of keeping it once he returned Bridget to the US.

He looked toward the monastery and saw Mi Mi with the ambassador racing away from him. The boat gained speed. Once the generals got their hands on Mi Mi, she was as good as dead.

Raindrops hissed into the water as the clouds overhead settled down on the lake. It had been raining in Washington the day Pete found out about Julie's death. The dark clouds above him now reminded him of every detail of that afternoon. His breathing came hard. He couldn't move. Exhausted, depressed and beaten, he just wanted to get out of there.

To his side, Pete heard the sounds of fighting from Bridget's boat. Beyond them, open lake beckoned to escape and freedom.

He stumbled toward the back of his boat and pulled at the starter on the engine. It caught and revved as he opened the throttle. He collapsed onto the flat wooden stern and lowered the propeller into the water. The boat moved forward. Pete turned the rudder toward the monastery and raced after Mi Mi.

Chapter Twenty-Three

Pete opened the throttle as far as it would go. The flat boat leveled up on a plane and started to gain on the ambassador's boat. The rain fell harder. Coming from the US, Pete had never experienced rain like this—so heavy it felt like a weight against his body. The wind picked up and whined past his ears. Hopefully, the people ahead of him couldn't hear Pete coming up behind them. It might be the only advantage Pete had.

They both raced beside the long line of military boats, but Pete didn't see any generals yet. He was still gaining. As he caught up to the back end of the other boat, no one had heard him yet.

The ambassador and Carter Smith were curled over, trying to hold umbrellas up against the monsoon. They didn't see Pete as he came alongside. With a swift jerk on the tiller, his boat slammed into the other one. The Marine driving looked up in surprise. He tried to compensate but over-steered. The boat wobbled from side to side, and Pete rammed it again. Wood cracked. This time, the shallow boat rolled far enough on its side to catch the water line and flip into the air. Chairs, umbrellas, boxes, and guns flew up like they'd bounced off a trampoline and then tumbled into the water along with Popham, Smith, the Marine, and Mi Mi.

Pete turned in a tight circle. The rain came down in silver sheets that churned the surface of the water. He stood in the boat in order to see. People from the line of boats were shouting at him. Water streamed down his face. "Mi Mi," he yelled.

His boat wallowed in place while Pete turned from one side to the other. He couldn't spot her anywhere. He saw Carter Smith gripping the side of his boat. Her eyes were rimmed in red, her hair plastered to her skull. In one hand she held a pistol while she pulled her body up with a free hand. She shouted something at Pete, but he couldn't hear the words. He saw her point the gun at him.

Pete tried to move forward but was too exhausted to take a step. He watched as she leveled the pistol at his head. Suddenly her body disappeared under the water. Pete wiped the rain out of his eyes and tried to see more clearly. Mi Mi popped up next to the boat. She must've pulled Smith down. Pete crawled to the side and lifted Mi Mi into the boat. They both fell back onto the floorboards. Six inches of rain water sloshed in the bottom. "Get going," Mi Mi shouted to him. "We're going to bloody sink."

As he tried to get back to the engine, Pete slipped on the wood. Rain bounced off the motor, and he worried it would stop running. He grabbed the handle and opened the throttle. To his relief, it roared in response, and the boat lurched ahead. With the flooding, it rode like a log in the water, but at least it moved.

They hurried toward the open lake while Pete kept the line of military boats to his right. Pete thought of Bridget. In the monsoon rain, he couldn't see very far ahead, but Bridget had been at the end.

When they reached the last boat, Pete slowed and looked around. He didn't see Bridget or her boat. Pete turned in circles while he searched. On the third swing around, he almost rammed Bridget's boat. Pete throttled back and, balancing himself, walked to the front. He reached out with his hand. "Come on," he called to Bridget. "You've got to hurry."

"Hey, Pete. You've got it all wrong." She didn't move.

Pete shouted again. "I'll get you home. Your father's worried sick. Come on."

"I'm not going."

Pete couldn't hear well in the rain. "Why not?"

"You don't have any idea, do you?"

"What the hell are you talking about? It's not your fault." His boat bumped into the side of Bridget's boat. He could see and hear her well.

She laughed slightly. "No, I'm not going back." She turned to face Pete. "When I started the audit on the timber company, I was shocked at how much money they were making."

"You're working with the generals?" Pete couldn't believe it. They'd never accept someone like her as a partner.

"Yes, because I'm the daughter of a congressman who found surplus military equipment. The generals needed my help getting it delivered."

"What the hell? Your father's selling the weapons?"

"All for national security. We teamed up with Free the Oxygen to provide security on the ground here." Her face contorted for a moment. "But it wasn't supposed to turn out with Jeff killed. We met with the NGO at the temple that morning, and I thought Jeff would agree to join us. He refused. And I had to leave with the soldiers from Free the Oxygen. There was nothing I could do. I guess they planted a Natural doll underneath him to make it look like the generals had killed Jeff."

"Maybe we can straighten this out back home. Come with me," Pete said again.

She shook her head. "Can't. Now I'll get Jeff's share—set for life."

"Don't you feel guilty?" Pete said.

Bridget's shoulders relaxed. She thought for a moment. "No. No, I don't. This is the biggest chance I'll ever have in my life. Can you imagine what it's like to be my age and look forward to auditing financial reports the rest of my life on a government salary? And, by the way, who am I hurting? This is all for the defense of these people. That's why my father secretly sold the equipment." She turned and crawled to the back of the boat. Across the water, she shouted, "And I'm sorry he used you, Pete. You're a decent guy, but he figured you wouldn't work so hard to find me. I'm surprised myself." With a quick tug on the engine's rope, it roared to life.

Then Mi Mi reminded him they had to escape before the military reacted. Pete looked down and saw the floorboards had submerged under water. He headed away from the other boats toward what he thought was open lake.

Mi Mi came back to sit beside him.

"Where are we going?" he said. "I can't see a damn thing." The world around him was a gray cloud, torn by sheets of falling rain. He didn't know where the floating farms were and had no idea what direction to go.

"Hurry," Mi Mi urged.

Pete idled slowly as he felt his way ahead. For all he knew, they were going in a circle and would end up heading back into the generals' boats. Then, from out of the gloom before them, Pete spotted a shape that resembled a boat. He saw two more. More military? He prepared to spin his boat to the side and get away.

At the last minute, Mi Mi shouted, "It's Kyaing!"

Four boats surrounded them as Daw Kyaing shouted across the water. "Can you follow us?"

Pete shouted back that his boat was slow from all the water flooded into it, but he would try to keep up with the others. Two boats straddled Pete on either side. They were filled with young women. Some ran the motors while others searched the water with binoculars—not that they could see much. Another boat ghosted up from behind them. Four women sat in it and had covered Moe with a rain jacket. They must have picked him up.

Daw Kyaing called to Mi Mi, "We will lead you out. Follow us." She turned forward in her Adirondack chair as her boat surged forward. Pete twisted the throttle and was able to keep up with the other boats. The flotilla slalomed through clumps of small islands, open water, and reed patches.

In fifteen minutes, Pete still couldn't see where they were going, but now the lead boat bore to the left and took them all up a narrow river. It twisted like a corkscrew. Along the banks, Pete could see an occasional house peeking out from the jungle behind it. Sagging palm trees hung over the water. The river branched, and the lead boat took the right fork. They picked up speed, and the rain started to slacken.

In forty-five minutes, Pete realized they had come out onto the lake again and were heading back for the town they'd left. Daw Kyaing called over from her boat that the rain would help hide them from the soldiers. They all limped back into Nyaung Shwe. The wind had dried them to some degree, but they were all cold and tired.

At the dock, two cars and some horse carts picked them up and hurried them to Daw Kyaing's house. Several bowls of hot *mohinga* helped everyone. Pete gulped more tea and felt his strength return.

Moe said, "When they threw me out of the boat, I almost drowned. Luckily, friends of Daw Kyaing rescue Moe."

Pete was gratified, but he knew they were still in great danger. As soon as the offloading of the weapons was completed, the Tatmadaw and the ambassador would probably come after them all.

As if to answer Pete, Moe moved to one of the bedrooms. He took the Nat doll with him and his book of numerology. Through an open door, Pete watched as Moe sat in a cross-legged meditative pose. Moe propped the doll before him and closed his eyes. When Pete looked back five minutes later, Moe was reading the book, making marks in it with a pencil. In another ten minutes, Moe came into the living room. He straightened and looked up at Pete. "It looks good—we will be all right. But you must leave country."

Pete admired his confidence. "Great for you, but how am I going to get out?"

"I have an idea," Mi Mi offered. "We can work with the NLD. I think we could even get Aung San Suu Kyi's help for you to leave. The embassy wouldn't dare cross her. It could create an international problem."

Pete said, "Okay." He looked over the table at Mi Mi. Her hair had dried in flat layers and her face drooped, but she'd never looked more beautiful to him. He'd come to respect her immensely and understood the cause she and so many others fought for here. His own life seemed small in comparison. He'd always worked alone, but here he'd seen a network of women who might even accomplish something in the end.

"We'll fly back to Yangon. When I get closer, I can get cell phone service and call ahead to party headquarters there," Mi Mi said.

By late afternoon, they were all airborne, flying in another small prop plane. Unlike before, Pete had never felt so happy to be in the old plane. They were not able to fly above the monsoon clouds, so the ride was rough most of the way. Pete didn't care. He was going home.

Part of him still felt troubled by his inability to rescue Bridget Holmes. Of course, it wasn't his fault. Instead, he'd take all the photos from Bridget's phone and those that Mi Mi had taken. When Pete got back, he could expose what had happened and the congress-man's complicity.

They landed at Yangon International Airport. Mi Mi told Pete to wait in the small lobby while she contacted the National Democracy League. Pete sat on a chair next to the money exchange where he'd met Carter Smith. How far he'd come since then.

Mi Mi came back and sat next to Pete. "I think it's all set. If we move fast, you can get out. As it turns out, there's not been an official request to detain you. We may not need the help of the NLD if we move bloody quick."

"The generals and the ambassador are probably still more interested in the weapons. But when that's done, they won't forget me," Pete said.

"Come on." Mi Mi stood up. "Let's get your tickets." She started to walk toward a low counter on the far side of the terminal. Pete followed.

"Just ship my stuff that I left at the hotel," Pete joked. They both knew how unreliable the mail was in the country.

They reached the counter and stood behind two people. Pete moved forward. At the window, he paused. He started to order two tickets because he hoped Mi Mi would come with him. She stepped up and said, "One ticket, please."

Pete sighed.

"I can guess what you're thinking," she said. They moved out of the line and stood close to each other.

"Why can't you come with me?" he said. A heavy weight pressed on his chest. "My mother was from Vietnam, but she made a good life in the US. You speak English well and are educated." He wished that he had known his mother better. Being in Southeast Asia made him feel closer to her in some way.

"Pete—"

"I love you, Mi Mi. I'm so slow that it took me a while to realize it, but it's true."

"It won't work. We both know that."

"All right," Pete took a deep breath. "I'll stay here with you."

Mi Mi put her palm on his chest. "You know that's impossible. When the ambassador and the generals get back, your life will be very short. You can't possibly stay."

Pete dropped his head. Thoughts swirled through his brain. The pressure in his chest increased.

Mi Mi said, "I'll be right back." She slipped between the people in the crowd. When she returned in ten minutes, she carried a brightly colored paper bag. She continued, "My work is here, Pete. You know that. We've accomplished so much. Aung San Suu Kyi is getting older; the party needs new leadership. And I haven't forgotten my dream to make my country an exporter of food. There is so much I can do here."

Pete felt the crowds surge around them, pressing closer as they moved into the waiting room for the flight to Taiwan. He felt the old ghosts pressing closer also. The woman he loved and had lost. New passengers came in from outside, bringing hot, humid air with them. Pete felt it and thought of the country he was about to leave, and all the mysteries it contained. The golden glitter that hid so many things underneath.

"Here, I have something for you." She handed him the bag.

He opened it, unwrapped some tissue paper, and pulled out a navy blue *longyi*. Pete held it up in front of him. The length was perfect. He glanced at his watch. "Do I have time to put it on?" He ran for the bathroom. He came back, pleased at how comfortable it felt. Maybe he'd start wearing one in Minneapolis.

"I can never thank you enough," Mi Mi whispered while she reached for his hand. "I'll always think of you and that time after the rally in Mandalay and it started raining while we were in the back seat of the taxi. I felt so close to you then."

Pete's eyes brimmed with moisture.

"Goodbye." Mi Mi lowered his hand and gave him a look with damp eyes.

Pete stumbled forward, ran his bag through the fake security machine, and walked outside onto the tarmac. He put on the NAS-CAR sunglasses. Thick, moist heat clamped around his body. He thought of Minnesota and how the new life of spring awaited him there. From a planter on the wall of the terminal, a burst of colors tumbled over the sides. Jasmine petals quivered in the heat. Bougainvillea grew uncontrollably and almost hid the Thazin orchid that still blossomed bravely—even this late in the season. And even though humans couldn't possibly hear it, maybe the other plants congratulated the orchid with thunderous applause.

Pete settled back into the seat on the Air China plane. Air conditioning whispered around him. Instead of covering up things like before, he'd expose all of this, including his old friend the congressman. As soon as he was airborne, Pete would e-mail Karen. He'd set up a time to meet with her and Tim. There was hope.

Music played from the plane's PA system. Pete heard something Asian—and he liked it. After his time here, its familiarity comforted him. Then Beatles lyrics came to him: *She's got a ticket to ride, she's got a ticket to ri-i-ide* . . . He hummed them quietly. Pete would visit the new restaurant with Karen and Tim. After all, "Ticket to Ride" had always been one of his favorite songs.

Colin T. Nelson has written four other books in addition to a short story included in a crime anthology. If you'd like to learn more about him or his writing, go to his web site at www.colintnelson.com.

Made in the USA
Lexington, KY
04 December 2015